THE LITTLE BEACH CAFÉ

SARAH HOPE

First published in 2018. This edition first published in Great Britain in 2023 by Boldwood Books Ltd.

Copyright © Sarah Hope, 2018

Cover Design by Head Design Ltd

Cover Photography: Shutterstock

The moral right of Sarah Hope to be identified as the author of this work has been asserted in accordance with the Copyright, Designs and Patents Act 1988.

All rights reserved. No part of this book may be reproduced in any form or by any electronic or mechanical means, including information storage and retrieval systems, without written permission from the author, except for the use of brief quotations in a book review.

This book is a work of fiction and, except in the case of historical fact, any resemblance to actual persons, living or dead, is purely coincidental.

Every effort has been made to obtain the necessary permissions with reference to copyright material, both illustrative and quoted. We apologise for any omissions in this respect and will be pleased to make the appropriate acknowledgements in any future edition.

A CIP catalogue record for this book is available from the British Library.

Paperback ISBN 978-1-80549-090-6

Large Print ISBN 978-1-80549-091-3

Hardback ISBN 978-1-80549-089-0

Ebook ISBN 978-1-80549-092-0

Kindle ISBN 978-1-80549-093-7

Audio CD ISBN 978-1-80549-084-5

MP3 CD ISBN 978-1-80549-086-9

Digital audio download ISBN 978-1-80549-088-3

Boldwood Books Ltd
23 Bowerdean Street
London SW6 3TN
www.boldwoodbooks.com

*For my children,
Let's change our stars.
xXx*

1

Pippa Jenkins flung her handbag onto the scratched laminate floor, ignoring the thud it made. So what if it woke her crabby neighbours? They were probably in a comatose state anyway, the amount of weed they smoked.

Sinking into the deflated cushions on the sofa, the sheen of rain covering her jacket soaked into the worn blue fabric, turning patches of it into royal blue smudges. She tossed the letters she'd scraped from the hallway floor onto the low coffee table in front of her and put her feet up, gently knocking the collection of empty crisp packets, toy cars and Lego bricks onto the floor.

Closing her eyes, she calculated that she had precisely six hours and fifteen minutes until her mum dropped Joshua off on her way to work so that Pippa could do the school run. After that, she had the grocery shopping to do and, hopefully, an hour spare to make a dent in the list of housework duties forever looming before she'd have to drag herself back to the restaurant to stand another twelve-hour shift.

There must be more to life, and motherhood, than this. Since

Joshua's dad had run off with the tart downstairs, she hardly even saw Joshua any more. Her mum dropped him off so she could take him to school and then after school, his care reverted back to her mum until the following morning. She used to have time to spend with him, to be a mummy, now all she seemed to be doing was working, cleaning and snatching an hour here or there to sleep.

She refused to open her eyes, she knew the living room was a complete mess, toys were still laying on the floor where they had been abandoned three days ago when it had been Pippa's day off and she had actually been able to see her son for more than an hour in one day. She could sense the clothes jeering her from the laundry basket, telling her that, yes, they had been clean but because she had forgotten to hang them up two days ago they would need washing again to get rid of the unmistakable musty, damp smell. She could almost feel the dust particles rising up from the TV stand, windowsills and the old pine cabinet she stacked toys inside, when they managed to get there, that was.

Pippa forced her eyes open, the continuous drill of the doorbell told her that her mum was outside with Joshua. Pushing herself up out of the sofa cushions, she pulled her coat tighter around her, she really must change the tone of her alarm so it actually did its job and woke her. That way she'd be able to put the heating on before Joshua was dropped off to change into his school uniform.

'Morning, Joshie. Hi, Mum. How's he been?' Pippa ruffled Joshua's light brown hair and picked him up, hugging him tightly.

'He's been a good boy, as usual. He's not had much sleep

though, I'm afraid. He had a bad dream and woke up crying for you.' Maggie slipped his book bag through the open door before kissing Joshua on the head.

'Thanks, Mum.'

'You're welcome. I'll pick you up from your club tonight, Joshua. Bye, love.' Maggie patted Pippa's arm and turned away, heading back down the stairs.

'Come on then, Joshie, we'd best get a wriggle on and get you ready for school.'

Shutting the door behind them, Pippa carried Joshua's small body to the sofa and sat down with him on her knee.

'Hey, Nana said you had a bad dream last night. Do you want to tell me about it?'

Joshua shook his head and bit his bottom lip.

'Oh, my little lad. You know dreams can't hurt you, don't you?' Pulling him closer, she wrapped her arms around his body.

Laying his head against her chest, he wound his small arms tightly around her neck. 'I just wanted you there, that's why I got upset, not because of the dream.'

'Oh, darling. It's my day off in two more days and then we get to spend the whole time together. Maybe we could go swimming and down the park? What do you think?'

'You never used to work this much. Not when Daddy was here.' Joshua yawned and rubbed his eyes.

'I know, but things change. It won't be like this forever.'

'Promise?' Joshua held out his little finger ready to link with Pippa's.

'I promise.' Pippa linked fingers with Joshua, mentally crossing her fingers at the same time. She still had at least two and a half thousand pounds worth of arrears to pay for the flat, thanks to Joshua's father's gambling problem. She should have seen it coming, she shouldn't have trusted him with the job of paying the rent, not after the first time. On the bright side, at least the rest of his debts were in his name only. 'Right, come on then, time to go and get your uniform on.'

'Are you getting changed too, Mummy?' Joshua swivelled around on her lap and looked into her eyes.

'Umm...' Pippa checked her watch. 'Wow, is that the time? No, we've only got ten minutes before the bus comes. Off you go and get changed and I'll make your packed lunch.' Pippa lowered Joshua to the floor and smoothed down the pale pink skirt with the small black apron she was still wearing.

* * *

As she rounded the open stairwell up to the flat, Pippa could feel the tension on her thin plastic shopping bags and knew she only had moments until the handles broke or the bottoms dropped out.

'Excuse me.' Pippa shuffled to the side and stepped around the young bloke who lived in the flat below. Why he chose to sit on the cold concrete steps to smoke never failed to amaze her. Pippa bit her tongue to stop herself from telling him he should be smoking that stuff either in his own flat or out in the open somewhere, not in the stairwell where young kids had to walk through and inhale his poisonous fumes. It just wasn't worth it. Last time she'd said anything he'd hurled a torrent of abuse and that night Joshua's bike had gone missing from outside the flat.

Once inside, she kicked the door shut and lowered the bags to the floor, a tin of beans rolling across the floor as the thin plastic finally gave up. After putting the milk and cheese in the fridge, she turned her back on the rest. She'd unpack it after a coffee.

With a mug of coffee in hand, Pippa flopped onto the sofa,

scooping up the letters from yesterday. She flicked through them, just as she had thought, bills, bills and more bills. All addressed to Mike, thank goodness.

Taking a sip of coffee, she flicked the TV on, settling on a generic morning show. She'd just have a few minutes to herself before the caffeine kicked in and she had to start on the housework.

* * *

'Drat.' Pippa woke up to a hammering on the front door, she must have dropped off. The dregs of cold coffee dribbled from the mug in her hand forming a new mark on the sofa. 'OK, I'm coming.'

Wiping the sleep from her eyes, she pulled the door open. Two men stood outside, one tall and slim, a cap pulled down, half covering his eyes, the other short and heavyset, a dragon tattoo curling above his shirt collar. Both wore the same dark blue jackets with white shirts.

'We're looking for Mike Cherington,' the heavyset one grumbled in a low voice.

'He doesn't live here any more. Can I ask who's looking for him?' Pippa kept her hand on the doorknob and slid her foot behind the half-open door, making sure she stood in the gap between the door and the wall.

'We're from Burton's Bailiffs, we're acting on behalf of The Framwell Garage. We're here to collect some bad debt owing to them.'

'The Framwell Garage? Where even is that?'

'Up north. Is Mike Cherington in?'

Great, so he was still running up debts and using their address. 'I've already told you, he doesn't live here any more.'

'Where might we find him?'

'I don't know. He ran off with the woman downstairs, leaving me and his kid in a whole load of debt thanks to his gambling addiction.' Stepping back she began to close the door.

'With all due respect, miss, we encounter a lot of clients who have supposedly left town. Now if you don't mind.' Mr Heavyset put his foot against the door before Pippa could close it.

'Seriously, he really isn't here. As I said, he ran off with the tart downstairs and I haven't seen him since. Believe me, if I knew where he was I would gladly tell you his exact whereabouts. In fact, I'd take you there myself so I could get him to repay the money he owes me. Now if *you* don't mind, please remove your foot so I can shut the door and get ready for work.'

'I'm afraid it's not as straightforward as that. You see, miss, we have it on good faith that Mike Cherington is on the tenancy agreement for this flat. Is that right?' Mr Heavyset waved a photocopy of the tenancy agreement in front of Pippa's face.

Grimacing, Pippa held tightly to the doorframe, her knuckles turning white. So much for client confidentiality. She bet that if she hadn't been so behind on the rent the bailiffs would never have been able to get hold of it.

'Which means, we have every right to seize goods on this premises unless you can prove without a doubt that they are yours.' A slow grin spread across Mr Heavyset's oily face.

'Only if I let you in, which I will not do.' Pippa grinned back, she knew her rights. 'Now, please remove your foot from my doorway so I can shut the door.'

'Well, not exactly. You see eighteen months ago the lovely Mike Cherington let us in and set up a repayment plan with us, agreeing to pay a certain amount each month until the debt was paid off. Unfortunately for you, he has stopped paying them

The Little Beach Café

which leads to us coming here and seizing his goods.' Mr Heavyset folded his arms in front of him.

'No, that can't be right.' Pippa looked from Mr Heavyset to Mr Thin and back again. That would have been just before he left. What would he have been doing up north? Pippa shrugged, maybe he had been visiting his sister or more likely spending some time away with the tart.

'I'm very sorry, miss, but it is. We have the paperwork to confirm Mike Cherington has deviated from the payment plan, and we also have the original documents with lists of goods to be taken if he were to fail to pay up.'

'He wouldn't do that. Not even Mike would stoop so low as to let people take our things.' Pippa shook her head.

'He has. Now if you would just step aside, please, miss.' Mr Heavyset stepped forward.

'No, no you can't.' How could Mike do this? How could he be so selfish? Wasn't it enough that he'd run off with Viv, who Pippa had stupidly thought was her friend and hadn't twigged that she'd only befriended Pippa to get to Mike? Oh no, he had not only left her for Viv or left her in debt with the estate agent, but he had also stitched her up with these people. He was such a coward. What had Pippa even ever seen in him?

'We can and we will.' Mr Heavyset thrust some official looking documents at her and pointed to Mike's signature.

Grabbing the documents, she skim-read the typed text. Sure enough, Mike had signed a disclaimer, giving his permission for the bailiffs to enter the property if he broke the contract.

'Oi, what do you think you're doing?' Within seconds of Pippa taking the documents in her hand, Mr Heavyset was through the door and standing in the middle of the living room, clipboard in hand.

'I'm sorry, miss, we're just doing our job.' Mr Thin smiled

apologetically at Pippa as he squeezed past her and joined Mr Heavyset. 'We've got a list of items to acquire to pay the debt that Mike Cherington previously agreed to. We'll be as quick as we can.'

'You can't,' Pippa's voice was a harsh whisper. They couldn't. Not her things, not her home.

'Right, let's get a move on with this now. TV, sound system and stereo from this room.' Mr Heavyset tapped his pen against the paper before pointing to the TV.

'Whoa, not the TV. You can take the sound system and the stereo, but I paid for the TV. You can't take that.' Pippa ran to the TV unit, spreading her arms in front of the modest flat screen TV.

'Mike Cherington knew what was on the list when he deviated from the payment plan. Unless you can prove it was bought with your cash solely, then it's ours to take.'

'It's five years old, what do you want me to do? Find a receipt?'

'A receipt will do, miss. If you could just show us proof of purchase then we will have no choice but to leave the TV.'

'I've just told you, it's five years old, at least. Of course, I haven't got a ruddy receipt for it.' Pippa's voice cracked as tears began to stream down her cheeks.

'Then we have no choice but to take the TV.' Mr Thin approached her. 'I really am sorry, we are just doing our jobs and trying to get our client's money back.'

Stepping to the side, she watched as Mr Thin unplugged the TV and lifted it up, carrying it out of the flat. What would she say to Joshua?

'Not that any of this will even come close to reimbursing what our client is owed.' Scribbling on his clipboard, Mr Heavyset hardly graced her with a glance.

* * *

Pippa stood in the middle of the living room and stared at the empty TV unit, the bare bookshelf that used to house Mike's stereo and the wires laying strewn across the floor. Sinking to the sofa, she folded her arms and lowered her head. She breathed in the warmth from the cocoon she had made with her arms. A slow, throaty laugh rose through her and escaped in a croaky bark. At least she could probably cross dusting off her list of chores to do now.

Her laugh turned into loud rasping sobs as she rocked herself forwards and backwards, forwards and backwards on the tatty sofa. What was she going to say to Joshua? How was she going to explain why everything of any value was missing? Why huge gaping spaces jeered at them where their electronics used to be? She certainly couldn't let him know that his waste-of-space father had as good as given their things away.

The chirpy ringtone from her mobile interrupted her thoughts.

'Yes?' Pippa cleared her throat. 'Sorry, hello.'

'Where the heck are you, Pippa Jenkins? I've got a private function to prepare for and I'm a waitress down!'

'Sorry, Mr Bert, I've just had a family emergency to deal with. I'll be there as soon as I can.' Pippa wiped her face with the end of her sleeve.

'You had better be.'

The dial tone hummed in Pippa's ear. Throwing her mobile onto the coffee table, she stood up.

Rifling through her wardrobe, she realised she didn't have another clean set of uniform. Her other one must be in the clean laundry basket, still waiting to be hung up or rewashed.

'Drat.' Pippa shook her coat off, draping it over the end of the bed, and sniffed her armpits. Going into the bathroom, she sprayed deodorant liberally under her arms, reapplied her make-up and ran the brush through her hair. That'd have to do. Slipping her coat back on, she made her way to the front door, trying not to look at the empty living room.

Pulling the front door open, she stepped out, straight into the path of the postman.

'Oh sorry, I didn't see you there.' Pippa looked up and stepped aside.

'No worries. Are you Pippa Jenkins?'

'Yes.' Pippa locked the door and pocketed her keys.

'I'm pretty sure I have a letter here for you.' He shuffled through the handful of letters he was holding.

'OK, thanks. Just pop it through the letter box for me, please? I'm just in a bit of a hurry.' Pippa forced a smile. She really had to get to the bus stop. Buses ran on the hour and the half hour, and it was almost twenty-five past. If she didn't hurry she'd miss the next one and be even later for work.

'Well, it's been posted through recorded delivery so I'll need you to scribble your signature. Yep, here it is.' He held out the letter and waited for her signature.

'Thank you.' Pippa took the brown envelope and scribbled her signature before turning and running down the stairwell, kicking aside the empty lager cans to save herself from tripping over them. At the bottom of the block of flats, she folded the letter and shoved it into her coat pocket before legging it to the end of the road. Turning the corner, she stopped, panting. She held on to the lamppost as she watched the bus turn the corner at the opposite end of the road. 'Drat.'

Catching her breath, she walked the rest of the way to the bus stop and perched on the filthy looking plastic bench. Digging around in her coat pocket, it dawned on her that she had left her mobile in the flat. She wouldn't even be able to ring the restaurant to warn them that she would be even later now.

Pippa nodded at the elderly lady who lived in the bungalow by the park at the end of the road and watched as she shuffled past.

She ran her hands through her hair and looked at her shoes. It was no good, Mr Bert would probably dock her wages for this. And to top it off, if there's one thing he hates more than tardiness, it's lack of communication. She dug her hands in her pockets and rooted around, double-checking that her mobile wasn't hiding under a mountain of dirty tissues and random small toys.

No, it definitely wasn't there. She pulled the brown envelope from her pocket, no doubt it was another late repayment letter for Mike. She probably shouldn't have signed for it, that would probably be used against her in some way. Turning the envelope over, she checked the name on it through the small address window. It was addressed to her. She knew she was behind on the rent, but the council tax and utilities were all up to date.

Pippa patted the envelope against her other hand, should she open it? Did she really need something else to worry about? She didn't have any more money to pay any other bills. She didn't even have enough to replace Joshua's tattered school trousers, let alone pay for the upcoming trip. Maybe she shouldn't open it, maybe she should become one of those people who hid unopened bills in a drawer somewhere.

Then again, she had the darn thing now, whoever she owed money to wouldn't know she hadn't opened it. She may as well face up to it. Pippa tore the envelope open and turned the letter over, holding her breath waiting to see the damage.

She scrunched up her nose, it wasn't a bill after all. Thank goodness. It was official though, it had a solicitor's watermark.

Pippa held her breath, her shaking hands making the words jumble in front of her eyes. It must be from Mike, what if he wanted to fight her for custody? He couldn't, not after leaving them in so much debt. Could he?

Pinching the bridge of her nose, her head thumping, she forced herself to read the letter.

'What?' She reread the letter. Her great aunt had left her a café on the South Coast! But she had passed away months ago, Pippa was sure of it. Her mum had gone to the funeral but Pippa hadn't been able to. Mr Bert had refused to give her any time off and Mike, they had still been together then, had laughed at her when she had said how guilty she felt, not being able to go and give her respects. He had told her to stop whining, that she had only met her great aunt a handful of times in her life, why would she want to go to some stuffy old ceremony full of other ancient pensioners ready to croak it? A shiver ran up her spine, she remembered the argument that had followed as if it had happened yesterday. Mike had shouted so loud at her that Joshua had hidden under his bed crying.

Mike had been wrong, of course, Pippa had wanted to go, she had wanted to meet her great aunt's friends. She may have only met her a few times in her life but they had been happy times, full of happy memories. Her mum, dad and her used to make the journey down to the coast once every year and Great Aunt Kathryn had always made them welcome.

She smiled. One year they had got stuck in traffic. It must have been a bank holiday maybe, and then there had been an accident and the motorway had been closed. Her dad's rusty Escort hadn't turned into the coastal café's car park until at least ten o'clock at night, way past closing time and, in hindsight, probably past Great Aunt Kathryn's bedtime. But, there she had been, sat in the café, smiling at them as they trudged in, tired and thirsty after their nightmare journey. Pippa remembered the mountain of ice cream, jelly, fruit and cream that her great aunt had whipped up for her before they had even taken their coats off. Nothing had been too much of a hassle for Great Aunt Kathryn, she'd always wanted to please everyone. She had been a kind and happy soul.

Pippa reread the letter. It was true. It was there in black and white, or black and off-white cream to be more precise. Great Aunt Kathryn had really and truly left her, Pippa Jenkins, The Little Beach Café of Pebble Road, Seaden Bay. Pippa read on, she had three months to claim the café before it would be auctioned off and the proceeds donated to the local nature reserve.

Closing her eyes, she pictured the gorgeous little café, the rows of freshly baked cakes and a freezer full of every flavour ice cream anyone could ever imagine, or at least every flavour the five-year-old Pippa could dream up of. Yes, it would be a perfect place to bring Joshua up. Walks on the beach, a school so close they could walk through fields to. No more buses or pokey flat. Fresh air. No need to dodge past people smoking weed and drinking at eleven in the morning on the stairwell.

Yes, life at The Little Beach Café would be perfect.

Pippa shook her head. If only life were that simple, jump in the car, or on a bus and train in Pippa's case, and arrive in their new idyllic life. Of course, the reality was so much different. She had bills to pay and a tenancy to keep up. Well no, that was a lie, since Mike hadn't been paying the rent the estate agent had forced them onto a month by month tenancy, no contract. Pippa assumed it was so that they could easily be kicked out if she failed to pay the rent again. But it was still impossible, Joshua had only just started school less than a year ago and had made some nice little friends. She had her job, which she needed to be able to pay the arrears.

Pippa folded the letter, pushing her fingers together to get perfect creases, and slipped it into her pocket. Standing up, she put her hand up to signal for the bus to stop.

* * *

'Please, Mr Bert, it was completely out of my control. I promise it won't happen again.' Her lips pursed as she set her jaw, she was determined not to cry, not in front of him.

'I'm sorry, Pippa, I've given you more chances than anyone else already. I need staff I can rely on, not someone flaky.' Mr Bert lifted his coffee mug to his lips, his peppered moustache collecting droplets of liquid.

'You can rely on me. Please? I need my job. I'm begging you.' Pippa clasped her hands in front of her.

'Pippa.' Mr Bert wiped his moustache with the back of his hand and stood up. 'With all due respect, I need someone who will be there for all shifts. Someone who I can call up at the last minute. With your boy so young, I know that's not possible.'

'You're sacking me because I'm a mum?' Pippa stared at the short, stubby man in front of her and shook her head.

'No, no. I'm sacking you because you've had three previous warnings for being late, or not turning up for work.'

'But I can't help that. I'm trying my best here, things have just been a bit difficult since Mike walked out. You know that.'

'I know, and I sympathise with you, I really do, but at the end of the day, sympathy and favours are not going to run my restaurant for me. I need staff.'

'But please, please, just give me one more chance? I need this job. I need it.'

Mr Bert shook his head and indicated the door. The conversation was over.

2

Peering out of the window, Pippa looked out at the dark countryside, naked twigs scratching the smeared glass of the bus window.

'What did you say, Joshie?' The rain pelting against the thin metal roof echoed around the vehicle making it difficult to hear him.

'When are we getting there?'

'It shouldn't be too much further. Ten, fifteen minutes maybe.' Pippa gripped the backrest of the seat in front of her with one hand and pulled Joshua closer with the other as the bus hit another pothole.

'Here you go, love.' An elderly man passed Pippa one of their bags that must have been thrown from the overhead shelf.

'Thank you, sorry.' Pippa smiled and squeezed the bag onto the pile of bags at their feet. Two suitcases, three strong carrier bags and a bin liner held all of their belongings. The ones they had chosen to bring anyway, the rest of their stuff lay at the flat where she had left them. She'd given the estate agent Mike's mobile number. Good luck to them if he answered. He never had for Pippa. Yes, he could deal with the rest of it. She grimaced at the thought of him, she felt a little guilty leaving everything for him to sort out but then, why should she? After all, he'd left her in the lurch big time, he deserved a little karma.

Pippa looked back at Joshua, singing along to the old portable CD player she'd found in the back of her wardrobe, swinging his short legs back and forth against the seat, and smiled. He'd been so excited to wear 'grown-up' headphones, he hadn't cared that they were bright pink. Using the palm of her hand, she wiped condensation from the window and watched the sheets of rain cascade from dark angry clouds into fields, cattle huddling together for warmth and protection.

The bus broke hard as they came up to another sharp corner on the windy country road and Pippa told herself for the hundredth time that the driver had driven this road hundreds of times before.

It would be so beautiful in the summer, not that it wasn't now. Even with the rotten weather, Pippa could see what a beautiful part of the country it was. She could almost picture her and Joshua walking through the fields, jumping over styles and picking wild blackberries from the hedgerows. Maybe they could even get a dog. Yes, that would be a good idea. It would encourage them to enjoy their new surroundings and make the most of countryside and seaside living. Joshua had always wanted a dog. In fact, so had Pippa, it had been Mike who had vetoed the idea, that and her ridiculously long working hours, of course.

'Can you smell the seaside yet, Joshie?' Pippa pulled the sliver of a window open and took a deep breath, the salty air laced with promise, filling her lungs, the smell of the sea brought inland with the rain. She'd made the right decision to accept Great Aunt Kathryn's café. Not that she'd had any choice in the matter, not after the estate agent had found out she'd lost her job and ended their tenancy. She still owed them money in arrears but they'd set up a payment plan for her. With the income from the busy café, especially with the holiday season not far ahead, all being well she'd be able to clear the debt within a year. Yes, Pippa smiled, she was looking forward to their new start, her chance to make things better for Joshua. To secure a more promising and happier future.

Turning away from the window she looked at Joshua, caught his eye and blew him a kiss. 'We'll go and check out your new school tomorrow, shall we?'

'Will you come?'

'Absolutely! And I'll be taking you to school and picking you up too from now on.'

'Really?' Joshua beamed.

'Really, really.' Pippa had never both taken him and picked him up from school in a single day. She'd even missed his very first class assembly because she hadn't been able to get time off to go and see it. Well, things were going to be different from now on. Yes, she'd have to get the café ready for opening, but then she would pop out to take Joshua to school. The lady who had worked for Great Aunt Kathryn had been as lovely too, maybe she was still working there. Maybe it was her who had been holding the fort since Great Aunt Kathryn had passed away. She definitely wouldn't mind taking care of the customers while Pippa did the school run.

'We're almost there now. Are you excited?'

'Yes.' Joshua bopped up and down and did a little dance in his seat.

Pippa laughed. 'Glad to hear it.'

The bus slowed down as they came into the village, a quaint sign greeted them, telling them that Seaden Bay was twinned with a village in France, not that Pippa could even take a wild guess at pronouncing it.

'Look at the pebbles on the garden walls. We're definitely close to the seaside now.' Pippa pointed to the low pebbled walls marking the pretty little front gardens of the cottages lining the street.

Turning left, they found themselves driving in line with the beachfront, only a path and metal railings separating the narrow road from the sand itself. The white of the waves caught the moonlight as they came bounding up the beach and rolled serenely down again.

The bus pulled to a stop at the side of the road.

'This is your stop, love.' The bearded bus driver twisted around in his seat and indicated Pippa to get up.

'Mine? Are you sure?'

'Yep. You said you wanted the closest stop to The Little Beach Café, right? Well, this is the last stop, the closest a vehicle as big as this is going to get to it.'

'Oh, right, OK.' Pippa stooped down and gripped hold of the bags and bin liner, dragging the suitcases out of the footwell. 'Come on then, Joshie. Let's start our new life!'

Joshua pulled the headphones down around his neck and pulled his hood up.

'Is the café straight ahead?' Pippa paused in front of the driver.

'Almost. If you go to the end of the road, you'll see a pathway worn into the slope of the sand dunes ahead, follow that up and back down and along and the café will be straight in front of you.' The driver pointed ahead.

'Thank you.'

'Just out of interest, love, you do know it's not open any more, don't you?'

'Oh yes. I'm guessing nothing is open at this time of the night in the village.' Pippa grinned as the driver chuckled back to her. Didn't he know that even in the city things weren't open twenty-four hours a day? Well, OK, they were, but she had enough common sense to know that things worked differently in a small coastal village.

The suitcases on their dainty wheels bumped down the bus steps straight into her ankles, slicing the skin. Wincing, she could almost feel the heat of the blood oozing through her socks.

'Which way, Mum?'

'Up here. The driver said there's a path through the sand dunes and it's up there. Here, can you just carry this bag please, Joshie? It's slipping from my fingers.' Pippa drew the suitcases to a stop and let the lightest carrier bag slide from her wrist into Joshua's small fingers. 'Thank you, darling.'

'I'm cold.'

'I know, poppet, but just look at that view,' Pippa called over her shoulder, hoping Joshua could hear her before the wind carried her voice inland. 'It's beautiful, isn't it?'

Joshua glanced towards the beach, holding his fluffy hood back from his face just long enough to see the moonlight illuminating the sand, glinting off of the pebbles sat at the top of the beach.

Pippa had forgotten how therapeutic the sound of the waves crashing onto the beach and being swallowed back by the vast ocean was. She hadn't been to the beach for years. It must have been three years ago, before Mike had started gambling and being all weird, since they had taken Joshua on a weekend break to Southend. He had only just turned two. Pippa remembered him waddling up the beach, his nappy sodden with sea water where he had fallen down whilst paddling and clasping two limpet shells. He probably didn't even remember.

They reached the end of the road and Pippa looked ahead. With the last street light behind her she could hardly make out the narrow pathway leading across the sand dunes.

'It's too dark, Mummy. We can't go down there.' Joshua bit the torn cuticle around his thumb, a habit he had begun since his father's disappearance.

'Yes, we can. One moment and I'll get the torch on my phone out.' Flipping the suitcases up, she pulled her phone out of her back pocket. 'Look, that's better, isn't it? We can see where we're going now.' Pippa held her phone and grabbed hold of the suitcase handles again causing the beam from the torch to shoot up towards the sky. Twisting her wrist at an unnatural angle she turned the phone, her grip precariously loose, and shone it towards the pathway. The light illuminated a bumpy track overgrown with the long coarse grass natural to sand dunes. 'Off we go then.'

'I can't, Mummy, I'm tired.' Joshua looked down at his feet, circling his ankle.

'I know you are, but this is the last stretch of our journey and I'll make you a lovely warm hot chocolate with cream and marshmallows when we get to the café, OK?'

'OK.'

'That's my boy.' She staggered up the curved dune, Joshua gripping onto the sleeve of her coat, the suitcases trundling reluctantly behind them.

As they reached the top of the sand dune, the wind whipped sand in a fury against their faces and Pippa reminded herself that they would soon be in the warm welcoming café of her childhood memories. They would soon be wrapped up under a duvet in bed and then the fun would begin in the morning. They could go and explore their new neighbourhood and go down to the beach to paddle and play before going to visit Joshua's new school. She knew it would be hard work running the café, but with the experience she'd picked up from years of waitressing for Mr Bert and learning some tricks of the trade from the staff who had been running it, she was sure they'd do just fine. The work-life balance here would be so much better than back in London. They would start living again instead of merely surviving.

Taking a deep breath of sea air, Pippa coughed out the sand, she wouldn't make that mistake again. Yes, life was pretty good at the moment. She lugged the suitcases up the slight incline, around a gnarled tree and back down towards the beach again.

'We must be close now, Joshie.' Pippa stood the suitcases up and held out her hand for Joshua, gently guiding him down from the sand dunes. Sweeping the phone's torch left and right it illuminated a wooden sign, slightly leant to the left, with the painted words almost unidentifiable from years of the onslaught from sand being thrown against it in winds such as these. 'Look, there's our sign, "The Little Beach Café"! And look! There's the café!'

They both stood there, Pippa holding on to the phone, Joshua huddled into her side, the wind whipping Pippa's wet hair into her eyes. Jerking her head, she shifted the wet strands of hair from her face. The small squat building stood to their right. It was pale blue just as Pippa remembered but it had seen better days, even from where she stood a few metres away she could clearly see it hadn't been painted for years, decades possibly. The paint was rubbed bare down to the wooden panels in some places and splintered, peeling in strips in others. The large windows positioned for diners to get the optimum sea view were covered in newspaper, curled up at the corners from the sun.

'It doesn't look like what you said it did,' the disappointment rasped through Joshua's voice.

'No, it doesn't. Maybe they've been having problems with the windows though. Let's go inside and take a look, shall we?'

Joshua nodded as Pippa grabbed hold of the suitcase handles again, tugging them across the sand and onto the grey paving slabs surrounding the squat building. First thing in the morning she'd have to come and sweep the stray sand from them, although with this wind she assumed it was a daily and thankless job.

Standing under the small porch, Pippa dug the key the solicitor had sent her from her coat pocket and twisted it in the lock. With a fair amount of pushing, the thin wooden door opened.

'Urgh, what's that smell?' Joshua recoiled back into the onslaught of the rain.

'It smells a bit musty, that's all. Hold on, let me find a light switch.' Pippa felt along the edge of the wall. 'There we go.'

The halogen tube lighting flickered to life baring the inside of the café. Red plastic tables were pushed against the walls, the chairs stacked precariously on top of them. The black-and-white checked floor tiles were dull with dust and the counter at the far end of the room was piled with clear plastic containers, the sort Pippa remembered gazing through at the scrummy home-made cakes underneath. Looking around, she could hardly imagine the scenes from her memory of the warm, friendly bustling café. In contrast, this room looked as though it had been taken straight from a movie set, filming about a ghost town.

'Yuck.' Joshua sidled up to his mum.

'It doesn't look as though it's been open for a while, does it, kid?'

Joshua shook his head.

'Never mind, it won't take much to get it going again, I'm sure.' Pippa swallowed hard. 'Let's go and have a look at the flat upstairs. We'll leave the bags here.' She took a chair down from one of the tables close to the counter and piled the bags on top, circling her wrists before wiping her now dusty hands down the front of her jeans. 'This way.'

They made their way around the back of the counter towards the pale blue door. Pippa remembered Great Aunt Kathryn bustling through, leading them to the flat and showing them where they would be staying for their holiday. She used a second key she had received through the post, its small paper label reading, 'Flat-Beach Café' and pulled the door open. The musty smell was even stronger here.

'I'm not going first,' Joshua whispered and hid behind Pippa.

'OK.' Pippa felt for the light switch and the small hallway was suddenly bathed in bright yellow light, illuminating the mustard coloured walls and the flower patterned brown carpet leading up towards the flat.

At the top of the stairs, Pippa opened a second door, this one glossed dark mustard to go with the walls. The door led straight into the living room, the yellow and brown flowered wallpaper brought back memories of her younger self trying to trace the petals trailing upwards. A brown sofa and matching chair were positioned around a dark brown rug, darker than the tea coloured carpet. A seventies sharp cornered sideboard stood against the far wall in front of the sofa, miniature ornaments of cottages and windmills depicting a village scene. A small old-fashioned boxed television was pushed towards the back of a clunky TV cabinet.

* * *

Pippa ran back downstairs, aware of how nervous Joshua must be feeling left alone in the unfamiliar flat. She pushed the door open into the café and went to grab the bags. She paused, bags in one hand and one of the suitcase handles in the other, she should check that she had locked the front door. However idyllic it seemed to live on the beachfront, she reminded herself that they were still in an unfamiliar village, alone on the beachfront.

Striding across the murky tiles she stopped halfway to the door. She could hear the wind and rain battering against the front window but there was also a different noise, a drip-drip-drip. It sounded more echoey, and closer.

'Mum, can you come up now?' Joshua's call was just audible from the flat above, the shake in his small voice clear.

'One moment, Joshie.'

In the two more strides to the front door, the dripping noise got increasingly louder. Maybe it was from outside after all?

'You're kidding me!' Pippa felt something cold and wet drop onto the top of her head. She reached up and rubbed the palm of her hand across her dark hair. Stepping back, she leant her head back to get a better view. 'Great, just great.'

The cream ceiling bulged in a patch at least half a metre across, the centre hanging lower than the rest which was where the water was dripping from, a puddle laying on the floor below. Pippa shook her head, how hadn't she noticed it earlier? She supposed she'd been too wrapped up in the realisation that the café hadn't been operating for months, if not years.

* * *

Back upstairs, bags and suitcases heaped in the corner of the living room, Pippa made her way around the small flat checking the ceiling for any leaks that could be coming from the roof and seeping downstairs into the café. The ceiling looked fine, it must have been coming from a leak in the small galley kitchen or the avocado green bathroom. She shrugged, at least it was localised and the roof was OK.

3

'Mum, is this OK?' Joshua looked up from the cupboard he was stacking plates into.

'Let's have a look. Yes, that's great, Joshie. Here's another one.' Pippa finished drying a royal blue plate with the checked tea towel and passed it to Joshua.

She plunged her chapped hands back into the hot soapy water, they were getting there. Between them, they'd already washed and sorted three cupboards full of pots, pans, plates and bowls. She'd also submitted a supermarket order of basic ingredients for various hot and cold drinks and sandwiches. Pippa smiled, she was looking forward to devising a new menu, but that could wait, first they'd open and get the customers back in. The quicker she could reopen the café, even just offering the basics, the sooner they'd have money coming in.

'So, what did you think of your new school then?'

'Loved it!' Joshua looked up at Pippa and grinned.

'So did I. Your new teacher was lovely, wasn't she? And the children in your class all look friendly.' They had visited shortly after nine and the headteacher had shown them around. They had walked along the beach and then across two fields to reach the school which had been a complete contrast to the trek through the city they had made a short few days ago to get to his old school. No more squeezing past teenagers, no more belching buses and irritable commuters.

'She was, she had kind eyes, not like Mr Hargreaves who always put everyone in detention. I can't wait to go on the obstacle course in the playground too.' Joshua stood up and came to stand next to Pippa at the sink. 'Did you see the wobbly bridge, Mum? It was massive, wasn't it? And they had a climbing wall!'

'I know. It did look awesome, didn't it?' The school was only tiny. There were only three classes in total; Reception, Years One and Two were taught together and so were Years Three and Four, and Five and Six. In the half an hour they had been there, Pippa had felt more warmth and seen more laughter and smiles from children and adults alike than she had ever witnessed at Joshua's old school.

'Afternoon.' The door to the café rattled open, knocking the small metal bell hanging from the ceiling.

Pippa jumped and turned around. 'Hello?'

'I'm Joe, the plumber.' A well-built man walked in and stood surveying the café. Dropping his heavy tool bag to the floor, he stood with his hands on his hips, his dark blue jeans a stark contrast to his white oil smeared T-shirt.

'Of course.' Drying her hands on the tea towel, Pippa came out from around the back of the counter and held her hand out. 'Thank you for coming out so quickly. I'm Pippa and this is Joshua.' Pippa indicated to Joshua whose head could just be seen above the top of the counter.

'You moved in here?' Joe took Pippa's proffered hand and

enveloped her small hand in his rough calloused one, his handshake strong and firm.

'We sure have. We got here yesterday.' Pippa automatically wiped her hand down the front of her jeans as soon as he released his grasp.

'Right, well, good luck with that then.'

'What do you mean?'

'I mean good luck with getting this place up and running and turning over a profit.'

'It shouldn't be too difficult, it's in a prime position and was always busy.' Pippa set her jaw. Who did he think he was, coming here and speaking to her like that?

'Years back maybe. I'm assuming you've not been into the village recently?' Joe smirked, his pale red lips showing through his dark stubble.

'No, but I remember what it was always like.'

'How long ago was that?' He knelt to his tool bag and drew out a torch, switching it on and shining it upwards towards the damp patch.

'Not that long ago.' Pippa crossed her arms in front of her. She didn't care if he doubted her, but still, how could a perfect stranger be so damn rude?

'You've definitely got a leak.'

'Some plumber you are,' Pippa muttered under her breath.

'I heard that. Can I take a look upstairs?' Joe turned on his heels and headed towards the door to the flat without waiting for an answer.

Pippa nodded at his back and rubbed her cheeks with the palms of her hands, hoping her blush would fade before he looked back. She followed Joe up the stairs and into the bathroom, watching sand spill from his clumpy beige boots. Pippa shrugged, there was no point asking him to take them off now, he'd only retaliate with some smart remark or other.

'Mum, can I have something to eat?' Joshua followed them up the stairs.

'In a minute, poppet.'

'OK.' Joshua stood in the bathroom doorway watching Joe as he, not so carefully, took the panel off of the side of the bath.

'Hello, mate, I'm Joe.' Leaning the plastic avocado bath panel against the wall he held out his hand for Joshua.

'Hello.'

'Why don't you go and get a bag of crisps?' Pippa bit her bottom lip, so Joe could be human after all then. She shrugged, maybe he'd just taken a dislike to her for whatever reason. Maybe she was just being sensitive.

'I need to take a look at these pipes of yours to see where the leak is coming from. I'll be a while so don't feel as though you've got to watch.'

'Right, of course.' Pippa turned on her heels, dragging her gaze away from him, and followed Joshua into the kitchen. That was her dismissed.

'Can I have the last pack of salt and vinegar, Mum? Please?' Kneeling in front of the kitchen cupboard, Joshua twisted around, a bag of crisps in his hand.

'Yes, and then come downstairs with me for a bit and help me, will you?'

* * *

Pulling the last of the newspaper off of the windows, Pippa scrunched it into a ball and threw it in the heap behind her. She turned and looked around the café, her hands on her hips. It was definitely starting to look like a café again now. The low afternoon sun poured in through the now clear, if not clean, windows and glinted off of the red plastic tables Pippa had pulled into place. The crockery, utensils and everything else had now been washed and restacked in the cupboards and the supermarket order would be delivered in the morning. She smiled, they should be able to open in a couple of days.

A tapping on the glass behind her caused her to jump and she jolted around, creaking her neck in the process. Raising her hand to her eyes, she peered into the sunlight. A man's face was pressed up against the glass, his knuckles gently tapping the glass.

'Can I help you?' Pippa swung the door open and smiled.

'Afternoon, I hope you don't mind me hammering on your glass like that, but I had to see for myself. There's been a rumour going around that this place was being reopened by a lovely looking lady, and from what I can gather, the rumours are true.' An infectious grin spread across his face.

Standing aside, Pippa stood aside to let him enter. He stepped inside, water glistened off of his bright yellow waders as he wiped his navy wellies on the cork matting.

'Well, the rumour that the café is reopening is true anyway.' She looked down at her feet and back up into his pale green eyes. She could feel a blush creeping up her neck.

'It's looking good in here. Are you opening in the morning?'

'Thanks. No, probably the next day.'

'Oh, that's a shame. I work on the boats and we've missed having somewhere to grab a bacon buttie after a morning's hard graft. Can I entice you to open for us tomorrow?'

'Well, um, I guess I could do bacon butties and coffee?'

'Brilliant, the boys will appreciate it. Shall I bring them in about ten?'

'Yes, yes. I'll make sure I have the bacon on.'

'Thank you, thank you. I'm Gus by the way and it's a pleasure to meet you.' Gus took Pippa's hand in hers and looked her in the eyes. 'It will be good to get some sense of community going again. Local businesses, supporting other local businesses.'

'Absolutely.' Pippa watched as he left, stopping and turning a few feet away to raise a hand to her.

'What are you grinning about? I'm afraid it's not great news.'

Pippa spun around to find Joe standing by the counter. For someone wearing such clumpy boots, he could sneak up surprisingly quietly.

'I'm opening a day earlier than expected and already have a group of customers waiting!'

'Umm, that wasn't Gus by any chance, was it?' Joe peered out of the window.

'Yes. Why?'

'You want to watch out for that one.'

'Why? What do you mean?' What was wrong with Joe? He had waltzed into the café as if he owned it, taken great delight in telling her the leak was a big problem, and had made it perfectly clear that he didn't believe that she could make a success of this. Not that she was the slightest bit bothered, of course, she hardly knew the bloke, and now he had the audacity to tell her to watch out for Gus, whatever that meant. Gus had seemed perfectly nice. He was polite, which meant he had a lot more going for him than Joe at any rate.

'Just tread carefully, that's all. He's trouble.'

'Right, OK.' Pippa shook her head, there was no point in getting into an argument with him. As far as she was concerned, he could do his job and leave.

'And besides, do you think it's wise to open earlier than you had planned to?'

'It's only a day earlier. And anyway, of what business is it of yours?' Pippa crossed her arms.

'Fair enough.' Joe turned away and Pippa could hear his boots clumping back up the stairs.

Right, if she were going to get this place fit to open by ten o'clock tomorrow morning she'd have to get a move on. She grabbed the window cleaner from underneath the sink and began on the windows adjacent to the door.

It was going to be so much fun running this place. Hard work. She knew that, but she would be doing it for her and Joshua, she wouldn't be working twelve-hour shifts to line Mr Bert's already full pockets. Plus, Joshua could help her in the café or just be chilling at a table while she served. They'd be together, that was her priority now.

The door to the flat slammed shut and Pippa spun around. Joe hefted his tool bag onto his shoulder and made his way to the front door.

'Where are you going? I thought you were going to fix the leak?' Pippa looked behind her, the drip, drip, drip continued, the puddle still expanding on the tiled floor.

'I need parts. I've turned off the water to the flat, so once the water sitting there has worked its way through the plasterboard it will stop.'

'Oh. So, there's no water upstairs at all? What about down here? What's actually wrong?' How would she and Joshua cope without any water upstairs?

'Nope, no water upstairs. Nothing else I could do. The water pipe to the bath is corroded, so I'll order a new one and come back when it's arrived.'

'When will that be? I've got a young son, we need water.' Joshua always used to come home from his old school muddy, or else that's what Pippa's mum would always complain. What were they supposed to do for a couple of days until the part came?

'A week? Two at the most. Your water will still work down here in the café.'

'Two weeks? Are you being serious? What about showers?'

'Look, I don't know what you're used to, but this isn't the city. There are public showers down at the beach a couple of miles away in the next town. If you're not happy with my services, you're welcome to get someone else in.' Joe shrugged his shoulders.

'No, no. Just please hurry them up if you can.' The only other plumber anywhere close had rubbish reviews on the internet. However much Joe annoyed her Pippa knew that he was good at his job.

Pippa closed the door behind him. What an obnoxious man! Pippa shook her head, she'd show him. She *would* open the café up tomorrow morning. She knew she had guaranteed customers already from what Gus had told her. She smiled, she couldn't wait to serve in her own café.

'Mum, when's dinner?' Joshua looked up from his colouring book.

'I'll put something on now if you're hungry. What do you fancy?'

'Can we have macaroni cheese, please?'

'Why not?' Pippa finished cleaning the last of the windows, carefully slipped the window cleaner back into the cleaning cupboard and washed her hands. She'd have to cook down here even though she had wanted to keep the café and their living quarters separate. Never mind, she supposed it wouldn't be for too long. As if Joe had been serious when he'd said the pipe could take up to two weeks to arrive. They might not be in a bustling city centre any more but they hadn't been thrown back in time to the Dark Ages. Pippa was certain he had just been awkward.

4

'Careful you don't get your trousers wet! Roll them up!' Pippa called across the sand to Joshua who had decided that paddling in the sea was of paramount importance on his first journey to his new school.

'OK.' Momentarily stooping to roll his trousers up to his knees he then continued to dance through the shallow water, oblivious when his right trouser leg rolled down to his ankles again.

Pippa shrugged, it would no doubt be dry by the time they got there anyway. She hefted Joshua's blue drawstring bag up higher onto her shoulder and smiled. She had been worried he was going to be nervous about starting, but he had bounded downstairs into the café fully dressed and raring to go before she had even woken him.

'Joshie, we need to go through the fields now, so come and get your socks and shoes on, please.'

'Can we walk this way every day, Mum? Please?' Flinging himself onto the sand in front of Pippa, he held his feet up, letting her dry them with a flannel she'd slipped into her handbag when he'd asked if they could walk the beach way.

'Of course, we can. It sure beats the smelly bus rides back in the city, doesn't it?'

'Yes.' With socks and shoes now on, Joshua ran ahead through the gap in the old sea wall and down the slope onto the narrow track between two fields.

* * *

'Ready?' Pippa looked down at Joshua, now holding her hand. He looked so small in his smart white polo shirt and black trousers.

Nodding, he pulled her through the open iron gates into the playground. Pockets of parents, ninety-nine per cent mums, stood in small groups chatting, watching their children run around and climb on the wooden obstacle course that circled the outside of the playground.

She paused, not sure where to position herself. They'd left with plenty of time to spare, Pippa's plan being to try to encourage Joshua to play with some of the children before he went into class.

'Why don't you go and play football with those boys over there?' Pippa pointed to a group of boys kicking a football against the back wall of the playground.

'No, they look older than me.' Joshua shuffled his feet and looked down.

'How about going and chatting to those children by the wobbly bridge then?'

He shook his head.

Swivelling around, Pippa noticed a mum and a son stood by Joshua's new classroom door. The boy looked nice enough and had a small bouncy ball he was throwing into the air while his mum tapped away on her mobile.

'Follow me.' Pippa let go of Joshua's hand, not wanting him to be singled out for still holding his mum's hand, and strolled across the playground, Joshua jogging beside her.

'Excuse me, please?' Pippa coughed, she never had been good at talking to new people, but needs must.

'Yes?' The woman looked up and tucked a stray strand of long dark hair behind her ear.

'My son, Joshua, is starting in Miss Camberly's class today, is your boy in her class too?'

'Yes. Max, come here. This is Joshua, he's the new boy Miss Camberly told you about yesterday. Why don't you go and play with him?'

Max shrugged and looked down at the small ball in his hand.

'Good idea. Go on, Joshua.' She gently pushed Joshua towards Max and watched as they walked a short distance away and began playing catch. 'Thank you, it's such a worry him starting a new school.'

The woman nodded, smiled and returned to her mobile.

Taking a deep breath, Pippa frowned. She hated small talk but if they were going to make this place a home, she'd have to get to know people too. 'Have you lived here long?'

The woman looked behind her, supposedly checking to see if Pippa were talking to her or the wall. 'All of Max's life.'

'Oh right, that's nice then.'

The woman nodded and then grinned, waving her hands in the air. Pippa watched as two other women walked across to them, ignored Pippa and hugged Max's mum. Taking a step away, Pippa stood awkwardly for a few minutes, unsure if she would be introduced, and then walked away. She shrugged, at least Joshua seemed happy enough playing with Max, who appeared the opposite of his mother and was chatting excitedly to Joshua.

* * *

Pippa smiled, the worry lines around her eyes relaxing and the furrow in her brow smoothing. Cupping her hands against the glass, she shielded her eyes from the glare of the sun. Joshua was OK. She could see him chattering to Max as he hung his bag on his peg. He twisted around and smiled sheepishly at his mum. Pippa waved.

'What do you think you're doing?' A gruff voice behind her startled Pippa and she twisted around, jolting her neck.

'Joe!' Pippa raised her hands to her cheeks, the heat instantly penetrating her skin.

'Got you!' Joe raised his hands in front of him as if to surrender.

'You sure did.' Pippa smiled back, unable to resist Joe's contagious grin, a small dimple gracing his left cheek. Pippa was sure he hadn't even slightly cracked a smile when he'd been at the café, she'd surely have remembered the way it transformed him.

'Is your little boy in Sparrow Class? Or are you trying to determine the PE bag trend of this term?'

'Very funny. It's Joshua's first day today. I was just making sure he was settling in OK. Why are you here anyway? Is there a leak or something?'

'Nope, my lad, Harley here,' Joe indicated to the wooden bridge behind them where a small boy was hanging upside down from the bars sporting a gelled spiky hairdo, 'is in Sparrow Class too. We were just running a little late.'

'As usual, Dad,' Harley called from where he hung.

'Yes, well, we'll be even later unless you stop with your bat impression and get over here before everyone goes into class and we have to go through the office.' Joe tapped on the window.

'Morning, Harley.' A slight woman with a dark brown bob opened the door and waited until Harley had given his dad a high five and slipped through, smiling at Pippa and Joe as she shut the door again.

'I didn't know you had a son.'

'You didn't ask. Are you still hellbent on opening your café today?'

'Yes.' Pippa crossed her arms, why had she been so stupid to think he'd just had a bad day yesterday? That he was actually really human after all? She checked her watch. 'In fact, I'd better get going now. Bye.'

Pippa marched away, aware that he was probably rolling his eyes at her. What gave him the right to judge her? He was just her plumber, he wouldn't even have been into the café if she hadn't asked him to do a job for her. She was hiring him, she was paying him. It was no business of his to judge her the way he did.

As she made her way back to the café along the beach, she took her shoes off and paddled in the shallow waters, her toes sinking into the wet sand as she walked. Gazing out across the ocean, she shielded her eyes against the bright sunlight. It was almost twenty past nine already, by the time she got back she would just about have time for a quick coffee before heating the grill ready for Gus and his workmates. Pippa smiled, she could do this. She could, would, make a success of Great Aunt Kathryn's café. She would make a home here for Joshua.

* * *

Pippa held her shaking hands in the pocket of her apron and plastered a smile on her face. This was it, she could see Gus, followed by about eight other men, walking across the decking towards the open door. Their bright yellow fisherman waders glistening in the sunlight. This was it, her first ever customers to her very own café.

Walking over to the grill, she checked that it was heating up properly and then switched the kettle on. She glanced back at the door, they were almost there. Piercing the bacon packet, she lay the slices onto the grill, sausages on one side, bacon on the other.

'Morning, Poppy!' Gus strode through the doors, a big grin on his face.

'Pippa. Morning and welcome to The Little Beach Café. What may I get you?' Pippa smiled and gently corrected him, a little put out that he hadn't remembered her name. But, hey, she supposed he'd remembered it began with a 'P', that must count for something.

'I'll have a bacon buttie and a mug of your strongest coffee please, Pippa?' Gus winked at her, awakening a flurry of butterflies in her tummy.

'You certainly can.' Pippa smiled as Gus perched on one of the bar stools to the right of the counter. Her first customer and her first sale.

Fifteen minutes later, nine fishermen were sat at the red plastic tables filling up on bacon and sausage sandwiches.

'Hey, thanks for bringing your mates in, Gus.'

'You're more than welcome. It's nice not having to traipse into the centre of the village just to grab a bite to eat at that poncy coffee shop or having to bring a pack up every day.'

'So, what do you think then? Do you think I can get it as busy as it used to be when Great Aunt Kathryn used to run it?'

'She was your Great Aunt?'

'Yes, she left it to me in her will.'

'I hadn't realised, I had assumed you'd bought it.'

'No. I remember coming here as a kid on our holidays. She always had the best choice of ice cream and would let me have as many scoops as I wanted.' Pippa smiled. Her Great Aunt Kathryn had been a kind lady, not just to herself and her family, but she remembered other children coming into the café and Great Aunt Kathryn always giving them an extra scoop of ice cream and piling the sprinkles on until they were almost streaming down the side of the cone.

'She was great, wasn't she? My mum would walk us home this way on the way home from school. We'd be allowed to choose an ice cream or a milkshake in the summer and a hot chocolate with cream and chocolate sprinkles in the winter.'

'I hope I can get this place buzzing again and make her proud.'

'I have every faith that you will.' Gus smiled at her and took her hand. 'Thank you again for such a good hearty breakfast, we'd better get back to the boats now. You'll be open again tomorrow?'

'Yes, of course.' Pippa watched as the men filed out, calling their appreciation, before starting to clear the tables and wipe down the grill.

* * *

'That's great, Joshua. I love the bright blue you've used for the sea on that one.' Pippa reached across the table and pointed to the waves Joshua was colouring in. 'It was a great idea of yours for us to make them instead of sending them to the printers. They go with our home-made and welcoming feel.'

'They do, don't they, Mum?' Joshua grinned and took a slurp of his strawberry milkshake.

'Absolutely!' Smiling back, she sieved through the pile of posters they had already completed. She'd put them up in the village after she dropped Joshua off at school in the morning. Business might be non-existent apart from the fishermen at the moment, but then no one else really knew that The Little Beach Café had reopened. These posters would change that.

'Mum...' Joshua put his pen down and clasped his hands on the table in front of him.

'Yes, poppet?'

'It doesn't matter.' Picking his pen up, he continued colouring the waves.

'What is it? Did something happen at school? I thought you said you'd had a good time and made lots of new friends?'

'I did. I just...'

'Go on...'

'Do you think Daddy will visit us here?' Joshua looked down at the table.

'Well,' Pippa coughed and gritted her teeth. 'I don't know, poppet.'

'Does he know we moved here? What if he tries to visit us at the flat? What if he thinks we're missing? What if I don't see him again?'

Pippa furrowed her brow and dug her nails into the palms of her hands. 'Sweetheart, I know this must be really hard for you. When we left I sent Daddy a message so he knows where we are when he feels ready to visit us.' Dragging her chair across the lino, she pulled Joshua into a hug. He didn't need to know the exact words in the text message she had sent Mike. He didn't need to know the expletives she had used and that she still felt as though she had let him off the hook lightly. He didn't need to know that she had told the spineless coward, his father, that she hoped one of the many companies he owed money to would take him to court. She couldn't bring herself to tell him that she very much doubted he would ever see his father again.

'When do you think he'll be ready to come and visit us?' Joshua's eyes filled with hope as he looked up at her.

'I don't know. I think he probably has a few things he needs to work through and sort out before he can get away to visit.' Pippa kissed the top of Joshua's hair. She swallowed, a lump stuck in her throat. She could deal with the hurt Mike had caused her, just about anyway, but what he had done and was still doing to Joshua, Pippa shook her head. How would he ever come to terms with his father leaving him?

Joshua nodded and wiped his eyes with the sleeve of his school jumper before looking back down at the poster he was colouring.

5

'Morning, Gus. What are you after today? Same as yesterday?' Rinsing the scone mixture off her hands, Pippa turned towards Gus.

'Yes, please. What are you baking there?' Gus leant over the counter, a broad smile igniting his pale green eyes.

'Scones. I'm going to start offering old-fashioned cream teas. I went down to the coffee shop in town yesterday, to check out the competition.'

'What did you think?'

'It was OK. Nice, and there's no way I can compete with them on the coffee and drinks front, so I thought I'd try and make this café into what it used to be. I'll serve old-fashioned, home-made, wholesome food, the opposite of the fancy coffees and pastries that they're selling in town.'

'Good idea! Now you just need to find a way to get the customers in.' Gus drummed his fingers on the counter.

'I'm way ahead of you.' Pippa reached under the counter and pulled out the pile of posters she and Joshua had created yesterday. 'What do you think?'

'Lovely. They're home-made too, I guess?'

'Yep, me and Joshua made them yesterday. I thought home-made-style posters to go with the home-made food we'll be selling. You think they're too childish?' Pippa grimaced. She knew she should have found a printing shop to do a more professional job, but in truth, she just didn't have the spare money. She had her last month's wages and that was it. Mike wasn't paying maintenance and although she should be getting some benefits from the government until this place started paying its way, it had all been suspended to be reviewed due to her change in circumstances. It could be weeks until it got reinstated.

'I see where you're going with them. They're good. Let's have a look through.' Gus shuffled through the stack of posters and held up one with cakes as the centrepiece. 'Now you're talking, these are going to go down a storm.'

'I hope so. I just need to get baking.' How hard could a cake be to make? She'd take a break to serve Gus and the other fishermen and then tackle a cake mixture. She remembered baking them with her mum when she was a little girl. They used to make birthday cakes together for her dad and grandparents. Admittedly, she hadn't made one since. Her mum had always been so excited to make Joshua's that she'd let her be. She'd have to try out a couple.

***

'Not again.' Pippa wiped the back of her hand across her forehead before trying to fish pieces of crushed eggshell from the bowl. The bright yellow cake mixture didn't exactly look like she remembered it had when she'd baked with her mum. Maybe it was because she was using real butter and not margarine?

Anyway, if she could just get rid of the lumps of congealed flour, she was sure it would turn out OK.

'That looks interesting.'

'Drat! Joe, you made me jump!' The metal fork rattled against the ceramic bowl and submerged into the gloppy mixture, eggshell and all.

'Sorry!' Joe chuckled, his dimple visible under a day's worth of dark stubble.

'It's not funny, I've lost my fork now.' Pippa frowned and began fishing out the fork with the wooden spoon. Maybe she'd forgotten to put some ingredient or such in, maybe that's why it looked so gloopy.

'Come here, you've got slime across your cheek.' Joe reached out and wiped Pippa's cheek with a napkin.

'Thanks. It's not slime. It's cake mixture.' Pippa set her jaw and stared at him.

'Of course, it is,' Joe chuckled. 'Sorry, I'm sure it will taste lovely when it's cooked.'

'It will.' She threw the fork into the sink and wiped her hands on the tea towel. 'I do know what I'm doing you know. I did work in a restaurant. A high-end restaurant. Where, I'll have you know, I was very well respected.' Pippa glared at him. There was no way she was going to admit that she used to pull double shifts carting fast food to speckly teenagers trying to impress the opposite sex and stuffy old business people who thought Mr Bert's tacky restaurant was posh enough to bring clients to, but cheap enough on their tight wallets.

'I'm sure you were.'

'Are you here to fix the pipes?'

'Nope, still waiting on the part.'

'Why are you here then? Literally just to poke fun at me?' Folding her arms, she scowled. He really was unbelievable.

'I can't lie that I wouldn't be tempted, but no, just after a milkshake.'

'Umm. What milkshake do you want? I'm trialling a latte flavoured one, if you want to give that a go?'

'Somehow I don't think Harley will fancy a latte milkshake. Plus, I could do without pumping him full of caffeine before his mum sees him.' Joe scrunched up his nose.

'Oh, I thought you meant for you. How is Harley? Has he been to the dentist or something?' Pippa slid the drinks menu across to Joe.

'No, he's just thirsty after walking home from school. Harley!' Joe glanced sideways at Pippa before turning to watch Harley bound in, football in hand.

'Dad, can I have a chocolate milkshake with extra cream, please?' Harley stood on tiptoes and leant his chin on the counter.

'You don't look poorly, Harley. Do you feel better after your walk on the beach?' Reaching up to the shelf on the wall behind the counter, she pulled the chocolate powder down.

'I'm not poorly,' Harley giggled and glanced at his dad.

'We'd best get marshmallows with that, please?' Joe ruffled Harley's hair and slid onto one of the red bar stools at the counter.

'Marshmallows? Right.' Pippa twisted around and glanced at the clock behind her again. Yep, it definitely said 2:15.

'Everything OK, Pippa?'

'Yes, yes.' Looking back at Joe, she shook her head.

The bell above the door tinkled, announcing new visitors. Great, Max and his phone obsessed mum strode up to the counter.

'Afternoon, Joe, lovely to see you and little Harley.' Charlotte patted Joe's arm.

The Little Beach Café

'Afternoon.' Joe shifted on his bar stool and smiled at Charlotte.

'I'll be with you in a moment.' Pippa smiled, so she could be human then. Maybe Pippa had just caught her on a bad day when she'd tried to talk to her in the playground on Joshua's first day.

'We'll be over there.' Charlotte's smile faded and was quickly replaced by a blazing glare as soon as she realised it was Pippa behind the counter. Taking Max's hand, she pulled him towards the table by the window.

Pippa shrugged. 'What time do you make it?'

'Time? It's 3:55. Why? What time does Joshua's club fin...'

'3:55? It can't be. The clock says it's 2:15.' Pippa waved her hands at the clock behind her, knocking the glass and milkshake powder across the counter, a fine brown dusting covering Joe's hands. How could she not have realised? 'Sorry, sorry. I need to go.'

'You go. I'll take care of this place.' Pushing his stool aside, Joe stood up, catching Pippa's apron as she raced to the door.

* * *

'Come here.' Pausing outside the café door, Pippa crouched down, holding her arms out. Joshua ran up to her and she enveloped him, burying her face in his windswept hair and took a deep breath. 'I really am sorry I was so late, Joshie. The clock had stopped and I just didn't realise the time.'

'That's OK, Mummy. At least you picked me up.' Grinning, he twisted out of her arms and pulled the door open. 'Is that Harley? Can I go play with him?'

Pippa nodded and watched him run over to where Harley sat at a table. She pushed the door closed behind her. Charlotte and

Max were still sat by the window, another mum and son had joined her. Max and the other boy, sat playing on their tablets while their mums chattered over a coffee.

Pippa had never been for a coffee with another mum before. It must be nice. She'd missed out on all of that. Mike had been laid off work three weeks before Pippa had given birth to Joshua and had never returned, leaving Pippa with no choice but to be the main breadwinner. She'd not had the chance to make any lifelong friends whilst watching the little ones playing at Toddler Group or even any School Gate friends.

This is what this move was supposed to be about. Time. Time to be around Joshua. Time to take him to school and back. Time to make some friends. To make a home. Instead, she'd failed at the first hurdle. She couldn't even pick her own child up at the right time.

Smirking, Charlotte twisted her heavily made-up face in Pippa's direction.

Turning away, Pippa looked at her feet. She knew she was a failure. She didn't need any confirmation from the likes of Charlotte. She, no doubt, had a husband who worked and provided for her and Max. She didn't have a clue what was going on in Pippa's life.

'Hey, you OK?'

Pippa startled and turned. Joe stood in front of her, her apron around his waist and the sleeves of his thin maroon jumper rolled up.

'Here, come and sit down for a bit. I'll get you a hot drink.' Joe cupped her elbow, leading her to a table by the counter.

She let herself be guided and sat watching as Joe first got Joshua and Harley a hot chocolate and a supermarket muffin each before placing a steaming hot coffee down on the table in front of her and slipping into the chair opposite.

'Why didn't you give the kids one of the cupcakes I had made?' Pippa wrapped her hands around the mug in front of her, the warmth seeping into her skin, slowly warming her hands.

'Have you tried them?' Joe grinned sheepishly and leant across, grabbing a cupcake from the counter and giving it to Pippa.

She folded the retro red and spotty cake case down and took a bite, spitting it back into the case straight away. 'Fair enough. I didn't realise they were that bad. How about the scones though? There's nothing wrong with those. Anyone can make a scone.'

'Umm, I'm sure they can, but maybe you'd been having a bad baking day. I served one and the customer complained it had almost broken her tooth.'

'Oh no! Seriously?'

'Afraid so. Don't worry, I charmed her and gave her a free coffee and she's not going to sue.'

'Let me guess, it was Charlotte, right?'

'Yep.'

Pippa sunk her head into her hands. 'I can't do anything right.'

'Hey, don't be so hard on yourself.' Cupping her chin with his fingers, he gently eased her face up so she was looking at him.

'I'm not. It's true. Look at this place. It's empty apart from the stupid cow from the playground who's probably only here to gloat and revel in my failure.'

'Stop it.' Joe wiped the tears rolling down her cheeks and stood up.

Pippa buried her head back in her hands, listening as he sent Joshua and Harley upstairs to watch TV, enticing them with a packet of crisps each. She then heard him telling Charlotte and her sidekick that he was closing up and offering their children a free muffin for the journey home.

'Here's a fresh one.' Joe sat back down opposite Pippa, sliding a steaming mug towards her.

'Thanks.' She rubbed her face before pulling the hot mug towards her.

'Don't beat yourself up about picking Joshua up late. We've all been there. We've all lost track of time or been caught up in traffic.'

'I bet you haven't been forty minutes late, though?' Pippa glanced up at Joe.

'Well, not forty, no, but it's not your fault the clock broke.'

'I should have realised when you walked in with Harley. I just assumed he'd been to an appointment or something. I didn't... I was almost an hour late to pick my son up. We've hardly been here two weeks and I'm already marked out as the flaky, unreliable mum who puts work before her own flesh and blood.'

'You're not marked out as anything of the sort. You've moved all this way and you're building a new life for you and Joshua. If anything, you'll be marked out as the brave mum who upped sticks to put her son first.'

'I'm not though. I'm still not putting him first. The whole idea of this move was to get out of the grotty flat in the middle of the city and to spend more time with him. But I'm not... I'm not spending more time with him.' She dried her eyes with a napkin. 'Yes, I'm here and he's here, but I'm always working. I'm not giving him any time. Any time with just me and him. Time with him as the focus instead of this place.'

'But you're doing it for him.' Joe reached his hands across the table and took Pippa's shaking hands into his strong steady ones, enveloping them and squeezing just enough to relieve the shaking.

The Little Beach Café

'I never should have come here. I should have stayed where I was. I should have carried on there. At least we had my mum to support us. At least I knew what I was doing. I should never have been so stupid to think I could come to this place. Somewhere I've not stepped foot in since I was eleven, and take over this.' Pippa waved her hand around her, encompassing the café in all its tired glory.

'It's very early days. Be a bit kinder to yourself. You've managed to get it up and running again in less than a week. Not many people would have been able to do that.'

'I didn't have a choice, did I? I didn't know it was going to be in such a state. When I got the letter I assumed it was still open. I should have just turned around and gone straight back. If I'd have begged for my old job back Mr Bert may have relented. What was I thinking?' Pippa pulled her hands free from Joe's grasp and ran her fingers through her hair. She couldn't do this. How stupid had she been? She'd have to move back in with her mum now and Mr Bert probably wouldn't give her her old job back. Well, he might, but would certainly make her beg and then be forever grateful to him for taking her back and exchanging long hours of hard graft for minimum wage. She wouldn't be able to rent again, not after having arrears. Her name would be blacklisted. She and Joshua would forever be living at her mum's house.

'Pippa, stop it.'

The seriousness of Joe's voice tore her away from her thoughts and she looked up, focusing through her tears on Joe's deep blue eyes and slight stubble. 'Sorry, I'm sorry. You probably need to go...'

'No, I don't need to go. But you need to stop being so self-destructive. Look around you. You and Joshua have come to a strange village far away from your family and you've taken on your Great Aunt's old café. You've got to have some faith in yourself. You can do this. You're always telling me how you've worked in the catering industry for years. This will be a walk in the park when you've let the foundations settle.'

'I was a waitress. Just a waitress. I didn't cook. I rarely even cooked at home because Joshua was with my mum all the time.' Pippa let out the sob that had caught in her throat.

'I did wonder. Especially after trying one of your cupcakes earlier.' A low, throaty laugh escaped and Joe's eye's creased with laughter lines.

'Oi, they weren't that bad.' Pippa couldn't help herself but smile.

'No, at least I didn't brave the scones and I still have all of my teeth intact.' Joe grinned, baring his teeth.

'That's very true. I shall continue buying in the cookies,' Pippa laughed. 'I guess at least if any budding comedians come by for a coffee or a cream tea, they'll find the inspiration they need to break out into the big time, a café owner who can't cook. It's just a shame it's actually my life and I've screwed up so dramatically.' Pushing the palms of her hands against her eyes, she promised herself she would not cry again. She would not. 'I just don't know how I'm going to tell Joshua we've got to leave. He's settled into his new school so well and he loves living near the beach. I don't want to be the one who drags him back to the city fog.'

'Give it a while, a few days at least. Things will turn around. You'll see.'

'I honestly don't see how. Plus, the longer we stay the more the bills are mounting up with no possible way of paying them off.'

'Just give it a little while and see how you feel then. You can't make any big decisions when you're feeling like this.' Joe rubbed Pippa's forearm.

'Thanks.' Pippa placed her hand against his. Maybe she'd got him all wrong. Maybe he was one of the good guys after all.

'Right, I had better get going. Harley's mum will be waiting.' Joe scraped his chair back and stood up.

Pippa shook her head. 'Yes, of course. I'll call them down. Thank you again for looking after this place.'

'No problem.'

* * *

Locking the café door, Pippa pulled the stripy blind down and leaned against it. She sank to the floor and pulled her knees up, wrapping her arms around them. Even she had thought she'd last longer than this here. Shaking her head, she tried to dislodge the feeling that she was letting Great Aunt Kathryn down. She'd tried her best, but her best wasn't good enough, as usual. There was no point staying here and getting into more debt because she couldn't provide what the customers wanted, no, deserved. It was a café after all, she needed to be able to provide food. She let out a throaty laugh. It was no good, she'd have to move in with her mum and try to get a job.

Standing up, she looked at herself in the mirror centred above the tables to her left. Her straggly hair was the colour of the driftwood framing the mirror. It too, had seen better days and Pippa should probably scrap it but she had always thought it added a particular charm to the room. Plus, it always reminded her of visiting the café before her dad passed away. He would pick her up and throw her onto his shoulders so that she could see her reflection. They would spend hours competing in Funny Face competitions. Pippa would scrunch her nose up, poke her tongue out and pull her ears forward with her fingers and he would laugh at her, call her his Funny Monster and pull her off his shoulders into a cuddle, tickling her until she could no longer breathe.

She often wondered what he would think of her now. Single mum, running from bailiffs and mounting debt. And now, leaving his grandson at school. She couldn't do this. Any of this any more. Maybe they had been better off in their scruffy flat with her working all the hours. At least she had been able to provide a roof over their heads. If she had continued to slog and show an attempt at paying off the arrears Mike had left them in, the estate agents might have let them continue living there. Plus, at least Joshua had been well looked after by her mum. Her mum had never left him at school wondering where she was for almost an hour. Pippa was certain of that.

As much as she loved this place and the potential it had, it wasn't her who could return it to its former glory. She could see that now. She wasn't up for this. She couldn't. She'd end up running it into the ground whilst running up more debts, her debts this time, not Mike's. She had to do the right thing.

She didn't have a choice.

Pippa laughed. Her green eyeshadow was smeared across her face in true panda fashion, highlighting their puffiness, and her foundation clumped around her nose. She ran the palm of her hand from her chin to her chest, was that only one double chin and not multiple? Yes, she had actually lost weight since being here. It must have been the meandering walks to school across the beach and through the fields. She'd miss those. She always thought of their walks as special Mummy and Joshua time. It had been a million times amazing being able to walk Joshua to school and back. To be able to talk to him about his day, to comment on the wildlife they could spot on the way. They were actually learning the names of the local birds. Joshua had found one of Great Aunt Kathryn's birdwatching books and, for the last week, had been carrying it to school and back, riffling through the pages every time they encountered a different species of bird. It was a far cry from always having their heads pointing down at the pavement, stepping around glass and needles.

She couldn't win. Whatever she did next would carve Joshua's future for him. But she couldn't stay here, her credit cards wouldn't hold much more. It wasn't as though she could look for a job here, rent and childcare around here would be astronomical. Plus, no estate agent would rent to her while she still had arrears at the old place.

No, she'd have to move back and try to make the most of a bad situation.

6

Closing the door to the headteacher's office, Pippa thanked the school receptionist and ventured into the rain. That had been harder than she had thought it would be. When Pippa had told Mrs Havish that they would be leaving in a couple of weeks, she had looked genuinely upset. She had told Pippa how well Joshua had settled in and how his academic achievement had already come on in leaps and bounds in the short two weeks that he had been attending.

Wiping the tears from her face, she knew herself how much Joshua had come on. His confidence in reading, especially, had improved so much. Joshua would now bring his reading book up to her whilst she pottered about in the café and read to her as she did the dishes or served the few customers who dared grace them with their presence. She couldn't once remember Joshua reading to her without her first nagging him to do so when he'd been at his old school. Here, the teachers were able to actually teach instead of constantly dealing with bad behaviour, resorting to crowd control. Maybe it was the fresh air, the fact that the school had more than adequate space for an amazing outside area. Maybe it was the fact that each class had its own Teaching Assistant instead of sharing one between year groups. Pippa didn't know, but she knew that whatever it was, it had definitely had a positive impact on Joshua's education and his mood as well. He had so much more energy now, he was all round a much happier little boy.

Pippa shook her head, their previous life in the city hadn't been all that bad, had it? No, it couldn't have been. Bile rose to her mouth just thinking about returning. She had to force herself to start focusing on the positives. They'd be with her mum again. That positive would certainly outweigh a lot of the negatives anyway. Both she and Joshua missed her. Talking on the phone each night was no comparison for seeing her.

* * *

Leaning her back against the low wall which surrounded the café's patio, she wiped the sand from her feet and slipped her trainers back on. That's another thing she'd miss, the coarse feeling of sand between her toes.

'About time too. I've been waiting over half an hour.'

'Oh, hello.' Pippa twisted around and made her way over to the front door. 'I'm really sorry, but I wasn't planning on opening today so I don't have much in, apart from bacon and sausages for the fishermen when they come by. I can make you a coffee or a tea though, if you'd like?'

'A coffee would be lovely, please? Get yourself one too and then we'll get to work. I'm Carol by the way.' Carol pushed herself up from the metal chair, using her wooden walking stick to help lever herself up and pushed her bobbed grey and white peppered hair behind her ears.

'Nice to meet you, Carol. What are you working on?' Pippa

fished in her jeans pocket for her bunch of keys and unlocked the door, holding it open as Carol shuffled through.

'Not me, we. We're going to be cooking, aren't we?' Carol looked back at Pippa before lowering herself at a table.

'Cooking? Do you want me to make you a bacon buttie?' Pippa pulled her windswept hair into a ponytail.

'He's not told you, has he?'

'Not told me? Who's not told me what?' Pippa went behind the counter and switched on the coffee machine.

'Joe. He didn't tell you I was coming.'

'No, should he have?' Pippa smiled, maybe this was his way of trying to make her feel better after yesterday. Maybe he thought if he sent a few customers her way it would make her feel more successful.

'I'm his mum.'

'Oh, right.' Pippa plonked two cups of coffee onto the table, the steaming brown liquid puddling on the checked tablecloth.

'You don't remember me, do you?'

'No, I... No, sorry, have we met?' Pippa slipped into the chair opposite Carol and mopped the coffee from the table, leaving a smear of brown.

'I used to work for your Great Aunt Kathryn. I remember you coming in with your mum and dad when you were a little girl.'

'Carol? Carol. I remember you made me that knickerbocker glory with the extra strawberries when I cut my knee that time!'

'That's it,' Carol chuckled. She had the same dimple on her right cheek as her son. 'It's funny what we remember from our childhood, isn't it?'

Pippa nodded and took a sip of coffee. 'Thank you for popping in.'

'I'm more than popping in. You have me here every day for as long as you need me.'

'I'm really sorry, but I'm closing up and moving back to London in a couple of weeks. And to be honest, even if I wasn't, I wouldn't have been able to afford to employ anyone.' Pippa scrunched her nose up.

'Oh, I don't need paying, my love. Well, maybe in coffee and the odd hot chocolate from time to time but, no, I'm not here for a job. I'm here to help you. To give you some friendly guidance. Joe mentioned you wanted to return the café to its former glory and offer the home-made cakes and cream teas we used to serve when Kathryn ran this place and so I thought I'd come and share the recipes we used to make.'

'Joe told you about my kitchen disasters yesterday, didn't he?' Pippa pulled at her T-shirt collar as a blush crept its way to her cheeks.

'He may have mentioned it in passing, but please don't be cross with him, he was only worried about you and has your best interests at heart.'

'I am more than a little rubbish at baking, to be honest.' Pippa smiled.

'Ah, so was I when I started working here. Kathryn taught me everything I know, so I'll just be passing the knowledge back to your family. But, if I'm stepping on your toes and you'd rather I didn't, I understand.' Carol patted Pippa's arm.

'Well, I am closing in a couple of weeks, I don't want to waste your time.'

'How about we do a deal then? I'll help you initially for these next two weeks and you don't make any decisions until then? We'll see if we can drum up a bit more business in those two weeks. If we can't, then, by all means, go ahead and go back to your old life, but if we can, you might reconsider?'

'I don't know if I can, I've just told Joshua's headteacher I'm pulling him out.' Pippa stared into her coffee cup.

'Pam Havish? Don't worry about her, she used to bring her own children in here when they were younger. I'll have a word with her and let her know you're not making any firm decisions quite yet.'

'I'm not sure.'

'You've not told Joshua about leaving yet, have you?'

Pippa shook her head. She had planned to wait and tell him as close to leaving day as possible. He'd be heartbroken to leave this place.

'That's settled then.' Carol drank the last of her coffee and stood, picking up both their cups. 'Come on then, let's get started. Let's show those expensive coffee chains how it's done.'

Behind the counter, Carol began taking bowls, measuring cups and spoons from the cupboards, while telling Pippa which ingredients they would need. Soon the counter was covered in equipment and ingredients.

'Right, I think we're ready to make a start now. I thought we could start with a basic Victoria sponge recipe, if that's OK? Have you got any fresh strawberries and cream? Don't worry if you haven't, we can improvise.'

'Yes, I've got fresh cream, and I think, I might have some strawberries I bought for Joshua's pudding upstairs.'

'Perfect. Grab a pen and notebook too and you can write the method down as we go so that you've got it for next time.'

Pippa ran upstairs to the flat and sifted through the bedside table, she was sure she had packed the notebook she had fruitlessly recorded her budget in each month, never being able to make the money going in balance with the money flooding out of the account. There it was, a blue notebook with pale pink butterflies fluttering across the cover.

Strawberries and notebook in hand, Pippa paused in the doorway to the living room and shook her head. Maybe, just maybe with Carol's help this place had a chance to pick up business and survive. Whether it was her and Joshua who could make this happen would take some time to find out.

* * *

'So, when did Great Aunt Kathryn close this place? I've got to admit, when we got here I was expecting it to still be open.' Pippa gently knocked the sieve against the side of the blue bowl and watched as the fine flour cascaded through the tiny holes and coated the butter and sugar mixture.

'Did you? That must have been a bit of a shock then! Let me think...' Carol closed the lid of the flour container and placed her hands on the work surface. 'It must have been five years ago. Ever since your Kathryn's heart op, which must have been ten years ago now, she was weaker than before and struggled to get around so much and then when my Bill passed away five years ago we made the decision to close. We just couldn't cope with all the work any more. Kathryn became so frail and needed time to rest and then when Bill went, I just couldn't cope with it all.'

'Oh no, I didn't realise she was poorly. Why didn't she let us know?'

'I'm not sure, to be honest. She was always such a fiercely independent lady and I think the idea of someone pitying her or mollycoddling her would have sent her running for the hills.'

'I feel awful, if I'd known there might have been something Mum and I could have done. She could have come and stayed with us for a while or something.'

'Don't feel bad, it was the way she wanted it. She wanted to duck out of life here, at her home and near the beach.'

'Even so, if we'd known...'

'No, she was happy right up until the end.'

'I always wanted to come and see her again but being with Mike, Joshua's dad, we just never had the money. I wish Joshua had met her.'

'She knew you would have done if you could have. She was proud of you, you know. Every time your mum rang her, Kathryn would spend days chatting about you to anyone who came in. Telling them she had a niece who worked in a posh restaurant in the city.'

'I was a waitress, just a waitress.' Pippa stared at the flour-dusted mixture in the bowl.

'Yes, a waitress dealing with those jumped-up people that I would imagine would go into a restaurant in the city. I don't know how you did it. Can't stand people like that.'

'Most of them were nice enough, there were only a few regulars who thought they were better than everyone else.'

'Even so, she was proud of you. She didn't much like that Mike of yours, though. And when your mum told her he had finally left you, well, that was the only time I ever heard her swear.'

'Really?' Pippa smiled. She couldn't imagine her Great Aunt Kathryn swearing. 'Why did she leave me the café? Do you know?'

'I think she wanted someone to carry on her legacy, to keep the café going.' Carol looked up at Pippa. 'But don't worry, she'd have understood completely if you want to go back to London.'

'Umm, I know she would. She was one of the kindest people I've known. I just don't know. My heart wants to stay, I just don't see how it's possible at the moment. It's eating up money I don't have, and if I don't start making a profit I'm not going to be able to pay my credit cards that I'm living on back.' Pippa shook her head. She had to face reality at some point; this was, and always would be, just a pipe dream.

'Let me help you. Let me show you how to bake and together we'll get this place turning a profit over. Wait and see.' Carol patted Pippa's floury hand.

'I hope so.'

'We will. By the way, I've asked Joe to pick Joshua up from school so we can work through. I hope that was OK?' Carol took the bowl from Pippa, held it under her arm and whisked, magically turning the sloppy yellow mixture into fluffy pale mountains.

* * *

'Hi, Mum.' Joshua and Harley ran into the café, Joe trailing behind them.

'Umm, something smells amazing!' Joe piled book bags, lunchboxes and coats onto one of the tables and strode up to the counter. 'Wow! Something looks amazing too!'

'Oi, hands off!' Laughing, she swiped Joe's fingers away from the huge Victoria sponge decorated with strawberries and cream. 'Thanks for picking Joshua up.'

'You're welcome. It looks as though my mum's kept you busy today. Where is she?'

'She's gone home. Yes, she's been amazing. I don't know whether to thank you or slap you!' Pippa smiled.

'Thank me, please! The boys have already worn me out by racing me along the beach all the way home.'

'Seriously, thank you. I was so angry with you when I found out you'd been gossiping about me, but now, well, I'm grateful that you did because look at everything we baked today.'

'I didn't gossip about you.' Leaning his forearms on the counter, he looked into Pippa's eyes. 'I would never gossip about you. I was just worried that you'd throw the towel in on this place without giving it a real chance.'

'Why would you care though? You've always been so critical of me and the fact that I was trying to get the café going again. Why the sudden change of heart?'

Joe shook his head. 'I'm sorry if I've come across that way.' He leant across further and took a deep breath, ready to say something else.

'Mum, can we have some of that cake, please? We're starving.' Joshua and Harley peered above the counter.

'Of course, you can.' Scrunching up her forehead, she looked away from Joe. Had she done something to annoy him? 'Do you want some hot chocolate too?'

7

Taking a deep breath, Pippa filled her lungs with the warm, salty sea air. This was as good as a million miles away from her old life in London. The air was not only laced with the unmistakeable seaside smell but was also pungent with hope, just as it had been that first night they had arrived.

Since Carol had begun helping her, Pippa had allowed herself to dream again, allowed herself to fantasise about how her and Joshua's life could be if they were successful in bringing more customers into the café, at making more, no some, profit.

It had only been two weeks and already the promise of home-made cakes and cream teas were enticing customers to venture in. Even the smug marrieds from the playground had begun using the café as their meeting place for coffee and cake on a Tuesday and Thursday, much to Charlotte's disgust, Pippa was sure, although she always seemed to perk up a bit when Joe happened to come in.

Standing still, she looked out to sea, the tide drawing the water up further inland. The white horses gently galloping towards Pippa's feet. Stepping closer, she let the warm water wash over her skin and curled her toes into the wet sand. She didn't want to leave. She couldn't imagine going back to London now, not after having a taste of this.

She missed her mum terribly and she knew Joshua did too. That was her only pull towards London now. She had been a massive part of their lives. On a week by week basis Joshua had probably spent more time with Pippa's mum than he had with her, so it was understandable that he missed her so much. Still, it was hard to see him cry for his nana, especially when there was nothing Pippa could do to help. Plus, if she was scathingly honest, it made her jealous and even more determined to put her all into making the café a success so it could be her, Pippa, who Joshua wanted at night. She wanted to fill that hole she had missed out on for so long thanks to the crushingly long hours she had worked in London.

Walking further into the sea, she let the shallow water lap at her ankles. She had no right to feel jealous of the bond between her mum and Joshua. Pippa knew she wouldn't have been able to provide a roof over Joshua's head if it hadn't been for her mum looking after him. Still, she was determined to try her best to change their stars. Her baking skills were more than marginally better than they were two weeks ago before Carol intervened and offered her time and skills. There was hope.

She dropped one of her flip-flops into the water. Bending down, she scooped it out and shook it dry. Her mum had promised to visit soon, she was just waiting to get some holiday time agreed at work and then she'd come down to visit.

'Pippa!'

Turning, she swept her hair away from of her face. 'Hi, Joe.'

'Are you on your way to pick up Joshua?'

'Yes, I'm not planning on being late again. Not an hour late at any rate,' Pippa laughed. 'Your mum's watching the café for me.'

'That's good then. I've got some great news for you!'
'Oh yes? What's that?'
'The part has come to fix your leak.'
'You mean I'll actually be able to have water upstairs now? I'll be able to get a drink without having to trek downstairs into the café in the middle of the night?'

Joe looked down at the sand at his feet. 'Sorry it's taken so long.'

'It's OK. I'm only joking. Well, half joking anyway, it *will* be nice to have water upstairs.' Pippa stole a sideways glance and nudged Joe's shoulder.

'I know.' Joe grinned back and pointed to the sea foaming at her ankles. 'Can I come in?'

'Of course.' Standing still, she let the warm water lap around her ankles as Joe slipped off his trainers and socks, rolling up his jeans.

'It's nice and warm.'

'You sound surprised. Don't tell me you don't usually paddle?'

'I haven't for a while, I've got to admit. So, my mum said that you were doing well with your baking.'

'She said that?'

'To be honest, I've noticed she's still got her teeth so I'm assuming you're improving.'

'Oi, I'll have you know I made a more than edible Victoria sponge this morning which didn't even dip in the middle when I got it out of the oven. Well, not that much anyway.' Pippa kicked and splashed water up Joe's leg.

'You'll be sorry for that!' Joe laughed, splashing her back.

Running ahead, Pippa laughed as Joe caught up with her and held her by the elbow, nudging her further into the sea.

'OK, OK, I'm sorry,' Pippa giggled as the sea lapped further up her legs.

Laughing, Joe twisted her around to face him. Pippa looked into his eyes and placed her hands on his forearms.

The shrill tone of Joe's phone rang, breaking the moment between them. Dropping her hands, she stepped back as Joe reached for his phone.

'Sorry,' Joe mouthed to her and turned, walking up the beach speaking into his phone.

Shaking her head, she stared into the horizon, the sea growing a deeper blue the further out it reached. What had just happened? Or what would have happened if Joe's phone hadn't rung? Pippa wrapped her arms around her and smiled. After a rocky start, Joe had been lovely to her, and to Joshua. He was a natural with Joshua, he really was. Of course, Pippa knew it was probably only because Harley was in the same class and Joe was glad of a new friend for him.

But, no, she was sure she wasn't imagining it, Joe had gone above and beyond to help Pippa. He had stepped in and looked after the café when she had rushed off to pick Joshua up when the clock had stopped and he'd sat and talked to her. Actually spent time talking to her and listening. When had anyone listened to her properly before? Apart from her mum, of course. It had been a long time, a really long time. And then there was the fact that he'd talked his mum out of retirement to help her get the café back to turning over a profit.

* * *

Leaning against the side wall of the playground, Pippa could see Charlotte and her clicky friends gossiping in front of the classroom doors, waiting for the bell to ring and the doors to open.

However much she tried to focus on the other parents in the playground, her eyes kept twitching involuntarily towards the gate. Where was he? Where was Joe? If he wasn't careful, he'd be late.

The shrill drill of the bell rang out and Pippa jerked her head back towards the door. Smiling, she watched the children bound out, filling the playground with shouts and laughter. Joshua and Harley came out side by side, deep in conversation.

'Hey, Mum.' Joshua ran towards her, threw his book bag at her feet and scuttled off towards the wobbly bridge.

She watched as Harley wove in and out of the swarms of parents and children and made his way to the back of the playground. He ran the last metre or so towards Joe who must have just sneaked in, jumping into his arms before wriggling out of his grasp and hugging the person standing next to him. Pippa narrowed her eyes, trying to get a better view. It was a woman, slim built with short bobbed dark hair. Who was she? She hadn't seen her before.

Joe looked across and raised his hand towards her. Pippa spun around, a deep blush creeping rapidly up her face. He'd spotted her watching him. Who was that woman? She was beautiful, whoever she was. Gulping, she realised it must be Harley's mum. How stupid had she been, thinking that Joe would ever take a second glance at her? His ex was stunning, not just plain stunning, but amazingly just-stepped-out-of-a-magazine stunning. Drab, frizzy-haired Pippa stood no chance.

'Come on, let's get back to the café,' Pippa called as she approached the bridge where Joshua and another boy were intent on seeing who could jump the hardest.

'Aw, can we just play for a bit, please?'

'No, sorry Joshua, but Carol is watching the café. But we can have a paddle along the beach.' Holding out her hand, she waited until she felt the warmth of Joshua's hand in hers and led him quickly through the school gates, keeping her head down as they passed Joe.

* * *

'Come on, Mum, race you to the sea!' As soon as they had climbed over the wooden style from the field, Joshua slipped off his shoes and ran towards the water, his black school shoes knocking against his side as he held them, swinging his arms to increase his momentum.

Plastering a smile on her face, Pippa half-heartedly jogged down to the water.

'Do you think Harley and Joe will pop by after school for their milkshake? If they do, can me and Harley play football on the beach with Joe? Please, Mum?' Joshua called over his shoulder towards her.

'I don't know, Joshie. They might not be coming by today.'

'But they always do. If they do, can I?'

'Maybe. Just wait and see.' She watched as Joshua retreated a little way up the beach and sunk to the ground, scooping handfuls of damp sand into a mound in front of him. It was true, Joe had been in the café almost every day for the past couple of weeks. 'What are you building?'

'A castle. But not the normal boring sandcastle everyone builds. It's a castle in the sky. Look, here are the clouds around it.' Joshua used his index finger to draw swirling clouds around the foot of his mound. 'And when you stand in the turret, the big big tower which will go here,' Joshua pointed to the front of his mound, 'you'll be able to see everything for miles and miles and miles.'

'Wow, that sounds fun. Do you think you'd be able to see the dolphins and sharks way out at sea?'

'Yes, but that's not what it's for.'

'What's it for?' Pippa knelt down beside Joshua and his cloud castle.

'It's so I can see Nana.' Joshua lowered his voice so that Pippa had to lean in close to hear him. 'And Daddy.'

'Oh right, well that sounds like a magic castle then, doesn't it?' Laying her arm around Joshua's shoulder, she pulled him close and kissed him on the head. 'I spoke to Nana today, she's going to try to get some time off work to come and see us in a few weeks maybe. And she wants you to ring her when we get home. She wants to hear all about your day at school.'

'OK. What about Daddy? When can I see him?' Joshua trailed a finger in the sand and wrote the word 'Dad' next to the foot of his cloud castle.

'I don't know, poppet.'

Joshua pulled away from Pippa's hug and stood up. 'I need to get some pebbles for the windows.'

Standing up, Pippa walked back into the shallow water. She swallowed the bile rising to her throat, did Mike realise what he was doing to his son? Did he even care? Probably not, he had always been selfish. When Joshua was born, Pippa had hoped fatherhood would change him but he'd still gone out down the pub with his mates most nights, dragging himself in after midnight. He'd perfected his timing so that he came back just when Pippa had finally managed to get Joshua off to sleep, waking him with his drunken rantings, slashing any hopes Pippa had of getting a few hours' sleep before her next shift at the restaurant.

Of course, Joshua didn't remember any of this, he'd been too young. He was still too young to make sense of any of it, only that he was here with Pippa and not his dad.

Looking out at the ocean, she watched as a ship in the far distance chugged its way towards the estuary in the town further along the coast. How selfish had she been for even thinking for a small moment that she could have feelings for Joe and, laughingly, that he might feel the same way. Men were all the same, they'd up and leave at some point in the future and cause all this pain, which was still there and still alive even after all this time. Kicking at the water as a wave curled its way towards her, Pippa bashed her toe on a pebble. Yep, that just about summed up her life at the moment. There was no way she could ever put Joshua through that again. No way. Yes, it still hurt her but for Joshua, it wasn't just about losing Mike, it was losing that person who was supposed to love him unconditionally, forever.

Joe might seem like one of the good guys but he already had form, he had split from his wife, Harley's mum. He was capable of letting people down, just like Mike. No, the best thing Pippa could do for Joshua, and herself, was to become independent, rely on no one and make their own happy memories.

* * *

'Hello, Joshie. Did you have a good time at school?' Carol threw the tea towel she was using to dry the dishes over her shoulder and welcomed Joshua with a hug.

'It was OK. Can I go watch TV, Mum?'

'Of course, you can. I'll bring you up a snack in a...' Before she had a chance to finish her sentence, Joshua had turned on his heels and ran up the stairs, the door to the flat banging shut behind him.

'Has he had a bad day?' Carol returned to behind the counter and began wiping the sides down.

'I think school was OK. He was happy enough when he came out. It was on the way home his mood changed. We walked along the beach and he stopped to build a sandcastle, only it wasn't a normal sandcastle it was one in the clouds so that he could see his dad.'

'Oh dear, love. That must have been hard for you to hear.' Carol patted her shoulder.

'It's just so unfair on him.' Pippa shook her head. 'It just caught me unaware that's all. Because he hadn't mentioned him for a while I stupidly thought we were getting on with our new life and, I guess, if I'm honest, I had hoped Joshie was starting to forget about him.'

'I'm afraid I don't think a child ever forgets a parent, however awful that person has been. But he'll move on, he'll start to think about him less and then one day he'll realise that he has all he needs right here with him already.' Carol placed a coffee, chocolate milkshake and a muffin on a tray in front of Pippa. 'Now, off you go upstairs and spend some time with your son.'

'Are you sure?'

'Of course, I am. He needs you more than I do. Now go so I can serve these customers.'

Pippa smiled and looked behind her, sure enough, Charlotte's perfect gaggle of school run friends were coming towards the door. Picking up the tray, she hurried up to the flat letting the door close shut behind her as she heard the bell announce the arrival of the smug marrieds.

* * *

Twenty minutes later, snuggled up on the sofa watching cartoons with Joshua, Pippa relaxed.

'Are you OK now, Joshie boy?' She kissed the top of his hair, his head resting in the nook under her chin.

'I'm OK.'

'Good. Daddy does love you. You know that, don't you?' She felt Joshua nod his head. 'And if you ever want to talk to me about him you can, OK?'

'Yes. I don't want to though. I know Daddy will come and see me soon. He's just busy that's all. Sam at school has a busy daddy too and he's fine with it.'

'Does he?' Smiling, Pippa was glad Joshua had found someone going through the same thing as him. Maybe Pippa could meet up with Sam's mum. Get to know her a bit, it would be nice to be able to talk to other people in the same situation.

'Yes, his daddy works on an oil rig. He's coming back for a while next month. Sam and his mum are going to throw him a massive party to welcome him home. Can we do that when Daddy comes home?' Joshua twisted and faced Pippa.

'We'll see.' Biting her bottom lip, she cursed Mike under her breath for the hundredth time that day.

* * *

'Hi, sorry to startle you, but my mum let me in.'

'Joe! Is Harley here? Can we play? Mum, can I go and play with Harley?' Joshua jumped off the sofa and ran out of the door.

'OK, just make sure you stay in the café,' Pippa called, hoping he'd hear her. She stood up and smoothed down her top. 'What are you doing here?'

'I've come to fix the leak. I got the part this morning. I told you, remember?'

The Little Beach Café

'Right, yes. Thanks. About time really.' Pippa strode out of the living room, Joe catching her by the arm as she passed him. Frozen to the spot, she looked down at Joe's gentle hand lying on her forearm.

'Are we OK?' Joe looked her straight in the eye.

'Of course.' She averted her eyes. 'I must go and help your mum with the dinnertime rush.' As she made her way down the stairs towards the café, Pippa could feel Joe watching her and she reminded herself it wasn't her who was in the wrong.

* * *

'Right, I'm off now. I'll see you in the morning and we're going to perfect scones tomorrow.' Carol smiled as she wrapped her thin floaty scarf around her shoulders and picked up her handbag.

'OK, lovely. Thank you again for everything.'

'Don't be daft, dear, it's a pleasure. Just try to cheer that grumpy bear up for me before you send him on his way, won't you?' Carol pointed towards the ceiling.

'What makes you think I can change his mood?' Pippa grumbled as she clattered plates and ice cream sundae dishes into the hot soapy water filling up the sink. The dishwasher was full, and she needed a distraction.

'He normally comes back from here in a happy mood.'

'I think he has other things on his mind rather than ice cream and milkshakes.'

'You may be right, ex-partners can be trying at times, but give it your best shot to take his mind off her, won't you? I don't want to have to have to listen to him sulking when he pops in for his dinner.'

Pippa forced herself to smile back and returned to scrubbing strawberry sauce from the dishes. So, it had been his ex then. He had certainly looked happy enough when he was with her. Maybe they were going to try again or something. Pippa shook her head, it wasn't her worry.

'What can I get you?' Pippa held a large smile on her face as she turned to Charlotte and her son.

* * *

'Mum, I'm bored.' Joshua sidled up behind the counter as Pippa finished wiping it down.

'I thought you were playing with Harley.'

'No, he went ages ago.' Joshua started tapping the side of the coffee machine.

'Don't do that, please. What do you mean, he's gone? He's not gone off without his dad, has he?' Pippa looked around the café.

'No, Joe went too. He asked me to tell you he's fixed the pipe.'

'I didn't see them go. Why didn't he come and tell me himself?' What was he playing at?

'You were busy serving and he didn't want to disturb you.'

'I see.' Pippa rubbed her jaw. She understood. 'Let's lock up and go upstairs now, shall we? You can have your first shower here!' It had been a nightmare not having water upstairs. Luckily, Carol had come to the rescue and let them use her shower instead of the communal ones at the beach, but it would be lovely now they wouldn't have to trek across the village every evening.

'Do I have to?'

'Yes, you do. Then we can have a snuggle on the sofa and watch a cartoon.'

'OK.' Joshua trudged upstairs.

8

'That's it, you're doing well. Just try not to get so much flour over yourself or me.' Carol held Pippa's hand over the sieve and guided it back to the middle of the mixing bowl.

'Sorry.'

'It's OK. Your mind seems to be wandering. Everything OK?'

'Yes, of course.' Pippa smiled and steadied the sieve, the white flour cascading down into the bowl, a small mound forming in the centre.

'Good morning, Joe.'

Jerking her head up, Pippa looked towards the door, the bell still tinkering to announce Joe's arrival.

'I need to go to check on Pebbles.' Carol untied her apron and hung it on the hook by the flat's door before patting Joe's arm on her way out.

'Hi, you OK?'

'Yes. You? Who's Pebbles?'

'My mum's cat.'

'Oh right, she's never had to pop out before.' Pippa finished shaking the flour into the bowl and lay a tea towel over it.

'I think it was to give us a bit of space.' Joe slid onto a stool, leaning his arms on the counter.

'Why would we need space?'

'I think I may have been a bit rude yesterday.'

'Yes, you were. You didn't even come to tell me you'd finished fixing the leak, I had to hear that from Joshua.'

'Sorry. You were busy serving though.'

'Hmm. It wouldn't have hurt you to wait or just to have called out.'

'I was an idiot. Sorry. I just didn't get very good vibes off you when I went up to the flat. I guess I thought you were annoyed with me for some reason.' Joe tipped out the salt shaker and ran his index finger through the white crystals. 'Did I?'

'Did you what?'

'Did I annoy you?' Joe looked up. His deep blue eyes staring into Pippa's.

'Well...' What was she supposed to say? That she thought they'd had 'a moment' and then he'd got a call and ran off to his ex? Was she supposed to say that seeing him with Harley's mum, who was everything Pippa wasn't, made her feel jealous? 'That's annoying me.' She tore her eyes away from Joe's gaze and looked pointedly at the salt spread out on the once clean counter.

'Sorry.' Joe gently swept the crystals across the counter into his other hand which he cupped just beneath the surface and threw it over his left shoulder. 'Oh, sorry, that probably didn't help, did it? It'll still be you sweeping it up. Although, at least it might give me some luck for this conversation.' Joe smiled sheepishly.

'You guessed it.' Despite her best efforts to keep a straight face, Pippa grinned back.

'Look, I am sorry. I was enjoying our walk. It was lovely to spend some time with you, just you. And I know I must have seemed rude rushing off like that.' Joe held her gaze. 'It was Harley's mum ringing to say that she was in the village and wanted to pick Harley up.'

'Right. It's OK, I understand.' Pippa ran her index finger over the last of the salt crystals remaining on the counter, gently dragging them into a tiny mound of her own. She shook her head, maybe she had overreacted. It was just the way he had been with his ex, all smiley and cheerful, and the way he had been with her, running off so quickly from the beach with no explanation and being in a major sulk when fixing the leak.

'I know I was all moody with you when I came to fix the leak. Me and Harley's mum had just had a bit of a disagreement and, well, I wasn't in the best of moods. Then, when you were off with me, I just... Anyway, sorry.' Joe stroked Pippa's hand with his thumb.

'It's OK. I had no right to be cross at you. I'm sorry too.'

'Shall we start again?'

Nodding, Pippa smiled. 'Do you want a coffee?'

'Go on then. We should have time for a quick drink before collecting the kids.'

* * *

'Now, where were we when we were rudely interrupted yesterday?' Joe paused, the foam of the sea lapping at his ankles.

'About here?'

'Come here then.' Joe gently tugged on Pippa's hand, pulling her into his arms.

'Have we got time?' Pippa looked down at her feet. She hadn't kissed anyone since Mike had upped and left. Even then, they hadn't kissed for ages, not properly. It had either been a peck on the cheek as she left for work or a drunken snog between the moments he stumbled through the front door until he collapsed on the sofa. His warm rancid breath making her want to heave and his wandering hands giving her the creeps. What if she couldn't remember how to kiss someone? What if she was rubbish? Did her breath smell?

'There's always time for a kiss.' Joe put his index finger under Pippa's chin and gently tilted her head back so that they were looking into each other's eyes. 'Is this what you want?' Joe's warm breath clouded Pippa's nose. She breathed in the earthy smell of their earlier coffee.

Nodding, she closed her eyes. Even with the million reasons why she shouldn't racing around in her head, she did. The warmth of Joe's lips found hers. Surprisingly his lips were smooth and soft, a stark contrast to the callousness of his hands. They stayed still, lips locked for a few moments before pulling away. Pippa smiled and buried her head in the crook of Joe's shoulder as he wrapped his strong arms around her.

'Was that OK?' Joe stepped back, still loosely holding Pippa's waist and smiled, his dimple appearing on his cheek.

'Oh, yes.'

'Good, because there's more where that came from.' Joe pulled her close to him again, his lips landing on hers.

* * *

Standing in the playground, the skin on Pippa's arm tingled, almost feeling how close Joe stood.

'Hi, Joshua, how was school?' Pippa asked, her question falling on deaf ears as Joshua threw his book bag at her and tore off towards the wobbly bridge, Harley a short distance behind.

'What are they like?' Joe dived to catch Harley's book bag as it came hurtling towards him.

'You would think they were never allowed on that thing at playtimes, the speed at which they leg it over there after school every day.' Pippa bent to pick up Joshua's book bag which had landed at her feet. 'I think I'm going to have to practise my catching skills at this rate.'

'Here, I think this flew out.' Joe picked up a piece of paper, looked at it and passed it to Pippa. 'You should get a stall.'

'What's that?'

'The Spring Fayre. You could serve cake and drinks. It had a really good turn out last year. I think you pay a tenner or something for the stall and then you get to keep anything you make. You'll earn loads. Plus, it'd be a great advertisement for the café.'

'I don't know, I don't think I'm confident enough to do something like that.' Pippa scrunched up her nose.

'What do you mean? You run the best café in town. Members of the dreaded scary public go in there all the time now.' Joe teased her.

'Very funny. You know what I mean though. It'll be busy and I won't have the counter to hide behind.'

'No, but you'll have a table to hide behind. Plus, surely the goal is to actually get the café to be busy and turn over a decent profit?'

'Well, yes, I guess so. It is. I do want the café to be busy. You know I want it to be like it was in its heyday.'

'There you go then. I'll keep an eye on the boys while you go round to the office and book a table.'

'What if it rains?'

'Then they'll move the tables into the hall.' Joe laid his hands on Pippa's shoulders and rotated her to face the school office.

'How will I get everything ready for it? I'll need to bake extra, and close the café for the day. I'll lose money.' Wringing her hands together, she looked back over her shoulder. She wasn't ready for this.

'Most of the village will be at the Spring Fayre anyway, you won't lose anything. Go on, no more excuses, this will be good for the café.'

'What if people don't like me?' Pippa grimaced. She knew it sounded feeble, but Mike had always put her down and teased her because she didn't have any friends. What if it was her and not the fact that she'd lost touch with them because Mike hadn't used to let her meet up with them? Whenever a social event which involved her friends had come up, he'd always said it was a waste of money and that they should spend time as a family instead of going out with other people. The fact that he'd always had money for going down the pub and getting wasted with his mates hadn't entered into it.

Joe stepped towards her, his mouth to her ear, his voice barely a whisper. 'How could anyone not like you?' Stepping back again, he raised his voice. 'This could be your chance to change your stars, as you call it.'

Pippa smiled and reluctantly headed towards the office. He was right, it could be the perfect opportunity to get word around about the café and to let people know they were a real competition to the chain coffee stores in the centre of the village.

* * *

'You OK, loves? Did you boys have a good day at school?' Carol greeted them from behind the counter at the café.

'It was fun, Grannie, we started practising for the Maypole Dance in PE today.'

'Ooh lovely, Harley. I can't wait to see that.' Smiling, Carol stroked her finger against his cheek.

The Little Beach Café

'Yes, we're going to be doing it at the Spring Fayre.' Harley grinned back.

'Fantastic. I do like the school's Spring Fayre!'

'Not only that, but Pippa has something to tell you about the Spring Fayre too, don't you, Pippa?' Joe put his hand on the small of her back and gently pushed Pippa forward.

'I do. I've booked a stall for the café.'

'That's a great idea.' Carol clapped her hands together. 'We can show off what we're offering here. Get some of those chain store coffee drinkers back here.'

'That's what Joe said. He said it would be good for business.' She smiled at him.

'It certainly will be. Now, let me get you two boys a milkshake and then maybe Joe will take you out for a kickabout on the beach while us girls write up a plan of action?'

* * *

'Did you sort things out with Joe earlier?' Carol placed two steaming lattes on the table and sat down opposite Pippa.

'Yes. Thank you.' Pippa felt the warm blush creep rapidly up her neck and looked down at her mug, the milky froth bubbling on the surface.

'Good, good. He was like a bear with a sore back when he came for dinner last night. At least he should be in a better mood now.' Carol smiled. 'Now, for this Spring Fayre, what do you think we should offer? The drinks we can serve up will be limited if we're on a pitch outside because we won't be able to plug the coffee machine in or anything, but we can use a couple of big urns to keep the water hot. I'm sure the old ones will be in the storeroom still.' Carol indicated behind her. 'Mind you, we'll have to test them to check they work still.'

'Yes, I hadn't thought of that.' Pippa wrote *Spring Fayre Action Plan* in bubble writing at the top of her notebook and underlined it. 'I guess we could ask for a table in the hall and then we'll be able to offer all our different coffees, but then most people will be outside if the weather's nice, won't they?'

'I think it'd be better to be outside, to be honest. We'd be in the thick of it then. Last year when I went along with Joe and Harley, most of the stalls were outside and the teachers had set games up for the children too so there were a lot of parents milling around. The perfect time for them to grab a coffee and a slice of cake, if you ask me.'

'OK cool, so we'll just offer normal coffee and tea and maybe hot chocolate then as the hot drinks?'

'I think so. We could always get a large menu printed to hang at the front of the table so people can see what they can get here back in the café?'

'Ooh yes, that's a brilliant idea. I'll ring round some printers to see if I can get some quotes.' Pippa wrote *'printers – menu'* on the notepad and circled it, drawing a large star next to it.

'What shall we sell for the children to drink? Again, we can't do milkshakes but we could offer flavoured milk if we take some cool boxes.'

Pippa tapped the pen on the notepad. 'Or we could offer free squash. If we're lucky it will be a nice day and the children will want a drink. Then when they get to our stall their parents may be tempted by the cakes and coffee?'

'I like your style of thinking. You're turning into quite the businesswoman, aren't you?' Carol smiled.

'Not quite.' Pippa laughed and shook her head. 'But, if we're lucky, we might just make some sales off the back of the free squash. Plus, if we keep everything at a reasonable price people might think about coming to the café in the future.'

'Perfect. Now, what cakes shall we do?'

Half an hour later, they had a list of the cakes they would need to bake nearer the time and had also decided to offer Cream Teas at a special price, tea, scones, butter, jam and cream included.

* * *

'How's the planning going?' Joe came into the café holding the football in his hands followed by Joshua and Harley, sweat trickling down their faces.

'Good, I think. I'm actually quite excited by the idea of it now.' Pippa smiled, tucking the pen in her ponytail, an old habit from her days as a waitress. 'I bet you boys are hungry, aren't you? Shall I see if I can rustle up some spaghetti Bolognese for dinner?'

'Can Harley stay for dinner then?' Joshua jumped up and down in excitement.

'Did you want to?' Pippa looked up at Joe.

'Go on, you may as well. It'll save you both eating me out of house and home later.' Carol patted Joe's arm and pulled Harley onto her lap, kissing the top of his forehead. 'Yuck, you're all sweaty.'

'Dad, please?'

'OK then. As long as you're sure you don't mind?'

'Brilliant. You'll stay too, won't you, Carol?' Pippa looked across at Carol who was holding Harley on her lap with one hand and drinking the last of her now cold latte with the other.

'No, thank you though, but I've got to get back to Pebbles. She's been at home on her own a long time now, bless her.'

'OK, if you're sure.' Pippa glanced across at Joe who rolled his eyes.

'Right, off you jump, Harley, I'm off home now. You be a good boy now and eat all of your veg for Pippa, won't you?'

Harley slid off Carol's lap and stuck his tongue out pointing his fingers down his throat making a gagging action.

'Oi, you! Don't be cheeky,' Joe chided.

'Why don't you boys go upstairs and watch a bit of telly before your dinner? Take the weight off your feet while your old parents make dinner, ay?' Carol patted Harley and Joshua on the heads before saying goodbye and leaving.

* * *

With Joshua and Harley safely upstairs, Joe leaned down and kissed Pippa on the lips. The tingle that ran across her skin, told her that she wanted more and she stood up into his embrace.

'You're gorgeous, you are. You know that, don't you?'

Pippa swatted the compliment away and pulled back, going behind the counter to begin making dinner.

'What can I do to help?' Joe joined her.

'You can peel some carrots, if you like.' Pippa indicated to the fridge, pulled open a drawer and handed him the peeler. 'Oh no, I've not even put the closed sign up yet.'

'I'll do it.' Joe went to the café door. 'After the Spring Fayre, you won't just be able to forget like that. You'll have loads of customers trying to get a last drink or cake out of you before they go home.'

'Let's hope so. Thank you for pushing me into booking the stall. If I hadn't done it straight away I probably wouldn't have.'

'You're very welcome. My skills of persuasion do some good at least.'

* * *

'What do you say, Harley?'

'Thank you for having me and thank you for dinner.'

'You're very welcome, Harley. Thank you both for staying.' After watching them make their way down the beach, she closed the door and pulled the latch up to lock it. 'Time for bed now, Joshua. Why don't you go upstairs and start getting ready while I finish cleaning up? I'll be up in a few minutes.'

'OK. Thanks for letting Harley and Joe stay for dinner. It was fun. Can they stay again another day?'

'Maybe. Now up you go.' Shooing Joshua upstairs, she began clearing the dinner dishes. Now they actually had water upstairs in the flat, they really should get in the habit of preparing dinner and eating upstairs.

* * *

Ten minutes later, Pippa double-checked the front door and followed Joshua up to the flat.

'Joshua, are you ready for bed yet?' She popped her head into his bedroom half expecting him to be playing with his cars rather than getting changed. 'Where are you, poppet?'

Going through to the living room, Pippa leaned against the doorframe and smiled. Joshua had dropped off to sleep on the sofa, still in his sandy jeans and T-shirt, curled up in the foetal position, thumb in his mouth.

'Oh, Joshie,' Pippa whispered under her breath. Gently, she lifted his legs and slid onto the end of the sofa, laying his legs back across her lap.

Joshua had been right, it had been lovely with Joe and Harley staying for the evening. Joshua had been in his element having another child to play with and it had been lovely having another adult to talk to. The fact that the adult happened to be Joe, had made it even better. Pippa smiled and hugged herself.

Maybe things would work out with Joe, maybe they would have a future together. Pippa shook her head, she really shouldn't let herself daydream like this, they had only kissed for the first time today. They hadn't even been on a date together. But he was lovely, perfect even. He was kind, thoughtful and seemed to actually care and want the best for Pippa and Joshua. Why else would he have encouraged her to book a stall at the Spring Fayre?

Leaning over, she stroked Joshua's cheek, his skin warm under her thumb. Most importantly, Joshua got on really well with him. And being a single parent too, Joe knew the obstacles they both faced. Yes, things could definitely be perfect.

Sliding out of her cocoon, she carried Joshua into his room.

'Night, night, sleep tight, Joshie.'

* * *

In the kitchen waiting for the kettle to boil, Pippa shook herself, she was being daft and thinking way, way ahead of where things actually were. Yes, her and Joe got on really well and definitely had feelings for each other, that much she was sure of, but it was silly to let herself get ahead of herself, even if for the first time in a very long time she actually felt a connection with someone.

9

'How are you doing with that Victoria sponge over there?'

'It seems OK. There isn't any mixture coming off on the knife when I put it in so that means it's cooked, right?' Pippa looked over her shoulder at Carol, took the cake tin out of the oven and stood up.

'That's right. Umm, looks lovely, pale but golden.'

Laying the cake tin on the counter, Pippa moved the cupcakes off of the cooling rack and tipped the cake tin upside down. Mentally crossing her fingers as she tapped the bottom.

'There you go, perfect.' Carol smiled as the cake fell to the cooling rack.

'First time for everything.' It was the first cake she'd managed to bake from scratch herself that hadn't fallen apart or sunk. 'We're doing well though, aren't we? After you've done that one, we've just got to bake the scones, a carrot cake and a lemon drizzle and then ice them.'

'Yep, if it stays this quiet in here too we should be finished by early evening and ready for the Spring Fayre tomorrow.' Carol beat the rich brown mixture peaking in hills in the blue ceramic bowl she was cradling in her arm.

'What's that noise?' A shrill tone rang through the café. 'Is that your mobile?'

'Mine? No. Maybe. No one ever usually rings me on that thing though.' Carol put the bowl down and searched through her fabric flower print handbag. 'Here it is.'

'I'm just popping upstairs,' Pippa whispered and softly closed the door to the flat behind her. She needed to put Joshua's school clothes from yesterday in the wash anyway. The café was empty so Carol could talk in privacy there.

* * *

Pippa looked at the clock above the mantelpiece in the small living room. It had been fifteen minutes. She tiptoed down the stairs and popped her head around the door to see if Carol had finished her call.

'Carol, is everything OK?' She hurried over to Carol where she sat at a table by the window clutching her phone in one hand and a scrunched up piece of kitchen roll in the other.

'It was my sister. Well, no, it wasn't, it was a nurse from her local hospital. She's had a fall.'

'Oh no, is she OK?' Sitting down next to her, she took Carol's shaking hand in hers.

'No, yes. I don't know. She's cracked her hip or something, I think. I'm not too sure, the line was pretty bad. The nurse said that she'd hit her head and was suffering from a concussion too.'

'How long will she have to be in the hospital for? Did the nurse say?'

'I think it depends on how bad her hip is. The nurse said they were waiting for an X-ray or scan or something.' Carol took one of the napkins tucked in the cutlery holder in the middle of the table and patted her eyes.

'Why don't you go and visit her?'

'I think I might need to. I feel awful for leaving you the day before the Spring Fayre though.'

'Don't worry about me. You need to think of your sister. Why don't you give Joe a call and let him know what's going on?'

* * *

'Mum, can we have some more chocolate milkshake, please? And what time is dinner?' A lock of Joshua's brown hair poked up above the counter as he clambered onto one of the stools.

Pippa looked up from her mixing bowl, smiled and tucked a loose piece of hair that had escaped from the extremely messy bun on the top of her head. 'Yes, of course. Let me just finish this and I'll get you both a milkshake. I'll do you a spot of dinner in a bit. OK?'

'OK, thanks.' Joshua jumped down and ran back to Harley who was sat at the table in front of the window drawing.

Stirring the gloopy pale mixture, she bit down on her bottom lip. She could do this, she was determined. Carol had given her specific instructions on how to make the lemon drizzle cake before Joe had taken her up north to visit her sister, and Joe had promised he would be back as soon as he had dropped her off, although that probably wouldn't be until late evening at best.

'Service, please.'

Pippa twisted sharply around, stood at the counter was Charlotte, her smug lips pursed together and the cosmetically tanned skin on her forehead crumpled around the bridge of her nose.

'Sorry, I didn't see you there.' Pippa rubbed the side of her neck, it felt as though she'd pulled a muscle when she'd twisted. 'How can I help you?'

'Can I have a top-up? And make it hot this time.' Charlotte pushed her coffee mug across the counter.

'Certainly.' Smiling, she took the mug. 'I'll bring it over for you.'

Resisting the urge to stick her tongue out at Charlotte's retreating back, Pippa got a clean mug and stabbed the button on the coffee machine. For someone that clearly disliked her, Charlotte spent an awful lot of time in the café. After Gus and the rest of the fishermen, Charlotte was the most regular customer they had. Pippa was sure she only came in to see her fail.

Resisting the urge to spit in Charlotte's coffee, she duly took it over to where she was sat at the back of the café.

'Here you go. Enjoy.'

Charlotte waved Pippa away, barely glancing from her phone screen. Pippa didn't dare ask where her perfect son was, probably at some super expensive and elite club or something. If the amount of time Charlotte spent sat alone in the café scrolling through her phone was anything to go by, then Max would end up in the *Guinness Book of Records* as the child who attended the most afterschool activities.

'You're welcome.' Pippa mouthed as she went over to Joshua and Harley, and ruffled Joshua's hair. 'How're your drawings coming along, boys?'

'Good, we've stuck all these pieces of paper together to make one huge picture.' Joshua spread his arms as wide as he could. 'Can you see what it is?'

'That's a good idea.' Tilting her head to the right, she tried to work out what scene the pictures depicted. 'Ooh, very good.'

Joshua grinned before returning to the serious business of completing the picture, his tongue sticking out in concentration.

Back behind the counter, she took a deep breath and leaned against the cupboards surveying the disorganised disarray of clutter. There were two full bowls of a pale mixture, both discarded, one too lumpy, the other too runny, a puddle of slimy liquid had dribbled down the side of one of the bowls forming a puddle on the counter, which would no doubt begin to weave its way down the cupboard doors. The plastic tubs of flour and sugar that she had so lovingly decanted packets into before opening the café, lay empty and abandoned on their sides.

'You'd better hope there's not an undercover health and safety inspector in the village today.' Charlotte twisted her coffee mug in her hand as if inspecting it.

'Well, no. I'd better hope not.' Pippa turned and grimaced. Could she ban people from the café, as they do on TV soaps? Taking the coffee mug from Charlotte's hand Pippa smiled. Unfortunately, Charlotte spent far too much money in here that without her custom Pippa worried the whole thing would collapse around her. 'Do you want to settle your bill?'

'Unless you want to let me have it for free?'

Pippa searched Charlotte's stern face for an indication that she had just attempted to crack a joke and laughed.

As Charlotte strode out, the small bell above the door tinkled to announce her departure while Pippa scrunched up her nose and collected the coins Charlotte had thrown down onto the counter.

'Mum, can we have dinner now? We're starving!'

'Yes, yes OK.' Pippa unravelled her hair and turned her back on the mess. 'Let's close the café and go upstairs for some dinner.' After dinner, she'd get the boys settled in front of a film and sort the mess out before starting on the lemon drizzle cake for the third time.

* * *

'How's it going? How's Harley been?' Joe closed the café door behind him, shutting out the cool night air.

'He's been fine. I didn't know what time you'd be back, so Joshua leant him some PJs and I made a little bed up in Joshua's room for him. They're both asleep.' Pippa took Joe's coat from him and pulled out a stool at the counter. 'You look shattered. Take a seat while I get you a coffee. How's your mum and your aunt?'

'I am. The traffic on the motorway was a nightmare on the way back. I think I must have gotten caught up in the commuter traffic from London.' Sliding onto the stool he wiped his brow with the back of his hand. 'Mum's fine. She was a bit shaky, but I waited until she was settled in at my aunt's place before I left. We got there too late for visiting times, but she'll get a taxi to the hospital in the morning.'

'Must have been a shock for her, getting that call I mean.' Pippa placed a steaming mug of coffee in front of him.

'Yes, I think it was. Thank you for having Harley.'

'You're welcome, he's been no trouble.'

'How is the prep going for the Spring Fayre tomorrow? You look as though you've got everything under control.'

'Umm, you wouldn't have said that about four hours ago when the counters were covered in the discarded cake mixture and I was rocking in the corner.'

'My mum feels really bad for letting you down. And I feel bad too, for talking you into this, thinking my mum would be here to help you.'

The Little Beach Café

'Don't worry. It can't be helped, and I'm a big girl anyway. I need to be able to handle these things.' She patted Joe's hand.

'Is there anything I can help you with now?' Twisting his hand around, he clasped Pippa's in his.

'If you really want something to do, you can decorate these cupcakes while I make the last batch of scones?' Pippa dried the blue ceramic bowl which had been drying on the rack.

'OK, I'll give it a go.' Rolling his sleeves up, he joined Pippa behind the counter. 'Are you ready after these?'

'Yes, well almost, I just need to get the tea, coffee, squash and cups together and ready. I've given up on the carrot cake though. I've baked two already and both had to go in the bin.'

'Fair enough, it looks like you've got plenty here anyway.' Joe looked around the small kitchen area, tins of cakes were stacked in a corner while the three cooling racks were filled with cupcakes. 'So, how are you feeling about tomorrow?'

'Honestly? I'm petrified,' Laughing, she tried to cover up the serious tone in her voice.

'Why? What have you got to be worried about?' Turning, he looked at her, the icing bag in hand.

'Seriously? Loads of reasons. What if no one comes to my stall? What if people don't like the look of my cakes? Or worse, don't like the taste of them? What if I poison someone?' Pippa grimaced, yes, she was joking but only half joking, poisoning someone through her baking was the prime subject and cause of the nightmares she'd been having recently.

'Your cakes look amazing. I'm sure they'll taste amazing too. You've learnt so much in the past few weeks about baking from my mum, you'll be absolutely fine. You've come a long way since you attempted to break Charlotte's tooth with one of your scones.' Joe pointed the icing bag at Pippa and chuckled.

'Oi, you promised you'd never speak of that incident again!' Grinning, she poured sugar into the bowl.

'And why on earth would people not flock to your stall when you have these on offer?' Joe swept his arm around the kitchen area, indicating the cakes and scones.

'I'm the new one though, aren't I? The outsider in the village. I've seen the way the other mums look at me in the playground, and the way the smug marrieds whisper when I walk past.'

'Now, you're definitely being paranoid. People may have been looking at you, gossiping even, when you first came to the village, but that would only have been out of sheer nosiness at who had come to open the café. And now, if they still do, which I very much doubt, it will be due to the lack of available village drama for the masses to talk about. Plus, they're most likely jealous that you've been brave enough to follow your dreams and take a risk while they stay at home tending to their lazy husbands and dearest children.'

Throwing a tea towel at him, Pippa grinned. 'Now, you're just taking the mickey. Honestly, you watch tomorrow, they do talk about me. And the way some of them stare at me makes me wonder whether I grow two heads when I go out in public.'

'You need to chill out. Not to mention take that massive chip off your shoulder. I know what you think they are thinking and you're completely wrong.' Joe folded the tea towel in half and flung it over his shoulder.

'What do you mean? I don't have a chip on my shoulder! I can't believe you said that!' Crossing her arms she scowled. The jokey atmosphere in the café suddenly turning chilly.

'You do. You think they're staring at you because you're a single mum, don't you?' Joe walked over and took Pippa's hand. 'I don't mean it as an insult. I felt the same way when me and

Harley's mum split. I thought everyone was looking at me and gossiping.'

'I have been a single mum for a while now, you know that, don't you?' Pippa pulled her hand away and leaned back against the counter.

'I know, but coming to a new place, this place, a small village where everyone generally does know everyone else's business. Single parenting is a lot less common than it probably was in London simply because the general population is a lot smaller here. I'm not saying there aren't narrow-minded people here, there are; we probably have more than our fair share of narrow-minded people living here if the truth is to be known, but that's not why they're staring at you.'

'I just don't feel accepted here, I guess. That's all. And for your information, I do not have a chip on my shoulder about being a single parent.' Turning around Pippa picked up an egg and smashed it against the edge of the mixing bowl.

'They're just curious, that's all. The playground parents are like that. Believe me, I've seen them stare and gossip at all the newcomers to the village, it's not just you and it's certainly not because you're a single parent. You know those women who hang around Charlotte? You must have seen the way they flock to her and hold on to her every word?'

Pippa nodded, her back still turned.

'It wasn't like that when she first came here. They gave her the steely stares and whispering behind hands treatment as they do to you.'

'Really? I assumed she'd been here forever?'

'No. I remember Harley was in nursery when she and her husband moved here. I think they were from Devon or somewhere, but wherever they were from the point is it took her a good few months to settle and be accepted by the other playground mums.'

'I didn't realise that. She always looks as though she's always been in the centre of the group.'

'That's my point. This village may appear prickly to outsiders, but once they've accepted you, you'll become family.'

'Umm, I'm not sure about that.' Twisting around, she looked back at him. Maybe he was right, maybe she did have a chip on her shoulder about being a single parent. Sometimes though it was difficult not to have. After she and Mike had split up the few friends who had still invited them out for drinks or get-togethers despite Mike's issues had shrunk away, it seemed that they either assumed that she'd feel uncomfortable around the happy couples, or more likely, her single status would make them feel uncomfortable. Pippa shook her head, did she even want to be accepted into the coven of playground mums?

'Of course, we could always give them something else to gossip about.' Smiling, Joe stepped closer towards Pippa and cradled her face in his hands.

'We could indeed,' Pippa mumbled as his lips met hers.

'Is this what you want?' Joe leaned back and looked into Pippa's eyes.

'Yes.'

With her hand in Joe's, Pippa let herself be guided upstairs.

10

'Did you want the water heater thing in the car too?' Joe popped his head through the front door to the café and called to Pippa who was gathering the last of the cake tins.

'You mean the urn? Yes, please. Here, Joshua, can you grab that pack of napkins from the counter please?'

'This one?'

'That's right, poppet. Thanks.' Cake tins in hand, she led the way out of the café, around the back and up to the driveway where Joe's car was parked.

'Here you go.' Joshua handed Pippa the napkins which she slid into the boot between the cake tins.

'Great, thank you. Right, Joshua, Harley, you two jump in and pop your seatbelts on, I'm just going to go and lock up the café and then we'll get a wriggle on. Are you both all excited to perform your Maypole Dance?'

'Yes!' Harley scrambled into the back of the car closely followed by Joshua.

* * *

'Are they both in the car ready?'

'Yes, ready and excited.' Pippa slid her arm around Joe's waist as he picked up the urn from the back of the stock cupboard.

'Hey, you.' Straightening up with his arms wrapped around the large metal cylinder, he kissed Pippa on the lips. 'And how are you feeling?'

'Petrified, but I'm trying to focus on being able to watch Joshua in the Maypole Dance. I missed his first school assembly because I couldn't get the time off work, so I can't wait to see him perform and to see how he's getting on with his classmates too.'

* * *

'How is everything? Are you happy with your plot?' Picking up a cupcake, Mrs Havish examined it before placing it back on the cake stand.

'Yes, it's great, thank you.' Had she just had her stall and cakes inspected? She had heard that Mrs Havish could be a bit of a perfectionist, was that why she had put the cake back and not eaten it? Were her cakes not good enough?

'You're welcome. These look lovely. I'm sure you'll be very busy.' Mrs Havish smiled before making her way to the next stall, a Tombola.

'That was high praise indeed.' Joe lifted his eyebrows.

'Mum, Mum, can we have a go on the Hook-a-Duck? Please?' Joshua bounded up, bringing himself to a stop inches away from where Pippa had balanced the lemon drizzle cake.

'Careful. Yes, when the fayre opens.'

'How long have we got? We've been here ages.'

'No we haven't.' Pippa checked her watch. 'They'll open the gates in another five minutes, why don't you go and play on the obstacle course until then?' She returned to rearranging the stall for the seventh time since she'd unpacked. Was it best to have the bigger cakes at the back and the cupcake stands at the front or did they hide the bigger cakes? Pippa bit down on her bottom lip, there was so much to think about.

'OK.'

'Joe, does this look all right? Do these cakes look squashed up? Can you see the scones from the front? Are you sure the sign telling people that the kids' squash is free is big enough?' Pippa twisted the cupcake stand around again, hoping the ones that had the most icing on were on show. Yes, she'd leave the cake stands at the front, the colourful icing of the cupcakes might entice people to buy.

'It all looks great. Stop worrying.'

'I can't help but worry. I've got a lot riding on this. Maybe it's too soon, maybe I shouldn't have signed up for this in the first place.' She wrung her hands in front of her. It was too soon, she still had so much to learn from Carol. What had she been thinking? She'd always lived by the old adage of 'walk before you run'.

'Too late. Smile, here come your first customers.'

'Hello, would you like to buy any cakes? Or how about a cup of squash for your little girl? The squash is free.' Plastering a smile on her face, Pippa told herself this was no different to the waitressing work she had been doing for the last nine years. She pushed the thought that this was probably make or break for her and Joshua's future at the café to the back of her mind.

'Would you like some squash, Josie?' The woman smiled at Pippa and took her purse from her bag. 'Can I get a squash and three of those cupcakes, please?'

'Certainly.' Pippa poured the squash, her hands shaking so much that the pale purple liquid ran down the sides of the plastic cup. 'Sorry, you're my first customer.'

'Thank you.' The woman took the cup and small cardboard

box of cupcakes. 'Josie, run over there and tell Daddy we have cupcakes.'

'Well done,' Joe breathed into Pippa's ear and stroked her forearm.

'Careful, someone might see.' Pippa glanced over to where Joshua and Harley were swinging upside down on the bars.

'Sorry, I really enjoyed last night.'

'So did I.' A slow grin spread across Pippa's face despite herself. 'We just need to be careful around the boys.'

'I know.' Joe stepped back and held up his hands. 'Is this far enough?'

'Very funny.' Scrunching up a paper bag, she threw it at him before turning to her next customer. 'Hello, how can I help you?'

* * *

'Mum, Mum, it's almost time for the Maypole Dance! We've got to go to our classes and get ready now.' Joshua rushed up to Pippa, his eyes glistening. 'You'll watch it, won't you?'

'Great! Come here.' Pippa pulled Joshua into a hug and kissed the top of his forehead. 'Of course, I'll watch it. I wouldn't miss it for the world. I can't wait. I'm proud of you, Joshie.'

'What for?' Joshua twisted around in Pippa's arms.

'For joining your new school and for settling in as well as you have. For everything.'

'Mummmm, I need to go.'

'OK, poppet, off you go. Enjoy yourself.' Straightening up, she watched as Joshua and Harley ran towards their classroom door. He seemed so much happier and more relaxed here than the old dingy school he had begun his education at.

* * *

Slipping the money bag into her pocket, Pippa joined the crowd of parents standing at the edge of the playground. The crowd naturally semi-circled around the Maypole.

'You OK? How's the stall going?' Joe joined her, placing the palm of his hand in the small of her back.

'Good thanks, half of the lemon drizzle cake has gone already so it turns out I can bake one even if it takes me three attempts.' Grinning, she turned to Joe. 'Did you have a good wander? What are the other stalls like?'

'OK, lots of games for the kids, obviously. There's another cake stall too.'

'Oh no. What's it like?'

'It's OK. Nothing compared to yours, of course.'

'Right, OK.'

'No, seriously. It's not a professional stall, it's just a group of local mums selling some home-made cakes and cookies.'

'I thought there was only going to be one cake stall. I remember Mrs Havish telling me that when I signed up. She said that they make sure they don't have stalls in direct competition with each other.' Local mums? How is that going to make her look? She'll still be the outsider, but now she'll be viewed as the outsider who tried to outdo local mums in a bake-off at the Spring Fayre. She'll never fit in here. Who had she been kidding? Why had she let Joe make her believe that this would be the turning point? That she'd be accepted once the playground parents had gotten to know her?

'I should think poor Mrs Havish was pushed into letting them set the stall up. It's Charlotte and her group of friends, so at least they're not from another café or coffee shop or anything. Look... here they come.' Joe pointed to the stream of excited children walking and skipping out of their classroom doors. 'Look, there's Harley and Joshua.'

'Oh yes.' Pippa used her hand to shield her eyes from the sun. Charlotte? Why on earth would she have wanted to run a cake stall? She'd known Pippa was coming today. She'd seen her bake the cakes and scones. Only yesterday she'd been in the café nursing her usual coffee by the window and Pippa had seen her glancing towards the kitchen area where Pippa had been baking numerous times. Had she been spying? Is that why she'd been spending almost every day in the café for hours at a time? What was her game?

'Don't worry about Charlotte and her wingmen, they're harmless. Forget about it and enjoy the Maypole Dance.'

Shaking her head, Pippa tried to push all thoughts of Charlotte out of her mind. She was here to watch Joshua dance and Charlotte. No, no one, was going to spoil that. It was the first time Pippa had been able to watch Joshua perform with school and trying to work out what Charlotte was playing at would have to wait until later. Waving at Joshua, she caught his eye and gave him the thumbs-up. She took a mental picture of the grin that spread across Joshua's face as he spotted her in the audience and promised herself she'd never forget the expression on his face.

Tapping her foot, Pippa watched as Joshua and Harley weaved in and out under the long ribbons hanging from the tall Maypole, skipping around their dance partners. Joshua's face flushed as his group paused and let the other half of their class skip under and through the ribbons they were holding until the brightly coloured fabric streams had been woven into a plait down the Maypole.

After coming forward to take a bow, Joshua and Harley's class ran to the side of the playground as another class took their places around the Maypole. Wiping her eyes, Pippa gave Joshua another thumbs-up.

'Are you crying?' Joe stared, the hint of a laugh thick in his voice.

'No.' Pippa turned away and pulled her hair across her face.

'You are. Here have this.'

Pippa took the tissue and wiped her eyes. 'Thank you.'

***

When the dancing was over and the children had been freed to run back to the Spring Fayre, the throng of doting parents, grandparents and friends slowly dispersed back into the huddle of stalls and games. Joshua skipped ahead towards the stall as Pippa followed.

'You were amazing, Joshie. You're such a good dancer.' Pippa ruffled his hair as he reached for a cup of squash.

'It was fun. Can I start going to a dance club? Owen goes to one. He's in my class, that boy over there in the bright yellow T-shirt. Do you see him?' Joshua pointed to a boy paying Hook-a-Duck.

'Yes, I see him.'

'Can I then? Can I go to the dance club with him? Please?' Joshua's deep brown eyes searched Pippa's.

'Maybe we can look into it and it can be something you can do when I'm earning a bit more money at the café.'

'Oh, please can I go now though? Please?'

'Soon. Just be patient.' It must be amazing to be one of those parents who can take their kids to any club they wish, but it just wasn't possible at the moment. The café was still haemorrhaging money, so anything she earnt was swallowed back into the business. She now had two credit cards maxed out just from buying supplies. The profit she made from the actual café barely covered the gas and electricity bills.

'Please, Mum? It's not fair otherwise, Owen goes, why can't I? Everyone in my class goes to at least one club a week. Max goes to three! He does swimming, football and something else, something where he does the karate chop like this. Look.' Joshua punched the stall, making the cakes shiver and the ready poured juice dribble over the edges of the plastic cups.

'Joshua, please? Here, take this pound and go and have a go on Hook-a-Duck with Harley.' Pippa placed a pound coin into Joshua's small hand and gently twisted him around so he was facing the Hook-a-Duck game.

'Mum, you've not answered me. Why can't I go?' Joshua stamped his feet and twisted back around to face his mum.

'Joshua, please don't. Not now. We'll talk about this later because, look, I've got customers to serve now.'

'Do you mind if Amelia has a cup of squash, please?' An elderly couple with a small girl sporting brown bouncing curls stood waiting.

'Yes, of course, sorry.' Pippa glanced across to Joshua as he strolled slowly towards Harley. 'Here you are, Amelia. I love your curls.'

'They're beautiful, aren't they?' The grey-haired woman patted the small girl on the top of her head. 'Now, do you want to choose some cakes for Mummy and Daddy?' The woman looked up at Pippa. 'Amelia's dad is at work and her mum isn't feeling well, is she, Amelia? So, it will be a nice surprise for her if we get her some cake, won't it?'

'Can I have that one, Nan? Please?' Amelia pointed to a cupcake mounded high with pink icing.

'Thank you.' Pippa waved as the small girl walked off clutching her box of cakes and turned to the next customer. A queue had formed, trailing across the playground to the other stall. It was probably the free squash, it had been a good idea.

Maybe she wasn't so useless at this business malarkey after all. Where was Joe though? He had promised to help her and she could certainly do with another pair of hands to serve. 'How can I help you?'

'Can I buy two slices of the chocolate cake, and can I be really cheeky and ask if you could put some squash in my little boy's beaker, please?' A young mum leaned over the top of her blue stroller and gently prised an empty orange beaker from her son's small chubby hands.

'Yes, of course.' Pippa smiled and took the beaker. 'Aw, he's lovely. How old is he?'

'Thank you, but don't let his angelic looks deceive you. He's one and a half and has just started walking. He's into everything at the moment.' The young mum took the beaker back and returned it to her son's grasping hands.

'Oh, I remember that time so well. You spend months watching their every move and wondering when they'll learn to walk and then, when they do, you wonder why you wished the time away when you could pop them in the middle of the living to run to the loo and they'd still be there when you got back.' Pippa laughed, it was such a long time since Joshua had been that age, but she still remembered it so well.

'You're absolutely right. I've not had a pee in peace in two months. I'm Rachel, by the way, and this is Archie. Nice to meet you.'

'And you both.'

* * *

Ten minutes later, the queue had dwindled down, the need for drinks and cakes after the Maypole dancing satisfied. Pippa lifted each of the cake tins she'd stacked underneath the stall, opened the metal lids and peeked inside. Each one was empty, she had been refilling the cupcake stands and scone platters throughout the morning but hadn't realised how often. Straightening up, she surveyed the stall, there was about a quarter of the Victoria sponge left, five scones and three cupcakes. One of the urns was completely empty, she'd drained that whilst trying to make a coffee before the Maypole performance. Pippa gently tilted the other one, she could feel the hot water sloshing about inside the metal casing. It must have about a quarter of its capacity left.

She bit down on her bottom lip. It was barely half past eleven, she'd probably end up closing before the lunchtime hunger took hold. She should have baked more cakes, scones and maybe invested in another urn. Why hadn't she? She'd be letting the school, Mrs Havish, down. Why hadn't she been more prepared?

'Stop chomping down on your lip.'

The tower of plastic cups she'd been counting tipped over and spewed across the table. 'Joe! You made me jump.'

'Sorry. Well, no, I'm not. It was my full intention to catch you unawares.' Joe joined her behind the stall, and placing his hands on her hips he gently moved her to the side before leaning across the stall and tidying up the scattered cups. 'Wow, it looks like you've been busy! You've sold loads.'

'I know. There was a crazy rush after the Maypole dancing. I feel awful though, at this rate I'll have to close early.' Pippa twisted a piece of her hair that had escaped her ponytail around her index finger.

'Why do you feel awful? That's a good thing if you sell out. It means this has been a success, surely?' Joe restacked the plastic cups and leaned his back against the stall folding his arms.

Pippa could feel his intense blue eyes searching her face and looked away. 'No, it's not. It means I've let Mrs Havish down. I'm going to be leaving her with an empty stall. I should have been more prepared and baked more.'

'Don't be daft. Come here.'

Pippa took a step towards Joe, they stood so close she could almost feel the warmth radiating from the bare skin on his arms. Joe lifted his arms and rested his hands on her shoulders.

'You've done well. Really, really well. This is your first stall and you've almost sold out, and that's due to you baking and selling good products, not because you weren't prepared. You had tonnes of stuff on here when the fayre opened. You've sold it because it was good, really good. You brought the customers in with the free squash for kids and they saw and bought your products. That shows you've got a brilliant business mind. You should be proud of yourself. You've made some money and you're getting the word out about the café.'

'I guess you're right. I like that way of thinking.' She smiled. Joe always knew how to put her in a better mood. He was a naturally positive person, whereas her, well, as her mum was always saying, she was a glass half empty kind of girl. Maybe she should start trying to look at life in a positive light now. She always used to be positive when she was a child, even as a teenager she'd been happy-go-lucky. Looking back, it had been in her early twenties when her outlook had shifted. When she'd met Mike.

She shook her head and watched Joe as he served customers, joking and chatting with them as he poured squash and bagged up scones. Why was she even letting Mike into her head today? She was hundreds of miles away from where she last saw him, and a million miles away emotionally from where she had been when they were in a relationship. If it could even have been called a relationship. She tried to push thoughts of him and the way he treated her out of her head but she couldn't get rid of the niggling doubt whispering in her ear that she would never be good enough for anyone like Joe. She hadn't been good enough for Mike, he'd always said that, and he had left her, hadn't he?

'You OK?'

Nodding, she stepped towards the stall. 'Can I help you?'

'Hi, yes. I hope so. I was chatting to you earlier about my little boy learning to walk.'

'Yes. I remember, Rachel, wasn't it? Rachel and Archie. Hello again, Archie.' Pippa waved to the small boy sat in his buggy waving his beaker in the air. 'Are you back for some more squash?'

'Yes, if that's OK, please? But that's not the only reason I'm here. I noticed your poster saying you're from The Little Beach Café?'

'That's right. Me and my son, Joshua, moved down here last month to run the café.' She pointed to Joshua where he and Harley were rolling down the small hill on the school playing field.

'Is the café in the village?' Rachel passed Archie a toy dinosaur from her bag.

'It's the old café on the beach, west side, past the sand dunes. You know the one?' An elderly lady who had bought some scones slipped them into her handbag and looked up.

'No, I didn't realise there was a café up that end of the beach.'

'Yes, yes. It was run by dear old Kathryn. A thriving little place it was in its day. Of course, it's been closed now for about five years, is that right, dear?' The elderly lady looked over at Pippa.

'Yes, about that. Kathryn was my great aunt.'

'Was she?' The lady stared at Pippa. 'I can see a likeness now you've said. You have her eyes.'

Smiling, she touched her cheek. It was nice to be likened to

The Little Beach Café

someone like Great Aunt Kathryn.'

'That's probably why I've not heard of it then. We only moved here about two years ago.'

'I best go, that's my little grandson calling me.' The elderly lady pointed across to where Charlotte's son, Max, was waving at her by the Raffle stall.

Pippa nodded and turned back to Rachel. 'We only opened last month, although it feels like we've been here a lot longer.'

'In that case, I've got a favour to ask, if that's OK?'

'Of course.' Pippa smiled at Archie.

'Well, feel free to say no, but there's a Toddler Group on at the village hall on Mondays and Thursdays and a few of us like to meet up afterwards for lunch. We used to go to the coffee shop in the centre of the village, but since the little ones from our group have become a bit more active we've not been made to feel very welcome.'

'Oh no, that's not good.'

'No, so we've been taking it in turns to meet up at each other's houses, but as you can imagine, it's not quite the same as having lunch out.'

'No, it's not, is it? You are all welcome to come to The Little Beach Café.'

'That's what I was going to ask. I know it's a bit awkward with toddlers, they're into everything at this age, so I wanted to ask if it was OK before we all land on you.'

'Of course, it is. It would be a pleasure to have you all. We have seating outside too, so on a nice day the little ones could even play on the beach.'

'That sounds lovely. There's about seven mums, one dad and ten little ones normally so it would be great to not have to carry on squeezing into someone's living room,' Rachel laughed. 'Thank you.'

'You're welcome. I look forward to seeing you all.' Pippa turned to Joe who had begun to pack away the spare cake boxes, paper bags and cups. 'Did you hear that?'

'Yes, you'll be busy on Monday!'

'I know. That's great though, isn't it? I've just got to make sure I make a good impression so that they tell their friends about the café and drum up even more business.' Pippa drummed her fingers against the gingham tablecloth covering the stall. 'I might see if I can pick up some colouring books and crayons, and maybe a few cheap toys to put out in the café. It might keep the children entertained.'

'That's a good idea. If the kids are being good, the parents are more likely to stay for longer and eat more.' Joe bit into the last of the cupcakes. 'These are lovely and, if I do say so myself, decorated beautifully.'

'They are indeed, and thanks again for helping. No, I didn't mean it like that, I actually meant it would be nice for Rachel and the others not to have to worry about keeping their kids entertained while having lunch. I'm not that shallow!' Laughing, she threw a napkin at Joe.

'I wasn't fishing for compliments on my decorating skills.' Joe scooped the napkin from the floor and threw it back.

'Not much! Right, let's get this cleared up and then we can check out the rest of the fayre.' Pippa packed away the cake stands and followed Joe to his car.

* * *

'Mum, why have you put everything away? Do we have to go now? Can't we stay for a bit longer? Please?' Joshua ran his hand along the empty stall. 'Harley's not going yet. Are you, Harley? He gets to stay for longer, don't you, Harley? It's not fair, I want to stay longer.' Joshua crossed his arms, staring up at Pippa, his eyes pleading.

'No one said anything about going, Joshie. I've just closed the stall because we ran out of things to sell. We can stay for a while longer.'

'Thanks, Mum. You're the best Mum in the world.' Joshua ran over, wrapping his arms around Pippa's waist. 'Can we go and look over that way now? Owen said there's a tattoo stall. Don't worry though, he says they're fake. Can I have one please, Mum, can I?'

'Why not? Come on then, you lead the way.'

Joshua slipped his hand into Pippa's and she let herself be pulled in the direction of the tattoo stall.

'Here it is.' Joshua stopped at the end of a queue of children snaking across the tarmac. 'They do glitter tattoos too. Are you going to get one?'

'Umm, maybe I will.' Why not? She glanced around. There were quite a number of craft stalls at this end of the playground.

'Can I have a drink, please?'

'We haven't got any more squash left, I'm afraid. Is there a water fountain in the school you can use?'

'No, we're not allowed to go back into the classroom, that was just to get ready for the Maypole dancing. But there's a stall over there selling drinks. Can I get one from there, please? I'm really, really thirsty.' Joshua held his throat as if he'd not had a drink in a week.

'Whereabouts?' She followed Joshua's finger as he pointed behind her. It was to the right of the tattoo stall. Cartons of juice were stacked in towers along the back of the stall, bowls of apples, bananas and oranges were surrounded by plates of cookies and cupcakes on a bright blue and white polka dot tablecloth. 'Yes, OK.'

'Thanks, Mum. Can I get a cookie too?' Joshua hopped from foot to foot.

'Hold on a moment.' Pippa stopped rummaging in her bag for her purse and looked at the group of three women standing behind the stall. Sure enough, just as Joe had said, Charlotte was one of them.

'Please, Mum.' Joshua tugged Pippa's sleeve.

'Yes, OK, here you go.'

* * *

Joshua slurped on his straw, drawing up the blackcurrant juice from its carton.

'Are you enjoying that?' Smiling, Pippa took a five-pound note from her purse. 'It's almost our turn now. Do you know which tattoo you want?'

'Spiderman!'

'Sounds good. Here we go.' Pippa cupped her arm around Joshua's shoulders, gently easing him towards the empty chair under the stall's canopy.

'Hello there. What can I do for you today? I'm guessing you're a superhero kind of a boy, is that right?' A middle-aged woman, hosting a sleeve of real tattoos and long brown hair, opened up a folder of fake tattoos for Joshua to pore over.

'Here, I'll take that and then you'll be able to look better.' Pippa took the empty carton from his hand and watched him turn page after page of tattoos, his tongue sticking out of the corner of his mouth and the skin on his forehead crumpling as he chose.

'You're the lady who has reopened the old café on the beach, aren't you?'

'Yes, that's right.' Pippa smiled.

'Nice to finally meet you in person. You've given the gossip gals over there quite a lot of work over the past few weeks.' She nodded towards the drink and snack stall and Charlotte and her friends who were gathered behind it. 'I'm Susie, by the way.'

'Hi, nice to meet you too. I'm Pippa and this is my son, Joshua.' Pippa took Susie's hand and noted she had a strong handshake. 'I don't think I've quite been accepted yet.' Grimacing, she looked over at Charlotte and her gang.

'Aw, don't worry about it. I moved here and opened a tattoo studio down the High Street last year, which wasn't exactly wanted or needed, apparently. If you believe playground gossip, that is.'

'Have you got children who come to this school then?'

'I sure do, Edith and Mabel over there. Or The Twins as they're often referred to, much to their disgust.'

Following Susie's gaze, Pippa saw two blonde haired girls practising gymnastics on a picnic blanket at the edge of the playing field behind the stall. 'They're lovely.'

'Not so much when they're still practising their handstands in their bedroom at eleven o'clock at night and each time they land "elegantly", as they say, another light bulb flickers out in the lounge underneath.' Susie shook her head and sighed.

'How long ago did you move here? If you don't mind me asking, of course.'

'Of course not. About a year and a half ago now.' Looking across the playground, Susie lifted her hand and waved at Charlotte, who waved back. 'See, give it time, even the hard-nosed PTA group have accepted me now. Of course, it does help that not only do I practise my skin painting skills on the people of the village, ever since the jewellers in the next village closed, I'm the only person to pierce the ears of their little darlings within a thirty-mile radius.'

'I'm sure I've started out on the wrong foot with Charlotte, though. I think I must have done something wrong in her eyes.' She glanced over again, she was sure she wasn't being paranoid when she saw the three of them huddled together, talking and looking over at her.

'No, I shouldn't think you have. They just don't like change. They're probably worried someone will join the school and take over their roles as Friends of the School or whatever they like to call themselves on the PTA nowadays.'

'Maybe.' Placing her hands on Joshua's shoulders, Pippa leaned over, looking at the tattoo choices he was mulling over. 'Which one are you going to go for then, Joshie?'

'That one, please?' Joshua looked up and grinned, pointing to a glittery Spiderman tattoo. 'Which one are you going to have?'

'Let's see, shall we?' Pippa flicked through the book until she was drawn to a shiny yellow sunflower.

'Are you having one too, Mum?' Susie slipped the two chosen tattoos from the folder before applying them. 'There, they both look amazing. A real one would suit you.'

'Maybe.' Pippa looked at the garish sunflower on her forearm and laughed. 'Maybe not one this bright though.'

'No, a nice small one with a watercolour wash would suit you. I offer ten per cent off to friends too.'

'Sounds nice, I'll bear that in mind if I ever manage to turn a profit at the café.'

'You will. New businesses always start off slow. You wait, you'll get there. This village needs a proper café that sells proper, decent food.'

'I hope so.' Smiling, Pippa held a five-pound note towards Susie, it was good to know that other newcomers had managed to start a business and be accepted by the community.

'Nah, you keep it. Give me a strong coffee on the house when I come into your café, if you like.' Waving her hand away, Susie grinned before calling over the next person in line.

'Thank you.' Taking Joshua's hand, Pippa guided him towards the craft stalls. A heart-shaped wooden chalkboard had caught her eye as they'd walked past earlier. It would look great hung behind the counter to advertise the selection of coffees they sold. Joe was right, it *was* a good thing, the stall selling out of cakes and drinks so quickly, it showed there was a need for the products that the café sold.

Maybe, in time of course, she could properly employ Carol and pay her a wage. She'd been amazing teaching Pippa to bake and Pippa knew, without doubt, that she was only just beginning her culinary journey; there was so much more Carol could teach her.

'Mum.' Joshua shook Pippa's sleeve.

'Sorry, I was miles away. What's the matter, Joshua?' Looking down at his messy brown hair, Pippa knew she could and would make a success of the café. There was nothing that could stop her, not when she had Joshua as her reason. She rolled her shoulders back, trying to work the knots out of them. This was the first time in years that she had been financially independent. She only had herself and Joshua to worry about. Gone were the days that she had to agonise over how much debt Mike was mounting up. There was no way on earth that she was planning on messing this up.

'Can I have a bit of money to go on the Tombola, please? There's this really awesome remote controlled car on there that no one's won yet. I might do, mightn't I? If I get the right number on my ticket? And there's a massive,' stretching out his arms as wide as he could, Joshua looked up at Pippa to make sure she was watching, 'bar of chocolate. If I win that, I'll give it to you though and we can have it for a film night, if you like?'

'That would be lovely, Joshie. Yes, here you go.' Placing a pound coin into Joshua's small palm, Pippa looked around. 'Have you seen Joe or Harley recently?'

'Yes, Harley is over there playing with Owen. I don't know where his dad is, I haven't seen him in ages.'

Pippa followed Joshua's finger as he pointed towards a group of children playing football on the field.

'OK, let's go and have a go on the Tombola then, shall we?'

'Can I go on my own? Look, everyone else is on their own in the line. Can you go and sit on the field like all the other parents? Please?'

'OK, I'll be right there then by the footie game, OK?'

Joshua nodded and marched towards the Tombola stall, his head held high with the trust Pippa had bestowed upon him by letting him go on his own.

Standing in the middle of the playground, she looked around at what remained of the Spring Fayre. Like hers, a few stalls had shut down for the day and most families were making the most of the sunshine and had taken to the field, picnic blankets scattered across the grass. She shook her head, it hadn't occurred to her that people would be making a day of it. She should have thought and brought a picnic for them to share.

Lowering herself to the grass, Pippa watched as Joshua handed over his money and took a ticket. Even from some distance away, she could see a massive grin spread across his face as he unravelled the ticket clutched in his hand. The lady behind the stall handed him the big bar of chocolate. Their luck was certainly changing down here. She laughed to herself as she watched Joshua hold the bar behind his back and run towards her.

Quickly turning her head away, she straightened her face.

'Mum, guess what I won?' Joshua jumped in front of her, his cheeks twitching in excitement.

'Oh, did you win something? I don't know, let me think.' Pippa scrunched up her forehead and tapped her chin with her finger. 'Did you win a bar of soap? No, maybe a jar of jam then?'

'No! Don't be silly. There weren't any bars of soaps or jars of jam there! I won this!' Reaching behind his back, he brought out the big bar of chocolate.

'Wow, that's great! Well done, you.' Pippa grinned and hugged him to her. 'Do you want to sit down and we'll have some of it now?'

'You can. Can I go and play football with Harley?'

'Of course, you can.'

'Are you sure you don't mind? Are you going to be OK by yourself?' Joshua twisted his ankle around in front of him and watched as his shoe made circles on the ground.

'Of course, I will. I might have a bit of chocolate though!' Smiling, Pippa watched as Joshua ran towards his friends before twisting around and looking at the other parents sat on the field. That's why Joshua had been so worried about leaving her on her own then. She was literally the only person sat alone. Couples lounged on checked blankets, small children playing on the grass to the side of them. Others huddled in groups, some squeezing onto their blankets not wanting to mark their clothes with the unmistakable green sap of freshly cut grass, others lying directly on the grass, catching the spring sunshine.

She gnawed on the nail of her index finger before reaching up and taking out her black hairband, letting her hair settle on her shoulders in a frizzy cascade before taming it and plaiting it back. It wasn't that she was the only single parent, she wasn't and she knew that, it was the fact that everyone else had friends or family to sit with that made her feel so alone. She had Joe, she knew that, but things were still very early days and, anyway, she hadn't even caught a glimpse of him for at least the last hour.

Brushing her hands across the grass in front of her, she told herself that it was normal for it to take a bit of time to settle in at a new place, to make friends, or even just acquaintances to say 'hello' to. Maybe next year she'd be one of those people sat with a group of friends.

Joshua scored a goal and ran into the centre of the area they were using as their pitch, his team members running towards him throwing high fives.

She'd made the right decision, moving down here. Life was good, the café was on the up, hopefully, Joshua was happy and settled at school and Pippa had met Joe. Things were good. She took a deep breath in, letting the warmth of the air around her fill her lungs. Now, if Joe was here with her things would be perfect.

* * *

'Mum, quick. Harley's hurt himself.'

Shaking herself from her thoughts, Pippa allowed herself to be pulled to standing before following Joshua across the field to where Harley lay on his back, clutching his knee to his chest.

'Harley, are you OK? Have you hurt your knee? Let's have a look, shall we?' Kneeling beside him, she gently moved Harley's hand. A small graze bled, blood flowing in a single stream down his leg.

'It hurts.'

'I know, sweetheart. It's OK. Let's get you over there and I can clean it up for you.' Pippa lifted Harley to his feet and led him towards where she was sat and her handbag. 'Pop yourself down and I'll get some antiseptic wipes out.'

With Pippa's help, Harley lowered himself onto the grass. 'I want Daddy.'

'He'll be here in a moment.' Twisting her neck, she looked across towards the playground, there were still people milling about and buying things from the few stalls which were still running. No sign of Joe, though. Turning back to Harley, she rummaged in her handbag and pulled out an antiseptic wipe.

'Will it hurt?' Harley held onto his knee.

'No, it might sting a little, but only for a second and it will clean all the mud and grass out. Look, you've got a blade of grass stuck in it. Are you trying to grow a football pitch on your knee?'

Harley laughed and then winced as Pippa wiped the graze clean.

'All done. See, it didn't hurt that much, did it? Now, do you want to rest your knee a little or are you OK to go back and play?'

'Can I go back and play? Where is Daddy?'

'I'm not sure, he can't have gone far though. He's probably looking around the stalls. You go and play and I'll go and have a quick look.' She watched as Harley ran off towards the football game, his injury all but forgotten.

* * *

Standing in the middle of the playground, Pippa looked up and down. Where on earth could Joe have got to?

'Hello, Pippa, I hear your stall did well?' Mrs Havish, who seemed to be circling the fayre paused in front of Pippa.

'Yes, it did, thank you. I'm really sorry I had to close early, I guess I just didn't realise how busy it would be.' Pippa wrung her hands in front of her.

'We do get busy at this time of the year. The Spring Fayre is usually busier than the Summer Fayre we hold on the last day of the summer term. Strange really.'

'I suppose people come to see their children dancing.'

'Yes, quite. But the children always put on a performance at the Summer Fayre too. I often wonder if it's because people have been starved of outside activities during the winter and come spring it gives people a little hope that the good weather is coming and it signifies the beginning of the countdown to summer.'

'Yes, that makes sense.' Pippa nodded. 'You've certainly been lucky with the weather today.'

'We certainly have. Were you looking for something?'

'I was just wondering where Joe, Harley's dad, had got to, that's all.' Feeling the heat rise to her cheeks, Pippa looked down at her shoes. She shouldn't have said anything. Was it obvious there was something going on between her and Joe now?

'I did see him walking towards the gate with Charlotte a few moments ago. Now, I'd better be off and see how the other stall-holders are doing.' Mrs Havish patted Pippa on the arm before wandering off towards the far end of the playground.

Joe was with Charlotte. Why would he be with her? And why would he be walking out of the gate, and leaving Harley with her? He hadn't even asked her to keep an eye on him. Obviously she didn't mind, Joe had helped her out enough over these last few days, but still, it would have been nice to have been asked.

Pippa glanced back at Joshua and Harley who were still concentrating on their football game and made her way to the gate. She wouldn't go out and she would still be able to see the boys from the gate, but she would just have a little wander over there and see if she could see them. Maybe Charlotte had needed something lifting from her car, Joe was the sort of guy who would offer to help after all.

As she neared the wrought-iron tall gate she spotted them. They were sat on the bench outside of the car park, by the side of the road. Standing still, she watched as Charlotte tipped her head down and Joe put his arm around her shoulders.

Taking a sharp breath in, Pippa turned and stumbled back through the gate. Why had she been so stupid to think that a man like Joe was interested in her? Any man in fact. But still, even if she had been naïve to begin to trust again, to begin to let Joe into her and Joshua's life, she still didn't deserve this. Did she? She didn't deserve him to so blatantly go off with another woman when he had offered up the day to help her with the stall. She thought they had planned to spend the day together. The four of them: her and Joshua, Joe and Harley.

* * *

Lowering herself back in her spot on the grass, Pippa plastered a smile on her face as Joshua waved to her, shouting that he had scored another goal. She gave him a thumbs-up before clasping her hands together in front of her, digging her nails into her palms.

She tried to focus on the physical pain, the sharpness of her nails piercing her skin, but she couldn't help telling herself that this was her fault. It must be. Mike had cheated on her, Joe clearly was. She must just be one of those women who gets cheated on. You hear about them, don't you? When she used to have the time to read trashy 'real-life' magazines she'd read about them, about women whose partners cheated on them, one after the other. It must be a signal she gave off. Maybe she looked like the sort who was too feeble to stand up for herself. Well, that wasn't her. She hadn't taken Mike back after she found out about his cheating and she certainly wouldn't be giving Joe another chance.

She shook her head, she'd known not to trust anyone again. She'd promised herself after Mike left that she wouldn't. She wouldn't ever, ever let another man in.

'Pippa, there you are. I've been looking all over for you.' Joe ambled across the playground towards the field, running his hand through his dark stubbly hair.

Of course, you have. Pippa could almost feel her eyes rolling involuntarily. There it was, the first lie. Or was it? He may have been lying to her all along. He probably had been.

'Did you have a wander around?' He flung himself down onto the grass next to her. His back against the grass, his knees pulled up. Reaching out, he tapped her on the thigh before lying back with his hands behind his head, squinting his eyes against the sun.

'Yes, thanks.' Stealing a quick glance at him, it suddenly hit her. Who had she been fooling? Or to be more specific, who had he been fooling? He was much better suited to someone like Charlotte. His athletic figure reflected hers, the well-kept stubble reflected her well-manicured and pristine nails and hair. She hadn't seen it before, she'd always seen him as the dishevelled plumber who just threw clothes on and sported the 'hadn't bothered to shave yesterday' shadow on his chin. But it was all thought out. It wasn't yesterday's stubble, he grew it that way. No wonder he had gone off with Charlotte. They were in the same league, unlike Pippa and him. Pippa was at least three leagues below him, with her saggy belly, dark under the eye circles and limp, often frizzy, hair.

'You OK?' Joe pulled himself up, leaning on his elbows.

Why had he left it for today though? That's what she didn't

understand. And why had he insisted on helping her with the stall? It just didn't make any sense. He'd gone out of his way to encourage her to sell at this fayre. Why?

'Charlotte's married.' The statement left Pippa's lips before she'd realised what she'd said, before her brain had processed the information. It all made sense, perfect sense. She was the cover. He had been using her.

'Sorry?' Turning his mouth down, Joe furrowed his forehead.

'I said, Harley hurt himself. He fell over and grazed his knee. He was asking where you were.' Concentrating on a blade of grass in front of her, she twisted it between her forefinger and middle finger.

'Did he? Is he OK?' Sitting up, Joe twisted his neck around to peer at the boys playing football to the side of them.

'He's fine. I cleaned him up.' The blade creased, its greenness fading in the lines she had created.

'Thank you.'

'It was just a graze.' She shrugged. 'I think I'm going to get going now.' Pippa let go of the blade, knowing that it will continue to grow but never quite be the straightest blade amongst its peers. Pushing herself to standing, she looked back at Joe. 'If it's not too much bother, could you drop my stuff that's in your car off later, please?'

'I'll come now too. They're winding the fayre down anyway.' Joe jumped up beside her.

Looking around, Pippa realised he was right, most of the stalls had been packed away and only a scattering of people were left spread out on the field, their picnic blankets flapping in the slight breeze that had become persistently stronger throughout the day. 'No, it's fine. I fancy a walk anyway.'

She turned her back on Joe before he could answer, instead heading towards the dwindling football game.

11

'Mum, why didn't we go in the car with Joe and Harley? Why couldn't we have stayed like they did?' Joshua trailed behind, dragging his feet in the sand.

'The Spring Fayre was closing anyway. Most of the stalls had already shut and there were only a few people left. You've not missed anything. Besides, I fancied a walk along the beach. I thought you would too.' Pausing to let Joshua catch up, she slipped her sandals off and braced herself for the cool rush of water around her ankles as she stepped into the sea.

'I did. I like walking on the beach, I just wanted to stay a bit longer.'

'Here, slip your trainers off and come and join me for a paddle.' Standing still, she let Joshua hold on to her for balance before holding out his trainers for Pippa to carry. 'You did really well in the Maypole Dance. I'm really proud of you.'

'I like it here. I'm glad we moved here. I miss Nana, though.' Joshua looked down at his feet, the white froth of the water covering his toes.

'I know you do. You used to spend a lot of time with her, didn't you?'

He nodded. 'I like spending more time with you though, but I do miss her. Why can't she just move down here too?'

'It would be lovely, but she's got her job back in London and she's got all of her friends there too.'

'But she's probably lonely. Especially in the evenings without me there. She used to say that I kept her busy and that she wouldn't know what to do without me.' Joshua looked out to sea, his eyes glistening with tears.

'Come here, Joshie.' Wrapping her arms around his small fragile shoulders, she followed his gaze out to sea too; a large boat was bobbing on the horizon. 'It's hard, isn't it? I miss her too, but it's only a couple of weeks until she comes to visit and we can make lots of happy memories to hold in our hearts until we see her again, OK?'

Nodding, Joshua wiped his eyes with the back of his hand and pulled away.

'You'll be able to show her the way to school, where your classroom is and how you can hang upside down without holding on when you're on the bars in the playground. Maybe, you can even invent a special smoothie just for Nana, you could choose which fruit you think she'll like and if you think she'll prefer it mixed with apple or orange juice. You can start practising and inventing tonight, if you like?'

'OK, stop talking about it now.' Joshua kicked the water up in front of him and walked on ahead.

Pressing the pads of her thumbs onto her eyelids, she waited until all she could see were stars before taking a deep breath. Today had been a business success, she had to remember that. Everything else may have fallen apart but it had been a success for the café.

She missed her mum too. She missed someone to chat to, to confide in and ask for advice. It wasn't the same on the phone and all she wanted now was a hug from her, telling her it would be all right and that Joe wasn't worth it. No man was.

Jogging, she caught up with Joshua. 'Shall we have a film night and get a takeaway pizza tonight?'

'I thought we couldn't afford takeaways? That's what you always say.' Joshua looked at the water lapping around his ankles.

'I think after the success of your Spring Fayre we can afford to treat ourselves for once, don't you?'

'I guess so.'

'Right, cheer up then. The first person to get to the café can choose the topping. On your marks. Get. Set. Go!'

Joshua ran ahead, Pippa following, their shoes bumping against her thigh as she tried her best not to trip on the wooden boards as they raced through the sand dunes to the patio in front of the café.

'I guess it's your choice then,' Pippa rasped out, bending down trying to catch her breath. She was fitter than she had been in London. Running the café was a lot more relaxed and easy-going than her old job as a waitress where she'd spent whole shifts on her feet rushing between customers and the kitchen non-stop. But here, she was getting more exercise in the form of walking Joshua to school and back every day.

* * *

Rubbing her eyes, Pippa yawned, she must have drifted off. Something had woken her. There it was again, the doorbell. Slowly, she pulled her arm from under Joshua's head and slid herself off the sofa, catching the empty pizza box as it slid to the floor. The film credits were still rolling. They must have been shattered, Pippa only remembered the beginning of the film and she knew Joshua had fallen asleep before her because she'd felt his head flop against her.

'One minute,' Pippa called out quietly as she padded down the stairs in her slippers.

She'd closed all of the blinds before they'd gone up for their pizza and film night so the café was dark, lit only by the moonlight shining in through the gap above the blind on the door. Pulling her pink pyjama top down, she unlocked and opened the door.

'Joe.' Why hadn't she just ignored the doorbell?

'Are you going to let me in? I've got some of your stuff here. The rest is in the car.'

Pippa slowly opened the door. She didn't have much choice, did she? He stumbled in, a pile of cake tins balancing in his arms. As he slipped through the doorway he leaned into Pippa, brushing her cheek with a kiss.

Stepping back, Pippa knocked into the table behind her, the edge of the table digging into the small of her back.

Joe placed the pile of tins carefully on the table nearest the door and stepped towards Pippa.

'Don't.' Holding her hands up, she stalled him.

'Are we OK?' Joe's arms swung back down to his sides, standing there as though everything was the same as it had been earlier that day.

'It doesn't matter. Thank you for bringing my things back. I'll come and help you with the rest.'

'Hey, it does matter. Come here.' Joe stepped forward towards her again.

'I'll grab my shoes and come and get my stuff.' Slipping away from him, she headed towards the back of the café.

'Don't be silly, you're in your PJs. I'll bring it round.' Joe squinted his eyes before turning his back and going back into the night.

* * *

'Right, that's the lot of it.' Joe placed the last of the carrier bags onto a table.

'Thank you.' Pippa continued placing the empty tins into the dishwasher, clanking metal on metal.

'Are you in a mood with me?'

Taking a deep breath, she straightened her back and clicked shut the dishwasher door. 'It doesn't matter.'

'That's the second time you've said that and you're still being funny with me, so it clearly does. Have I done something to upset you?'

Pippa dried her hands on the tea towel before folding it and putting it back on the counter. 'I saw you with Charlotte.'

'What?' Joe ran his fingers through his hair. 'So what if you saw me with Charlotte? I don't understand.'

Did she really have to spell it out to him? Looking down, she moved the tea towel an inch to the right. 'I saw you with your arm around her. I was cheated on by my ex. I can't, and I won't, go through that again. Can you just leave now?'

'What? Pippa, look at me.' Stepping towards her, Joe placed his finger under her chin, lifting it gently so she was looking into his eyes. 'I would never cheat on you.'

'I saw you.' He was good at this, at lying. He kept his eyes so still. Not like Mike. Pippa had always known when he had been lying because he'd never been able to look at her straight, his eyes would flicker and he would chew his thumbnail, always his thumbnail. Taking a step back, she pulled her chin away from him. 'Please go.'

'Just hear me out. Come and sit down and let me explain.' Joe stood with his arm outstretched to the table to the side of the counter. 'Please?'

Dropping her eyelids, she looked away.

'Pippa, please?' Joe pulled a chair out from the table and sat down.

Shaking her head, Pippa did as Joe asked and slipped into the chair opposite him.

'You saw me put my arm around Charlotte when we were sat on the bench outside the school, right?'

'Yes, you can't deny it. I saw you with my own eyes.' It was her turn to look him in the eye.

'She was upset, I was comforting her. That's all. Nothing more and nothing less.' He spread his hands across the table, palms facing upwards.

'I knew you'd do that.' She traced her index finger across the table in front of her, tracing a star.

'Do what?'

'Make up some excuse. You all do.'

'I'm not making up anything. It's what happened. She was upset so I put my arm around her, just like anyone else would. And what do you mean "you all do"?'

'You. Men in general. You all make up some excuse to try and wriggle out of it.' She'd heard enough of this. Mike had made excuse after excuse to try and put her off the scent of him having an affair with the tart downstairs. She was not going to go through that again. Back then, she'd been naïve. She'd rather have believed every single lie he had told instead of face up to the truth that he was making a fool of her. Well, she was different now. She was stronger. She'd learnt from her mistakes and she'd never let another man treat her the way Mike had. No way. Pushing her chair back, she stood up. 'I think it's time you left.'

'No, not until you've heard me out. Please, sit down and let me explain properly.'

'What's the point?' Pippa shrugged her shoulders. She couldn't put herself through this again. Mike was Joshua's father, she had felt she had no choice but to believe his lies and stay with him for as long as she could, but with Joe it was different. And more importantly, she couldn't let Joshua see his mother go through another failed relationship.

'The point is, I've done nothing wrong. I promise. And if you let me explain, you'll see that too. Just give me five minutes and I'll show you I'm not like those other men you're talking about. I'll show you we're not all bad. Far from it. Plus, I have real feelings for you.' Joe looked down at his hands which were clasped in front of him and back up to Pippa. 'And I think you have them for me too. At least, I hope you do.'

'Five minutes.' Slipping back into her seat, she crossed her arms. This excuse had better be good.

'I'm good friends with Charlotte's husband, John. Or I used to be. You may have seen him at the school gates?'

Pippa shook her head. She knew Charlotte was married by the humongous diamond ring she wore on her ring finger, but she'd never actually seen him.

'Well, like I said, I used to be good friends with him. That was until I found out he was having an affair.'

'Her husband is cheating on her?' Perfect Charlotte? She was stunning. If she couldn't keep a man, what hope was there for the average woman?

'Yes. About a month ago I saw him out on a "date" with another woman.' Joe curled his fingers into quotation marks as he said the word 'date'. 'Charlotte obviously had to know what he was up to. I had gotten to know her quite well from when me and Harley's mum were together, and we used to go for meals together. I couldn't bear to see her taken advantage of like that.'

'So you told her today? Why did you leave it for a month? Why did you let her husband play around behind her back for so long?' Typical, one immoral male sticking up for another.

'No, I didn't tell her today. I didn't tell her at all. I spoke to John the day after I'd seen him and told him to tell her or I would. He told her.'

'So you decided to make your move today?'

Joe ignored Pippa's sarcasm and shook his head. 'John turned up at the Spring Fayre with his mistress. The idiot. I mean what a thing to do, it was hardly fair on Charlotte or Max. So I took her out of the school grounds for a while. She was understandably really upset, which is when I put my arm around her. That was all.'

'Right, OK.' Pippa looked down at her hands, the nail on her middle finger was completely ragged. She didn't even remember biting it.

'I might not be perfect, but I can promise you one thing, I am not a cheater. I have never cheated and I can promise you I never would. I do kind of feel responsible for Charlotte going through all of this though. If I hadn't given John an ultimatum he might not have left her. Not so soon anyway. So I feel awful for her, which is why I make sure I'm there to help her if she needs it.'

'You did the right thing.'

'Putting my arm around her? It's just a natural reaction when trying to comfort someone I guess.'

'No, I mean you did the right thing giving her husband an ultimatum, it would have come out at some point. Maybe months, or even years, down the line he would have told her or left her for his mistress and that would have hurt more, knowing that he had been lying to her all that time. So you did the right thing by making John tell her. I wish someone had told me.' Pippa let Joe take her hands into his, his calloused thumb stroking hers.

'I wish someone had told me too.' He looked down at their hands, intertwined.

'Your wife had an affair?'

'She did indeed.'

'Sorry, I didn't realise. I wouldn't have accused you of cheating if I'd known.'

'You weren't to know.'

'Well, I'm sorry.' How could she have read him so wrong? 'I feel completely paranoid now.'

'It's OK. I know what it's like to be hurt by the one person you think you can rely on. So I know why you jumped to that conclusion when you saw me and Charlotte together.'

'It's no excuse though. I guess I just find it hard to trust anyone. After Mike left I promised I would never put myself in the position of having to trust anyone again.'

'Me neither. But please try to trust me. I won't hurt you, I promise.' Joe squeezed Pippa's hands.

'Umm.' His clasp made her feel safe. Maybe she *could* trust him. They had so much in common, they had both been cheated on and were both the main carers of their children. Maybe she should take a chance.

Joe stood up and leaned across the table, curling his index finger to indicate to Pippa that she should do the same. Pushing the chair back, Pippa stood up meeting him halfway. Joe's lips were warm on hers. Pulling away and linking his fingers with hers, he led her around the table until they were stood in front of each other. Running his fingers through her hair, he pulled her towards him again, this time the kiss was harder and faster than it had been before.

He lifted his head slightly, a centimetre, if that, away from her. 'I think I've fallen for you.'

'Me too.' She had. She knew that then. That was why she had felt so crushed when she had seen him with Charlotte. Her stomach flipped as she realised how she actually felt for him. She hadn't felt like this since she had first met Mike all of those years ago.

12

Running the pink brush through her shower-wet hair, Pippa watched in the mirror as Joe walked behind her into the bathroom.

'Morning, gorgeous.' Wrapping his arms around her waist, Joe gently kissed her neck.

'Morning to you, too.' She twisted in his arms before kissing him on the lips.

'I've got to go and pick Harley up from his mum's before she has to leave for work. I'll pop by after school pick up, if you like, though? Or of course, I'll see you at the school?'

'That'd be nice. Maybe we could have a late picnic on the beach with the boys once I close the café up?'

'Already looking forward to it. I'll let myself out.' He gave her a final kiss before leaving.

Turning back to face her reflection in the mirror, she placed the brush on the little shelf underneath the mirror and picked up her bottle of foundation. How could she ever have doubted him? He was one of the good guys. It would be so lovely when they could tell the boys about their relationship, it would mean an end to the snatched moments of intimacy when they were asleep or at school. Maybe one day Joe and Harley could move in and they could be a real little family. Pippa smiled. After Mike had left she never thought she'd meet anyone else, definitely not someone she felt so comfortable around and who she could see a real future with anyway.

Picking up her mobile she checked the time. She had ten minutes before she would have to wake Joshua and bribe him to get ready for school while she went downstairs and started preparing the café for opening. It was the day the Toddler Group parents and children were due to pop by. Pippa dotted foundation across her face before rubbing it in, she thought she had everything in place. She'd already baked extra cupcakes. She'd popped to the local supermarket with Joshua and picked up some colouring books and chunky crayons that she'd leave on the tables and Joe had dropped off some of Harley's old toys to leave in a basket in the corner of the café. She brushed blusher across her cheeks, she didn't think there was anything else she could have done.

* * *

'Could I have an iced coffee, please?'

'Carol!' Pippa sprang up from where she was putting mixing bowls away in the cupboard under the counter.

'Sorry, love, did I startle you?'

'Yes. But in a good way. It's lovely to see you. How's your sister?'

'You can ask her yourself later. I've persuaded her to come and stay with me for a few weeks. I'm hoping she'll decide she loves it here as much as I do and decide to move here, but we'll just have to wait and see.' Carol pulled herself up onto one of the stools in front of the counter.

'How's her hip?' Pippa placed an iced coffee down on the counter before turning back to make herself one.

'She hadn't broken it in the end, thankfully. She's just very bruised and still feeling quite fragile at the moment. I wouldn't want her rattling around in her house all by herself, at least with her here I can keep an eye on her.'

'Good idea.' She turned back to face Carol, leaned against the back counter and sipped her iced coffee. It would be good to have her back, even if she couldn't come back to work, just to have her to talk to and sound ideas off of would be nice.

'So, what's new here? How did the Spring Fayre go?'

'Amazingly well, surprisingly. We sold out of all the cakes and scones well before the end of the fayre.' Pippa left out the part about the misunderstanding between her and Joe. Carol was Joe's mum, he could tell her the nitty-gritty details if he wanted to. 'Oh, and we've drummed up some more business, thanks to getting the word out about the café. We've got a group of parents and little ones dropping by after Toddler Group around lunchtime today.'

'That's great news. Right, what needs doing?' Carol slipped off the stool and took her apron from the hook hanging by the door to the flat, slipping it over her head she joined Pippa behind the counter.

'It's OK, you should be spending time with your sister, not helping out here.'

'Nonsense, I should think my sister's had enough of me chattering on, for the moment anyway.'

'Are you sure? OK, thanks. Well, I baked extra cupcakes for the toddlers so they need icing and, of course, we'll have the fishermen wanting their late breakfast in about half an hour, so that needs to be prepared too.' Lifting the lids to the cake tins, Pippa started placing the cupcakes on the counter ready to decorate.

'They look delicious. I always knew there was a master baker inside of you waiting to come out.'

'I don't know about that, but what I do know is, I wouldn't have even been able to make the cake mixture without you!' She had to admit they did look and smell good.

'I'm sure you would have worked it out for yourself. Shall I take charge of those and you can prepare the breakfasts?'

'Yes OK.' Pippa pierced the sausage skins before putting them under the grill, they'd be at least six of the men wanting a full English breakfast and, over the last few weeks, Pippa had definitely learnt that preparation was key.

* * *

'That was lovely as always. I'm sure your breakfasts get better each day.' Gus grinned, leaning his forearms on the counter. 'Of course, it does help that the chef is as gorgeous as you.'

'I'm sure your comments get more charming every day.' Pippa grinned back.

'Only because your beauty does.'

Laughing, Pippa gave Gus his change. 'I'll see you tomorrow.'

'Already looking forward to it.' Gus waved, shouted out his goodbyes to the few remaining fishermen who were scraping the last pieces of food from their plates and left.

'You shouldn't encourage him.' Carol twisted around to look at Pippa, icing bag in hand.

'Ah, he's harmless enough.'

'Umm.' Shaking her head, Carol iced the last cupcake before placing it on the cake stand.

Frowning, Pippa went to clear the plates from the tables.

Why was Carol always so disapproving of Gus? She was always tutting in his direction or avoiding serving him. It was true, he was a bit smarmy and overly confident, but he didn't mean anything by it. He had been nothing but supportive since the café had opened and Pippa owed a lot of business to him. Not only did he bring his crew in every morning but on more than one occasion a customer had mentioned that Gus had recommended the café to them. The least Carol could do would be to put aside any personal opinions of him and serve him professionally.

She shook her head, it was wrong for her to even think badly of Carol, she was doing all of this out of goodwill, Pippa wasn't paying her. Hopefully though, if business continued to improve she should be able to offer her a permanent position with a salary in a couple of months.

* * *

'Wow, they look amazing.' Slipping behind the counter, Pippa loaded her pile of plates into the dishwasher.

'Thank you. Is this them coming now?'

Jerking her head up, Pippa saw a group of parents and children coming towards the door. There must have been at least twelve women and one man, five buggies and a handful of toddlers bouncing along holding their parents' hands.

'Rachel, hi. Morning, everyone.' Drying her hands on a tea towel Pippa walked over to greet them. 'Thank you so much for coming to check us out. We've got colouring sheets and crayons on the tables for the little ones and a box of toys just over in that corner. The menus are on the tables, so I'll give you a few minutes to settle and then come over and take your orders, if you like?'

'That's great, thank you. That's it, Archie, you can go and get a toy to play with if you like. It's a lovely idea to have toys and colouring, thank you so much for that, we might actually be able to finish a coffee in relative peace.'

'You're welcome, it's lovely to see so many people in here.' Pippa smiled back.

'There's a few more of us than I told you about. When I mentioned that we were coming here a few others decided to come along.'

'No problem. I'll let you settle yourselves and be back in a moment.'

* * *

'You stay this side of the counter, poppet. Look, why don't you see if you can colour this tiger in?' Grabbing a pack of crayons and a colouring sheet in one hand, Pippa held out her other hand and led a little girl of about three back towards the tables.

'Maddie, come and sit next to Mummy.' A woman with long curly black hair pulled a chair out next to her and patted the seat before lifting little Maddie, almost a miniature mirror image of herself, up onto it. 'Ooh a tiger, are you going to colour the tiger in? Thank you.' The woman looked over at Pippa and smiled.

'You're very welcome.' Returning to the counter, Pippa looked down at the small notepad in her hand. 'Right, we've got two jacket potatoes, four paninis, three sandwiches, two bagels and a soup.'

'Let's get cracking then. I'll take the jacket potatoes and the soup. You might as well start on the paninis and I'll help you when I've got these in.'

'Good idea. I think this is the busiest we've ever been.'

'It certainly is, but we'll manage. They've all got their coffees and teas so I'm sure they'll be happy chatting while we get their lunch ready. Are the children not having anything?'

'Yes, sorry I'd written their orders on a different page so I knew they were smaller portions. Here they are, cheese or ham sandwiches mostly.' Pippa pulled butter, ham cheese and mayo from the fridge before slicing the paninis open.

'Let's have a look.' Carol wiped her hands on the tea towel slung over her shoulder and skim read the orders.

'Do you think we should get some of those cardboard lunchboxes in and start doing a special little lunch for children? You know, the ones where they can choose so many items to go in their lunchbox? And we could start offering chips and fish fingers or chicken nuggets or something?'

'That's a great idea. It'd be good to capture the afterschool market too. I know we have quite a few people who pop in for ice creams or something on their way past, if we offered some meals aimed at children we might entice a few of them to stay longer.'

'I'll get some next time I go to the wholesalers then.'

'I think you may have found your niche, The Little Beach Café: A Family Friendly Choice.' Carol used her hand to show an imaginary sign in an arch. 'Those pompous coffee chains in the village certainly don't offer anything aimed at children, so I think you could be onto something.'

'You're right, I think we may have found our niche. The café used to be popular with families when Great Aunt Kathryn owned it, didn't it?'

'Yes, in the height of the summer the queue would be trailing out of the door after school, and in the summer holidays all the tourists would flock here for their ice creams, drinks and lunches. Of course, that was when the village was more of a tourist hotspot, when people were more interested in spending their holidays sitting on the beach or exploring the local villages rather than these big holiday park things.'

'Excuse me, can I grab a cloth, please? We've had a little accident with a glass of juice.'

'Don't worry, I'll come and clean it up.'

* * *

'That was manic, but great fun.' Pippa threw the dishcloth on the counter and swung up onto a bar stool.

'I think it went well. Rachel said they'd be back next week anyway.' Carol smiled as she loaded the last cup into the dishwasher. 'A few of them mentioned how child-friendly we were here and that we didn't make them feel awkward with the little ones running around.'

'They were so cute, weren't they? It'd be great if it does become a regular thing. I'm going to grab a coffee and have a look at ordering some plastic beakers and plates for the children. Do you want a coffee?' Pippa slid off of the bar stool and joined Carol behind the counter.

'No, I'm OK, thank you. I might pop home and check on Silv, if you don't need me for a bit? I'll make sure I'm back so you can collect Joshua at school pick up though.'

'OK, thanks. Say hi to her from me.' Balancing a latte, a cupcake and her notebook on a tray, Pippa made her way to the table closest to the counter and sank into a chair. Wiping some spilt latte from the tray, she pulled her phone from her pocket. She was sure she'd heard a ping earlier. Yep, it was Joe.

Sorry I can't make it tonight. Harley staying at his mum's. Will try tomo.

Taking a sip of latte, Pippa swallowed hard. She'd been looking forward to seeing Joe that evening. Maybe he'd taken on an extra call now that Harley was staying at his mum's. She couldn't blame him for working extra hours when he had the chance. It was a shame though. She'd half expected him to pop in whilst the Toddler Group parents had been there. He'd said he might do if he had time between jobs. She shook her head, maybe the jobs had been more complicated than he'd expected. They'd just have to make the most of seeing each other tomorrow. He was sure to pop in tomorrow morning on the way back from dropping Harley off at school.

* * *

The tinkle of the bell above the door shook her from her thoughts. Downing the last dregs of latte, Pippa looked up, took a deep breath and made her way to the counter.

'Hi, Charlotte. What can I get you?'

'A minute to look at your menu, if it's not too much to ask.' She lowered her head and stared at the menu, her dark hair shielding her face.

'Of course not.' Pippa reminded herself what Charlotte was going through and how she must be feeling. Although, she was sure she hadn't been this rude to people when she'd found out Mike had run off with his tart. Heartbroken, yes, but she certainly hadn't used it as an excuse to be plain bad-mannered to all she ran in to.

'I'll have the iced coffee.'

'Coming right up.'

A shrill tring rang from Charlotte's shoulder bag which she deftly swung around, unzipped and prised a thin black phone from. Pointing to Pippa and then to the table by the window, she stalked away whispering into her phone.

'You're very welcome.' Pippa muttered under her breath and gritted her teeth.

* * *

'Here you are.' Placing the glass of iced coffee on the table in front of Charlotte, Pippa began backing away.

'I don't care what he says. He only wants custody so he can move back into the house and not part with any of his precious money by paying maintenance. Yes, I'll get you the paperwork. Now, please, ring me back when you've spoken to his solicitor.' Charlotte slapped her phone down onto the table with such force the iced coffee sploshed perilously close to the rim of the glass before burying her head in her hands, a long, high pitched sob piercing through the quiet café.

Pippa dithered on the spot, one second turning back towards Charlotte, the next taking a step towards the counter. She'd never seen Charlotte let down her frosty façade before. If she was honest, she hadn't quite believed Joe when he'd told her how upset she had been at the Spring Fayre, she hadn't been able to picture Charlotte being capable of any type of normal human emotion.

That sob though, it was pitiful. A memory of when she had entered the flat and found Mike's drawers half emptied, unwanted pants and T-shirts flung onto the floor around the bedroom, a note scribbled on the back of an envelope telling her that he had left, flashed into her head. The memory of the lost, desolate feeling that had swept through her body that day made Pippa's spine chill and she retraced her steps towards Charlotte. Sitting down next to her, she reached her arm around Charlotte's bony shoulder and pulled her close. Charlotte lowered her head onto Pippa's shoulder, her hair bouncing up and down as she took deep, shuddering breaths.

Should she say something? Try to tell her it would be OK? Pippa shook her head. There was nothing she could say that could take away the pain Charlotte was feeling. She knew that. She remembered feeling so angry every time someone had told her that Mike wasn't worth it or that she was better off without him. Yes, she was better off without him and no, he hadn't been worth the ton of tears she'd shed but at the time all she'd wanted to do whenever someone had said that to her was to scream at the top of her voice that it was OK for them, their partner, love of their life, hadn't broken their heart, it was OK for them to tell her meaningless platitudes when it wasn't their life being pulled apart at the seams. No, there was nothing she could say that would make it any easier for Charlotte to bear. There was nothing anyone could do or say that would ease the passage from securely married to completely alone.

'I'm sorry,' Charlotte swallowed her sobs, her voice sounding hoarse.

'That's OK. Here.' Pulling a paper napkin from the cutlery pot in the middle of the table, Pippa passed it to Charlotte.

'Thanks.' Sweeping her hair back away from her face, Charlotte wiped the tears from her cheeks. 'I really am sorry. I should never have broken down like that.'

'Please don't apologise. It's better out than in as they say. Are you OK?' Why had she asked that? Of course, the poor woman wasn't OK. Her marriage had just broken down. 'I know it feels like the end of the world now, but things will get better. I promise.'

'What do you mean? Has Joe been spreading rumours about

me?' Charlotte whipped her head around, her eyes circled with black mascara.

'What?' Of course, she wasn't supposed to know anything, Joe had told her in confidence and only after she had accused him of having an affair with Charlotte. 'I just overheard you on the phone. I'm sorry if I jumped to the wrong conclusion.' Holding her breath, Pippa watched as Charlotte's jaw hardened, her eyes narrowing as she peered at her through her tear-soaked eyelashes. Joe would never forgive her if she betrayed his confidence. Pippa pushed back her chair and stood up, she had definitely crossed the line.

'He had an affair. Probably still is.'

Slipping back into her seat, Pippa let her breath out. She believed her. 'Sorry to hear that.'

'Fifteen years of putting up with him, twelve of those married to the selfish pig, and this is how he repays me.'

Gingerly, Pippa put her arm around Charlotte's shoulder again as she sank her head back onto the table.

'Fifteen years. The best years of my life I've dedicated to him. I could have had a career, made something of myself. Instead, I gave everything up to follow him around the world on his stupid business trips. What am I supposed to do now? A shrivelled up old woman like me who can't get rid of the scars left behind by the caesarean however much "magic",' Charlotte lifted her head, faced Pippa and used her index fingers to exaggerate two inverted commas, 'scar fading cream, ointment and serum I have used. No one will want me now. No one. I'll be left on the shelf and become the single mum on the playground everyone stares pitifully at whilst secretly cheering that at least it's not them.'

Charlotte lifted her head again and wiped her eyes before looking at Pippa. 'Sorry, I don't mean that people gossip about you or pity you because you're a single mum. They don't. When you first arrived they did but now, I think they generally admire you, taking on this café on your own. I guess I mean I don't want to be that woman whose husband left her for a younger, better model, you know what I mean?'

'It's OK. I know what you mean. Joshua's dad left me for another woman too. I got home from work one day and he was gone.'

'That's awful.'

'I know. He was a rat, but looking back, I probably should have left him years before. He was a complete chauvinistic waste of space. I just hadn't seen it while we were together. At the time though, I felt as though my whole world had fallen apart. It felt as though someone had picked me and my bubble of life up and shaken it so everything fell out of place. It will take a while, but you will be able to get through this.'

'I don't see how. He wants custody of Max so that he can keep the house and not pay maintenance. He near enough admitted that was the reason, it's not as though he spends any time with his son at the moment, and when he does he normally sticks a film on for him so that he can do a conference call or something.' Charlotte sniffed and took a slurp from her iced coffee.

'What are you going to do?'

'I've got my solicitor on the case. She's the best there is in family law and works at my dad's firm. Apparently, I have a strong case because he spends so long away from the home with work he will have to prove how he can care for Max full-time while keeping things stable, like his school and afterschool activities. And she thinks being as I gave up my career to care for the family home and Max, I could even push to keep the house and get spousal maintenance as well as child maintenance.'

'That sounds promising then?'

'Yes. I know it does, but it still doesn't stop me worrying

about what could happen. I mean, my solicitor is good, really really good, but he'll have a damn good solicitor on his case too. There's a lot that could go wrong.'

'It must be terrifying. I guess you just need to trust that she knows what she's doing.'

'I know. She even thinks that after we outline our case and what he stands to lose if I win, I will be able to make him a deal and say that I'll drop my claim for spousal maintenance and he might drop the case.' Charlotte took a shuddering breath before blowing her nose.

'That sounds positive then.' Pippa re-centred the cutlery pot. Although Mike running off had been cowardly and pure selfish on his part, not to mention horrendous for Pippa, it sounded like she'd had an easy time of it compared to poor Charlotte. She had never had any financial support from Mike for Joshua, but at least he hadn't tried to use his son as a lever to get possession of the home or for financial benefits.

'How do you do it?'

'Sorry?' Pippa snapped back into the present and looked at Charlotte.

'How do you cope with being a... single mum?' Charlotte almost spat the words 'single mum', making Pippa recoil.

'Mike, Joshua's dad, just upped and left one day. Before I went to work he was sat in the kitchen eating his toast as usual. I remember having to look away and bite my tongue because he was getting crumbs all over the kitchen floor which I'd only mopped the night before. And when I got home, he was gone. He hadn't left a note or anything, obviously, I wasn't even worthy of that in his eyes. A few of his clothes had been taken. To be honest, I assumed he'd just gone to stay at a mum's house, he did that a lot you see, just left for a few days. Looking back, he probably hadn't been at his mother's, he'd probably been off and about with his mistress.' Pippa grimaced, she'd been so naïve, all the signs had been there, glaringly obvious in fact.

'He didn't even tell you? How long until you realised he wasn't coming back?'

'Oh, not long. About half an hour after I'd got back, the neighbour who lived in the flat below came running up, shouting that Mike had run off with his girlfriend and I must know where they were. Of course, I didn't. I still don't know where he is.'

'He doesn't see Joshua? At all?' Charlotte picked at the scrunched-up tissue in her fist.

'Nope. He hasn't even called. It has been really tough on Joshua. Especially at first, because it was his dad who did most of the childcare while I worked and suddenly he wasn't there any more. He still asks about him but the move down here has definitely helped. It's taken his mind off of things I think.'

'At least Max will still see his dad, I guess.'

'Yes, it should make the transition easier hopefully.'

'Just as long as I can win the custody battle, of course.' Charlotte smiled bitterly before frowning and staring at the tissue in her hand.

'You will.'

'How do you cope with everyone staring and knowing your business though? I'm so worried about telling the girls. I don't want their pity. I can barely face their smug faces each morning anyway, I just couldn't cope with them pitying me because my husband's left me.'

'I'm sure they won't pity you. They'll be worried about you for sure, but that's completely different than pitying you. They're your friends, they care about you.'

'Maybe. I'm supposed to be meeting them here in a few

minutes, you won't say anything, will you? I will tell them, just in my own time.'

'Of course, I won't. Why don't you go and clean yourself up and I'll get you a fresh iced coffee?' Standing up, Pippa scraped her chair back and picked up the abandoned iced coffee.

'Thank you.'

'You're welcome and anytime you want to talk, just shout. You will get through this and be happier for it. You're a strong person, I thought that the first time I met you on the playground.'

* * *

Back behind the counter, Pippa pulled her mobile from the apron pocket, still no text from Joe.

'Afternoon, what can I get you?' Putting her mobile, screen down, next to the coffee machine, Pippa smiled as Charlotte's crew tottered towards her, their high heels tap-tapping on the lino.

'Afternoon. I'll just have a glass of spring water and a small salad, please? Hold the dressing though, I'm trying to lose a few pounds before my Lawrence's work ball on Saturday. He thinks he's going to hear about his promotion beforehand you see, so I must look my best.' Sadie flicked her long brown hair and smiled over her shoulder at her friends standing beside her.

'That's absolutely fine. I'll bring it over.' This would be a long couple of hours before the school pick up. Taking a deep breath, Pippa reminded herself that it shouldn't matter who she served, as long as they were bringing money into her business she should be grateful.

13

'It was lovely meeting your sister yesterday. How is she today?'

'She's quite a character, isn't she? I'm enjoying having her around though, the house does get lonely sometimes.' Wiping the counter, Carol collected the crumbs before shaking the dishcloth off into the bin.

'Are you sure you don't mind looking after Joshua later while me and Joe go out?' Joe had promised her his mum was more than happy to have both the boys while they went out on a proper date but she couldn't help feeling a bit uncomfortable. Carol already did so much to help her.

'About that, I'm afraid Joe asked me to tell you he couldn't make it tonight.' Carol stopped what she was doing to look at Pippa.

'Oh, OK.' Why hadn't he told her himself? And why couldn't he make it? She hadn't seen him for almost a week now, not properly anyway, and he'd been quite distant when she had ran into him on the school run. That was why he'd arranged for them to go on a proper date that night, to make up for it.

'Harley's not been himself since he found out about his mum

and I think Joe just wants to spend some time with him, to reassure him.'

'Right, what's happened to his mum?' Pippa furrowed her brow, Joe hadn't said anything to her, she was sure of that. Joe hardly spoke two words about Harley's mum so she was sure she'd have remembered if he'd told her.

'Didn't Joe tell you? The bloke she ran off with has dumped her. Serves her right if you ask me, but she's been trying to muscle in on Harley and wanting to spend more time with him. Of course, normally it would be a good thing, a mother wanting to spend time with her son, but after her near enough abandoning him and barely seeing him once a week when she was with the homewrecker, Joe's obviously worried about upsetting Harley's routine if she gets back with her fellow or finds someone else to latch on to and drops him again.'

'Oh bless him. Poor Harley, it must be confusing for him.'

'Yes, it is. She thinks she can just pop over to the house whenever she feels like it. Then, of course, she promises him she'll take him out for a meal or on a trip out or whatever. She doesn't consider the fact that he has his football club to go to or that he's just had dinner or it's his bedtime. It's like watching her play tug of war with the poor mite.' Carol shook her head and emptied a can of beans into a saucepan.

'So she's been popping round to Joe's quite a bit then?' Pippa pulled out the grill, the sausages were almost done.

'Yes, as far as I know, she's been around every evening this week. Yesterday evening Joe came over to mine just to get away from her. She just thinks she can pick off where she left off with her relationship with Harley, and she can't. It's not fair on him.'

'No, no it's not.' Pippa swallowed a bitter taste in her mouth. Why hadn't he come round to the café to get out of his house last night?

'Here come the rabble.' Carol stirred the beans before ladling them onto the plates.

'Hello, ladies. How are we on this fine morning?' Gus unzipped his yellow plastic overalls, pulling it down to his waist revealing a tight-fitting navy T-shirt.

'Fine.' Carol turned around, giving her attention to one of the other fishermen.

'How about you?' Leaning his elbows on the counter, Gus grinned at Pippa.

'I'm good thanks. And how is life treating you?' Smiling, Pippa shared the sausages onto the plates.

'Had a bit of a rough start to the week, but things are looking up after coming in here.' Gus leaned across and pinched a sausage from the plate nearest to him.

'Oi.' Swatting his hand away, she wished she could do the same to his chat-up lines. 'I noticed you weren't out fishing, did you take some time off?'

'Yes, but enough of my problems, let me stare a little longer at the great views in here before I taste your delicious brekkie.'

Laughing politely, Pippa turned to collect the fried bread and spotted Joe at the far end of the counter. Smiling, she waved at him. Joe grinned back and wriggled his fingers in a self-conscious wave.

'That fried bread looks tasty, of course, it's not the only thing in here to look tasty.' Gus stroked Pippa's hand as she loaded the plates in front of her.

'Hey, I'm serving.' Pulling her hand away from him sharply, she watched as the last piece of fried bread fell to the floor.

'Sorry, I crossed the line. I'll wait for my grub at the table.'

Frowning, Pippa looked back towards where Joe had been standing. 'Carol, where did Joe go?'

'He left, love.'

'Drat.' Pippa whispered under her breath, he must have been called away.

* * *

'I'm glad they're gone, well not all of them I guess. I'm just glad Gus has gone, he sometimes gives me the creeps a bit.' Rounding the counter, Pippa weaved her way through the tables, kicking chairs back under and stacking the debris left over from the fishermen's breakfast onto a tray held in her left hand.

'He certainly can be. I'm glad you're not being brought in by his charm, he's not good news. I saw the way he was trying to flirt with you.' Carol shook her head and tutted. 'And so soon after dumping Mia too.'

'He did say he was going through a tough patch, that's why he's not been in the last few days. He's had the time off work to sort things out or obviously to try and get over his relationship breaking down.'

'Sorting things out? Getting over his relationship? My arse.' Carol snorted.

'Oh.' Pippa paused on her way back to the dishwasher, she'd never heard Carol talk like that about anyone before.

'He dumped Mia by text and swanned off on a last-minute holiday to Spain.'

'Spain?' Had she heard right? Carol was ramming the mugs into the dishwasher so frantically Pippa was surprised she hadn't broken any of them. Yet.

'Yes, Spain. He breaks up a marriage, makes his mistress distance herself from her child and then, bam! Breaks up with her and has the audacity to swan off to Spain, probably to escape any confrontation he deserves from her. I'm sorry, but it's one thing messing around with another human being's life, but when there's a child involved, it's downright cruel. Poor Harley doesn't know whether he's coming or going at the moment.'

'Harley?' After pushing one of the plates back into the centre of the tray to balance it, Pippa wiped her red ketchup-stained finger on the dishcloth she had hooked in the crock of her little finger.

'Yes.' Carol straightened slowly, her hand on the small of her back. 'Oh, you didn't know?'

'Know what?'

'It was Gus who was having an affair with Harley's mum. Mia is Joe's ex.'

'Oh.' The tray clattered as Pippa thudded it slightly too hard down on the counter. 'He never said.'

'Didn't he?'

'No, I would have remembered that.' Why would Joe not have mentioned Gus had stolen his wife from him? Thinking back, Joe had always been frosty towards Gus and he'd made some comment when she had first called him out to sort the leak out and Gus had popped by. Pippa shook her head, how could she not have picked up on something? And more to the point, why hadn't he told her?

* * *

Pippa flicked the channels again. Why was there never anything on TV? Maybe Joshua was right, maybe she should look into paying for one of those subscription TV packages.

She tapped her phone with her index finger. Should she message him? She didn't want to come across as too needy but she did want to know where she stood. She understood he must be preoccupied with Mia being back on the scene, but the night after the Spring Fayre had been lovely. More than lovely. A warm blush crept up her neck. It had felt right. It had felt as though they were meant to be. Pippa grimaced, even thinking about describing their time together as 'meant to be' echoed like a cliché in her head, but it was true. It had felt right. She had felt at home in his arms. They had fitted.

Cradling her phone in the palm of her hand, Pippa spun her apps to messages and clicked on his name. She'd just message him casually and see if he mentioned anything. She could feel herself falling for him, her feelings intensifying, and she needed to know if he felt the same way. Plus, if he knew she was beside him, willing and happy to support him with Harley's mum, then it might just take a bit of stress off of him. She probably should have messaged or rung him earlier, as soon as Carol had told her what was going on. Why had she left it so long?

Hi, how's it going?

It's good thanks. Harley's been asleep for ages so just chilling. How about you?

Same. Trying to find something to watch.

Missing you.

You too.

Really enjoyed Friday.

Me too.

Pippa paused, her index finger hovering over the glowing screen. She took a deep breath and typed.

So can I ask you a question?

Of course.

What are we?

What do you mean?

Well…can you see a future for us?

She probably didn't even need to ask. If the way he acted around her was anything to go by, then, of course, he wanted a future together. Then again, he had been pretty distant but that was only because of everything going on with Harley and his mum, wasn't it?

Pippa scrunched up her nose. Why wasn't he messaging back straight away? He had been before, maybe she shouldn't have asked. Maybe it was too soon to put a label on them. Maybe it had meant nothing to him. Maybe she meant nothing. Or maybe Harley had woken up or he'd popped to the loo or something. She was probably overthinking everything.

She watched as the light from her phone faded, the screensaver kicking in.

Can I ring you?

Pippa grabbed her phone.

Yes.

'Hi.'
'Hello, you,' Joe's voice breathed down the line.

Pippa smiled, she loved the way he began their conversations.

'How are you? Your mum mentioned the problems you've been having with Harley's mum.' Twisting her hair, she hoped she hadn't just landed Carol in trouble.

'She said she'd told you.'

'How come you didn't tell me yourself instead of making excuses?' Did that sound a bit accusing? 'I mean, you didn't have to, of course, but when she told me, I felt bad. Maybe I could have helped, been someone to rant to about it.' Pippa laughed trying to keep the conversation casual.

'I probably should have done but I didn't want to put it on you.'

'You wouldn't have.'

'Maybe.'

'And you know you could have come round here this evening if you'd wanted. Harley could have had a sleepover with Joshua and we could have caught up.' She'd had to say it, it was bugging her why he hadn't thought of it if he'd known they didn't have plans.

'It's been a bit of tough week, I just wanted to keep Harley in his routine.'

'That's fair enough. Probably a good idea.' They could have made sure the kids had had an early night if that was all he was worried about. 'Hey, that was a fleeting visit earlier.'

'I know, I came in to say hi then I saw you with Gus, and I guess, it made me feel weird.'

'I was just serving him breakfast. The fishermen come in for their brekkie. It's good business.' Had he felt jealous? So he does feel something then?

'I know and I accept that. It's just hard not to be tempted to knock his block off every time I see him.' Joe laughed although Pippa could tell he was being at least a bit serious.

'Fair enough.' Why did she keep saying that? And why wasn't he answering the question he'd rung her to answer? Taking a deep breath, Pippa guessed she'd just have to ask again. 'So?'

'So, what?'

'So, continuing on from our texts...' Come on remember. It was embarrassing enough.

'What about them?'

Was he doing this on purpose? Did he like hearing her squirm? He was such a tease. 'I asked you if you could see a future with us.'

Silence.

'Joe?' Was he teasing her again? If so, she'd pay him back later. Maybe she'd remind him on every anniversary how he'd teased her at the beginning of their relationship. When would they tell the boys? When would he and Harley move in? Or would they move to his or get someplace new? She could rent out the flat above the café for a bit of extra income if he wanted them to have their own place together, a new start. She slapped her forehead, she was getting way ahead of herself here. It was just that she didn't feel she really needed to ask the question. The way she'd felt in Joe's arms had been confirmation enough.

'Pippa, look, you don't want a relationship with me. Not really.'

'Pardon?' Automatically she put her hand protectively over her heart.

'It's been fun, but you don't want a relationship with someone like me.'

'What do you mean?'

'I mean, it wouldn't be fair on you. I'm a single dad with my own business, I don't have much time for relationships. It wouldn't be fair on you to accept the limited amount of time I could offer you.'

'I'm a single mum with my own business too, remember? I know what it's like not to have much time. I thought you enjoyed spending time together? We've spent enough time together over the past few weeks so time can't be that much of an issue anyway.' What did he mean? She knew what she would be getting into, he must realise that. She was understanding of time issues and everything else that went hand in hand with being a single parent.

'I have really enjoyed spending time with you and getting to know you better.'

'Right...' Pippa picked at a yellow stain on the arm of the sofa. It was crusty. Joshua must have split some ice cream on it earlier. 'But you can't see a future for us?'

'I think things have become more complicated. You deserve better than me. You deserve more. I'd like to be friends though. I really mean that. You understand, don't you?'

Pippa swallowed, a raw taste of bile rising to her mouth. 'Yes, of course, I understand. I have to go now, Joshua's just woken up.'

She clicked the phone off, letting the silence surround her, the thick suffocating smell of loneliness enveloping her body. Pulling her knees to her chest, she bit down on her bottom lip. She would not cry. Shaking her head, she visualised the thoughts of her 'future' with Joe pouring out of her mind. Squeezing her eyes tight shut, she felt a rush of heat flood her face.

How could she have been so presumptuous? It was the first time since Mike that she'd even come close to trusting another man. She had been so so sure that he'd felt the same way as her. He'd spoken about experiences they'd share in the future. She covered her face with her hands, trying to block everything out.

He'd even asked her if she wanted any more children. She remembered it so clearly. They'd torn themselves apart from each other after an afternoon together and gone into the café to make themselves a coffee. They'd had to duck behind the counter as someone had knocked on the door, how they hadn't seen the closed sign she didn't know.

'Would you have any more kids?' Sat back on his haunches, Joe had leaned forward towards her too far to whisper and he'd had to grab hold of a cupboard door to stop himself falling into her.

'I don't know. I think so. I mean I'm completely happy and lucky to have Joshua, but I'd always pictured myself having more. I don't know. I guess I'd be happy either way.' She hadn't told him that she'd already named their future children; Josephine, after her dad naturally, and Harper, just because she liked the name. She remembered thinking that she didn't want to scare him off, but at the same time feeling silly because she had known nothing would. That they were meant to be together. 'How about you?'

'There can never be enough children in the world, can there? Yes, I would.' He had grinned at her, kissed her on the nose and peeked above the counter before pulling her to her feet.

Had he led her on that day? Or had he changed his mind? If so, why?

Pippa clenched her fists. Of course, Harley's mum. That was the only thing that had changed, Mia had been dumped by Gus. And now he wanted her back.

Rolling onto her side, Pippa dug her teeth into her fist and let the tears flow.

14

Turning the sausages under the grill, Pippa heard the bell above the café door tinkle.

'Hi, Carol.' She straightened up and tried to suppress the blush she could feel creeping up her neck. Had Joe told her about their conversation?

'Hi, love, how are you doing?' With a gentle thud, Carol dumped her handbag on the counter.

'I'm fine, thanks. How are you? How's Silv?'

'Getting stronger and more stroppy every day.' Carol opened her mouth, closed it and opened it again. 'Joe told me he has called things off with you. Are you OK?'

'Joe? Yes, he did. Never mind though, I kind of figure it's the wrong time to get into anything serious now anyway. Not with the café going from strength to strength.' Pippa picked up the cutlery container from the dishwasher and went to refill the pots on the tables. Blinking, she batted back the tears, willing them not to embarrass her. Carol would think she was completely soppy, crying over a non-relationship that had actually barely begun.

'I hope this isn't going to change anything or make things awkward between us.'

Pippa felt Carol's hand on her shoulder, turned and smiled.

'Of course not.'

'Good.' Carol rubbed her hands together before picking her bag up again. 'And just for the record, I think he's being stupid letting you go.'

Pippa smiled again, a real smile this time. Trust Carol not to mince her words.

* * *

'Mum, can Harley come and play?' Joshua panted, his hands on his knees, before running back into the sea again.

'Not today, sweetie.'

'Why not?'

'Because he's busy today.'

'That's what you said yesterday.'

'Well, I think he's spending more time with his mum now after school, so he will be a bit busier from now on.' Pippa dug her toe into the sand and drew a heart, immediately kicking sand back over it.

'I don't know if I believe you.' Joshua flopped down on the sand at her feet. His uniform would be covered in the stuff, she'd have to get a wash on as soon as they got home. His other school shorts and T-shirt were still in the dirty washing pile too.

'Pardon?'

'I said, I don't know if I believe you. Harley said his dad told him that we were busy yesterday. Well, we weren't, were we?'

'I do have the café to run you know.'

'I know that, but him and Joe could have come round to ours like they always used to. We could have played, couldn't we?'

'Umm.'

'Mum?'

'Yes?'

'Are you even listening to me? I said that me and Harley could have played at the café like we always did anyway.'

'I'm sorry, Joshua. It's not that easy.'

'It always used to be.' Joshua stared into the ocean before looking back up at Pippa. 'Can we play here for a bit?'

'Yes, go on then.' Lowering herself to the sand, Pippa watched Joshua drag a large flat pebble through the sand making a series of complicated roads. She'd have to ask Carol to have a word with Joe and see if they can't just be friends, or else civil to each other, for the sake of Joshua and Harley. They hadn't even known that a relationship had been on the cards between their parents, it wasn't fair on them to suffer the consequences.

* * *

'Pippa, hello.'

Pippa paused and pulled up the lever of the coffee machine, the mug underneath barely half full and twisted around. 'Joe.'

'Thank you for having Harley round to play and I *am* sorry if I gave you mixed signals.'

Mixed signals? There had been no mixed signals. All she'd been doing since last week was going over everything that had happened between her and Joe, and she definitely knew that there had been no mixed signals. What they had had together, even for only the briefest of times, had been something. She was certain of that.

She'd come to the conclusion that he still had feelings for Mia. It made perfect sense and was the only explanation she could think of. It had been when she'd turned up that Joe had gone all funny and backtracked. She didn't blame him, not any more anyway. As far as she was aware, he had been happily married to Mia when she'd ran off with Gus so it stood to reason that he would still be in love with her and wanted her back.

Pippa shook her head. 'It's fine. Can we just forget about it all though please and start again? The boys are such good friends, it would be a real shame if this impacted on them.'

Joe cleared his throat. 'I couldn't agree more.'

'Good. I'll just go and call them. They're playing upstairs.' Pippa backed away and closed the adjoining door between the flat and café behind her.

Sinking onto a step halfway up the stairs, she sunk her teeth into her index finger and closed her eyes. This was going to be harder than she thought. Taking a deep breath, she slid herself up the wall to standing and plastered a smile on her face.

'Boys, Harley your dad's here. Time to go home.' Pippa surveyed the room, the coffee table had been pushed to the side and toy cars stood in lines, weaving across the room. A box stood on its side, parking spaces drawn on in the telltale zig-zaggy lines of a child in a hurry. It seemed the cars were queuing for a space. 'It looks as though you've had fun though.'

'Yes we have, but Harley's car has broken down and I need to get through all this traffic to fix it. So can we just have a few more minutes please, please, please?' Joshua indicated a blue car on its side by the fireplace.

'Umm, I think Joe is in a bit of a hurry. Sorry. But maybe we can invite Harley back another day.'

'Can we ask him? Come on, Harley, let's go ask your dad.'

'Joshua...' The boys ran down the stairs leaving Pippa standing alone in the middle of the car covered living room. Turning on her feet, she forced herself to follow them down the stairs. Poor Mrs Garey was still waiting for her mocha.

Halfway down the stairs, Joshua and Harley hurtled their way back up.

'Joe said yes. Harley can stay for a bit, if it's OK with you. It is, isn't it? OK with you? Thanks, Mum.' By the time he'd finished the sentence, Joshua was nowhere to be seen.

Taking a deep breath, Pippa put her head down and headed straight for the coffee machine. She'd make Mrs Garey's mocha and focus on work. With any luck, Joe would have gone for a walk or something.

'Pippa.'

'Yes. Damn.' She wiped the dark liquid from her wrist off on a tea towel and refilled the mug, for the third time now. 'Yes?'

'Are you trying to avoid me?'

Pippa laughed, how could she possibly avoid him when he was sat squarely in the middle of the counter?

'Had you wanted me to tell the boys I was busy and they couldn't play longer?'

'No, why would you think that?'

'You just seem a bit... jumpy, that's all.' Joe laid his hands palm down on the counter.

'Sorry, I'm just tired, that's all.' That one normally worked when she couldn't think of another excuse. 'I'm going to take Mrs Garey her mocha now and then I'll make you one and you can sit at the table by the window and enjoy the view while you wait, if you like? Good.'

'OK, if that's what you want.'

* * *

'Pippa, what's going on between you two?' Charlotte slid her empty coffee mug onto the counter.

'Who? Refill?' Pippa waved the mug in front of her.

'I think I will, yes. Don't give me that innocent crap, you know who I'm talking about.' Charlotte looked pointedly over at Joe before staring back at Pippa.

'Oh, nothing.' Waving her hand dismissively, Pippa turned her back and refilled the mug.

'Correct me if I'm wrong, but I'm sure it was you who gave me the "oh, it's better to talk about your problems" spiel? So talk. I'm listening, and I have a whole coffee to finish before I'm going anywhere.' Charlotte hopped onto a stool and crossed her arms.

'OK, OK.' Holding up her arms, Pippa surrendered, Charlotte would only continue the interrogation ruthlessly, so she might as well open up sooner rather than later. 'Me and Joe kind of had this thing going. Or I thought we did, anyway.'

'You both kept that quiet! Joe spent ages talking to me when John turned up at the Spring Fayre, he didn't mention anything.'

'Yes, well, as it turns out he didn't think it was anything, which probably explains why he didn't mention anything to you.'

'So this is why?' Charlotte waved her free hands between Pippa and Joe.

'Yes. To be fair, he's trying to be friendly about it but, I can't.' Shrugging, Pippa picked up the dishcloth and wiped the spotless counter.

'Because you thought it was going somewhere?'

'Nailed it in one.' Studying an imaginary spot on the counter, Pippa felt Charlotte's hand on her arm and smiled up at her. 'I thought we had something special. He was the first man since Mike that I'd even liked in that way, let alone thought I could trust.'

'I'm sorry. It's crap when that happens.'

'It is crap, you're right.'

'And he showed no sign at all that it wasn't just a casual thing?'

'No, he even spoke about the future. As if we'd be together in the future, I mean.'

'And nothing changed between you?'

'No. Apart from his wife splitting from the man she ran off with.'

'Oh.' Charlotte shook her head.

'Oh, what?' Jerking her head up, she looked into Charlotte's eyes.

'Just that, well, he was really cut up when she left. Me and John were really worried about him actually.'

'And you think he wants her back?' Pippa put her hand to her neck and coughed. It felt as though she had something stuck in her throat.

'Probably not. That was over two years ago now.' Charlotte waved her hand in front of her as if she was trying to bat the words lingering in the air away from them. 'It's just me being stupid. And bitter. Remember my husband's been sleeping around, I'm just thinking they're all the same. Joe's not. Joe's lovely. He...'

'It's OK. I've been thinking the exact same. Whether he knows he's finished with me because he wants her back yet or whether it's subconscious, I don't know. But that's why, and I've just got to get over him.' Smiling, she watched as Joe stretched his long legs under the table, placed his hands behind his head and leaned back. She would miss him though. 'I think I'm just destined to be single. No one would want me anyway.'

'Don't talk daft, you'll find someone. We both will. Hopefully.'

'Maybe.'

15

'School was brilliant today! We had the firefighters come in and we were even allowed to go into the fire engine and have a look! It was amazing! Can Harley come round and celebrate with a massive ice cream sundae?' Joshua threw his book bag at Pippa's feet and ran over to Harley where he was stood with Joe.

'Don't worry about it, Joshie, I'll pick your things up and wouldn't it be nice if you could wait for me to answer? Not all of the time, but every once in a while maybe?' Muttering under her breath, Pippa bent and retrieved the book bag, opening it to check Joshua's water bottle hadn't smashed.

She'd planned a nice film night for the evening. She'd even bought a pic 'n' mix for them both from the tourist shop further up the beach and bought the new Lego DVD Joshua had been nagging her for. She didn't want Harley over. If Harley came, Joe normally tagged along and even now she found it difficult not to daydream about how their lives would have turned out if Joe hadn't called things off.

'Hey, Pippa, are you sure it's OK if we come over? Joshua's invited us for dinner, is that right?' Joe grinned at her.

'Dinner? Yes, of course.' Smiling, she gritted her teeth. How could Joe always be so cheerful when they were together? Probably because she had meant nothing to him anyway.

'And a massive ice cream sundae for pudding!' Joshua piped up, jumping up and down. 'Come on, Harley, let's run on ahead. Are we going the beach way?'

'We can do.' Pippa called to their backs. 'Just wait for us when you get to the road!'

'Do you think they heard?' Joe nudged Pippa's elbow and laughed.

'I think they heard. Whether they chose to listen is another thing entirely.'

* * *

'Thank you, Mrs Garey. Now have a lovely evening.' Pippa watched Mrs Garey totter down the path and turned the sign to 'CLOSED'. Placing her fingertips to her forehead, she tried to ease the threat of a migraine and mentally ticked off what she could cook for dinner. There wasn't much in the freezer in the flat and she didn't like dipping into the café stores because it muddled the inventory, but she might have to tonight. She didn't think fish finger sandwiches would cut a celebration meal and she didn't want to order a takeaway, which was what it would have been if it had been just her and Joshua, because then Joe would realise that she hadn't planned on inviting them back.

'Mum, can I have a drink?'

'Please? Yes, here you go.' Placing a glass of water in front of him, Pippa wiped the sweat from Joshua's hot forehead, his hair sticking up at the front. 'Are you having fun?'

'Yes. We've been racing on the beach. Do you know where my football is? Joe said if I could find it he'll play footie with us.'

'Yes, it's upstairs under your bed.'

'Thanks, Mum.' Joshua gave Pippa a quick hug before running upstairs, his small feet pounding on the stairs.

* * *

Two minutes later, he was back down, football cradled in the crook of his arm as he ran back through the café.

'Enjoy!'

'Oh, Mum, what are we having for dinner?' Joshua paused, door ajar and looked back at Pippa.

'What do you think everybody would like? Chips and chicken nuggets or jacket potatoes with tuna and sweetcorn?'

'Jacket potatoes with lots and lots of tuna and sweetcorn please!'

'OK.' Pippa went to the window and watched as he ran up to Joe who high fived him before taking the ball and kicking it back towards Joshua who had run slightly away.

Joe was so good with him. And Joshua really looked up to him. Pippa shook her head and walked away. She should make a start on dinner. Yesterday, Charlotte had mentioned that she'd seen Joe at the supermarket with Mia at the weekend.

* * *

'Mum, Mum.'

Pippa banged her head on the open cupboard door at just the same time as the café door slammed shut.

'Mum, Daddy's outside! Daddy's walking up the beach! He's come to see me!' Joshua's screeched, catching his breath between each word.

'Don't be daft, Joshie.' Rubbing her head, Pippa was sure she could feel a bruise forming already.

'No. He really is!'

'Joshie, sweetie. I'm trying to get dinner.' Looking over at Joshua's flushed red face, his eyes glinting, Pippa cursed Mike once again for hurting his son. 'Come here.' Walking towards him and opening her arms, Pippa pulled him into a hug, kissing his forehead. 'I know you miss your Dad but...'

Pushing his hands against her stomach, Joshua stood back, looking up at her. 'It really is him. Come and have a look if you don't believe me.'

'He seems pretty set that it's his dad.' Joe came running into the café, Harley behind him. 'As soon as he saw him come round the corner down by the beach huts, he said he had to come and tell you.'

'OK.' Flinging her arms up in the air, Pippa began walking towards the door. 'I'll go and check if that'll make you feel better, Joshie?'

Joshua nodded, his brown hair bouncing on his head, which reminded Pippa she was supposed to have rung the barbers for an appointment.

'Right, you stay in here.' Pausing at the door, Pippa put her hand up to silence the protests. 'And I'll go and have a look.' She rolled her eyes at Joe and mouthed, 'I'll only be a minute.'

Outside, she shielded her eyes from the brilliant glow of the sunset reflecting on the blue ocean. She'd stay out here a minute or two, just to make Joshua feel that she had taken him seriously. She'd have to think of something to tell him. She couldn't tell him that there was no way in a million years that his dad would bother to come and see him.

Taking a deep breath, Pippa let the warm air, laced with the distinctive saltiness of the sea, envelop her. Life could actually be good here, more than good, if business continued growing. She'd get some flyers printed to entice the holidaymakers to come and experience an authentic cream tea and home-made cakes.

'No, no, no.' To begin with, the words escaped as a whisper, getting louder and louder as he got closer. It was definitely him, Mike. The closer he got, the more she was sure of this. Dead sure. He was wearing his uniform dark skinny jeans with rips at the knees with a pale blue T-shirt. She'd always thought he was too old to wear ripped skinny jeans.

'Hello, Pippa.'

He was there, right in front of her now. She could see the wrinkles around his eyes. They looked like laughter lines. They were new.

'No, this can't be happening. You can't be here.' Backing away, the handrail leading up to the café felt cool and hard on the small of her back.

'Pippa, listen. I can explain.'

'I don't want to hear it. Just go.' Turning, she collided with Joe who had appeared by her side.

'Is everything OK?' Joe crossed his arms, staring down into Mike's eyes. He was only a couple of inches taller, but he seemed to tower over him.

'Hey, mate, I just want to talk to her.' Mike stepped back and held his hands up.

'Pippa?' Joe looked at her.

'No, it's fine.'

'I only want a chance to apologise, to make things right.'

'Mike, just go. Please?'

'Dad! Daddy! I knew it was you! I told you, didn't I, Mum? I said it was Daddy!' Joshua ran between them straight into Mike's open arms.

'Buddy! I've missed you so so much.'

'Me too, Daddy, I've missed you. Why didn't you come any sooner then? If you missed me?' Joshua leaned back, his arms still around Mike's neck and looked into his eyes.

'I didn't know where you'd moved to, did I? Mummy forgot to tell me, didn't she?'

'Mum? Did you?' Joshua's small voice came out barely a whisper.

'I did.' Pippa rubbed Joshua's back and narrowed her eyes at Mike. 'Daddy knows that, don't you, Mike?'

'Let's not worry about that. It's all boring adult talk anyway, and I want to catch up with you now, buddy. Now jump down and show me around your café, how about a tour? Would that be a good idea?' Lowering Joshua to the floor, Mike whispered to Pippa, 'I'm here to make it all up to the both of you, Pippa. If you just let me.'

Gritting her teeth, Pippa stood back to let Mike and Joshua pass and leaned against the handrail.

'Are you OK? Why did you just let him into your café?' Joe leaned back next to Pippa, the handrail shaking slightly against his weight.

'He's Joshua's dad, isn't he? What else am I supposed to do?'

'Daddy, can I go and show Joshua's dad around too?' Harley, who had been observing from a short distance away approached them.

'Is Mike safe with the boys?' Joe leaned in and spoke quietly.

'Yes, he's harmless enough. An eejit, but a harmless eejit.'

'Go on then.'

They both watched Harley run up the path and into the café.

'What are you going to do?'

'I don't know. Once he's tried to explain his actions he'll likely be on his way. It's just so unsettling for Joshua. But they don't see it, do they? Not the parents who walk away in the first place and not get in touch.'

'No, they don't.'

'Anyway, he'll probably be gone by the morning. We best go and see what they're up to.' Pushing away from the handrail, Pippa paused and waited for Joe to join her. 'Thanks for coming to see if everything was OK.'

'Anytime.'

* * *

'Thank you for letting me stay for dinner, I appreciate it.' Mike paused by the front door to the café.

'I didn't really have much choice. I hinted enough but couldn't really ask you outright to leave in front of Joshua, could I?' Crossing her arms, Pippa looked at him. He had shaved his blonde hair so it was barely visible against his scalp. It suited him, she had to admit that. And he'd obviously been doing something, he had a healthy glow on his cheeks, maybe his new job was based outside. He'd worked as a labourer when they had been together. Well, 'worked' was probably too strong a word, but he had dipped his toes into the labouring world even if he'd only lasted one morning.

'Actually, could I have a quiet word with you now that Joshua is asleep? Please?' His green eyes bore into her.

'Why not?' She indicated the table by the window and they both sat opposite each other.

'I know what I did, walking out on you and Joshua, was inexcusable but I was in a really bad place.'

'You ran off with the slapper downstairs! You weren't in a "bad place", you'd been shagging her behind my back for months.'

'That's not true. It was a silly mistake. I hadn't been thinking straight.'

'It wasn't just a silly mistake.' Pippa spread her hands, palms down in front of her on the table. 'The evening you left, I had Dom, do you remember him? Shirley's boyfriend? Well, he barged his way into the flat, shouting the odds, wanting to know where you were. Anyway, Shirley had had the courtesy of leaving him a note saying that she had been having an affair with you for six months already. So don't give me that spin about it being a rash decision and you hadn't been "thinking straight". You had known exactly what you were doing.'

'It had just all got on top of me. Not being able to provide for my family had been really hard.' Mike reached out, his skin warm against Pippa's hand.

'That was your own doing. The number of times the Job Centre had lined up interviews for you that you didn't attend and the number of jobs you started and then left on the same day...' Shaking her head, Pippa moved her hands away from his and laid them in her lap.

'I just hadn't seen a way out of the financial rubbish we'd got ourselves into. I thought the only choice I had was to leave, to give you and Joshua a fresh start.'

'Are you being serious?' A deep hollow guffaw escaped Pippa's throat. 'It was you who had gotten us into all of the financial mess. It was you who had time and time again gone down the bookies with the rent money, you who had hidden all of the utility bills, promising me that you had paid them with the money I had given you to pay them. The money I had earned by working all the bloody hours under the sun.'

'I know, I feel so ashamed that I behaved that way, but I had a gambling problem. I've been getting help, my counsellor thinks me running off with Shirley was all part of that. I never stopped loving you, Pippa, it was the gambling that made me run off with her.'

'Right, of course. And I suppose it was "the gambling",' Pippa curled her index fingers mimicking inverted commas, 'that stopped you from being capable of thinking about the consequences of abandoning your partner and young son with a ton of debt?'

'You can laugh, but it was. It really was. I never ever stopped loving you both. And look, it didn't do you any harm, did it? Look at you, lording it up round here. A café, beach on your doorstep. I did you a favour really, wouldn't you say?'

'You left us in real trouble. I don't think you actually realise how much you did us over.'

'I do. I really do. I'm so sorry.' Reaching out, Mike left his hands lying on the table between them.

'The rent hadn't been paid in four months. I had to beg that snotty nosed woman from the estate agents to let us stay and she only agreed if I started paying off the arrears. The electricity got cut at one point too. I can tell you, that's not much fun with a five-year-old in the middle of winter.'

'I'm sorry.'

Pippa batted away Mike's apology with her hand. 'Over the following months, I worked all the hours I could. Joshua practically lived with my mum. I hardly even saw my own son.'

'I...'

'And then the bailiffs turned up. They took everything.' Closing her eyes, she could still picture them, could smell the sickly sweat of the bolshy one. Automatically, she rubbed the shoulder she had hurt when they had pushed her aside.

'I didn't know the bailiffs had come.'

Narrowing her eyes, she looked at Mike.

'I didn't. I swear.'

'What did you think would happen when you stopped paying your repayment plan? That everyone would let you off, pat you on the back and let you get on with your life? No consequences?'

'Where were they from? The bailiffs?'

'That's the really insulting part, they were from some garage up north. We didn't even have a car.' She shook her head. 'Was it for your tart's car? Or did you buy a car so that you could run off together? Was that it?' Pippa looked down at her hands. 'You had planned on running off all along, hadn't you? The debt was nothing to do with me, Joshua or the flat. At all.'

'Oh.' Looking down at the table, Mike made a pathetic noise.

'Is that all you've got to say?'

'I've said I'm sorry, there's not much else I can say.' He looked up. 'But, hey, at least things turned out well in the end! You should be thanking me really. If I hadn't have left, you may never have moved down here!'

'I think you should go now.' Scraping back her chair, Pippa stood up, her hands clasped tightly behind her back.

'It was a joke! That's all, just a joke. I know I've put you through some really difficult times and I am really really sorry about that.'

'Please go.' Holding the front door open, Pippa watched as Mike reluctantly stood up and slid his chair back under the table.

'Let me make this up to you.' Pausing in front of her, he put his hand gently on her arm. 'Please?'

'Mike, it's not as easy as that. The amount of stress you've put me through, the amount of debt you left us in. You didn't give me, and more importantly, Joshua a second thought when you ran off into the sunset with your floozy. It was that close,' Pulling her arm away from him, Pippa held up her hand, her thumb and index finger almost touching. 'That close to me and Joshie being kicked out onto the streets. How the hell are you going to make up for that?'

'I will. Everything's different now.'

'How? How is everything different?'

'Because I realise what a waste of space I actually was. And I've changed.'

'OK, right then.'

'No, really I have.'

'I'll believe that when I see it.'

'OK, deal. You'll see, I'll be back tomorrow and the day after and the day after. I will make this up to you. And Joshua.'

Pippa nodded, rolling her eyes. 'Bye.'

'No, see you, not bye.' Mike grinned and began walking down the path.

'Mike?'

'Yes?' Pausing, he looked back.

'If you haven't changed, if you don't really mean it, then please, for Joshua's sake, don't bother coming back tomorrow.'

Turning his back on her, Mike saluted scout style and continued walking away.

Slipping into the cool night air, Pippa watched as he trailed his way through the sand dunes until he was out of sight. Perching on a chair, she looked up across the ocean, the reflection from the stars dancing on the gently bobbing water. Was he being sincere? Was he really sorry for what he had done? What he had put them both through?

She ran her finger along the edge of the table. She couldn't risk Joshua being hurt so badly by him again. He had been so upset when Mike had left and just when she thought he was getting used to not seeing his dad he would get upset again. Only the other day, Joshua had run up to her after school, pulled her into a quiet corner of the playground so they were not visible and hugged her tightly before asking why his daddy didn't love him any more.

No, Pippa would have to work out quickly if Mike was serious about being a permanent part of Joshua's life or not. She couldn't watch her son's heart being broken all over again.

* * *

After locking up the café, she tiptoed upstairs to the flat and popped her head around Joshua's bedroom door. Standing in the doorway, she watched the slight rise and fall of his duvet before turning her back again.

'Mum?'

'Yes, sweetie?'

'Can you come and sit with me for a bit?'

'Of course, I can.' Making her way towards Joshua's bed, she was careful not to stand on any Lego or toy cars that lay strewn across the beige carpet. 'I thought you were asleep.'

'I was. I had a bad dream.' Crawling out from under his duvet, he lay his head in Pippa's lap.

'Oh, darling. What was it about?' She stroked Joshua's hair from his eyes.

'I don't want to talk about it.'

'OK. Just remember it was just a dream, and dreams can't hurt you.'

Joshua nodded and put his thumb in his mouth.

'Will Daddy leave me again?'

'Daddy loves you and always will. It wasn't you Daddy left, he just had to go away last time.'

'But will he go away again?'

Pippa took a deep breath, she didn't want to lie to him and tell him that no, his father would stick around and actually have contact with his only son, but on the other hand, she couldn't make any false promises either. He probably wouldn't even come back to see him tomorrow. 'Honestly, I don't know, Joshie.'

'Really?' Joshua rolled onto his back, his eyes wide, staring at Pippa. 'I don't want Daddy to leave again. I want him to stay. Harley has his daddy, why can't my daddy love me like Harley's daddy loves him?'

'Oh, Joshie, Daddy does love you. He loves you more than he loves anything else in the whole wide world, but sometimes he has to go away to do other things.'

'I don't want him to go. I want him to stay here forever.'

'I know.' Leaning down, she kissed him on the forehead. 'Why don't you try to go back to sleep now? It's very late and you'll be tired tomorrow.'

'Will he come to visit me tomorrow?'

'Shall we wait and see?' Pippa gritted her teeth, how dare Mike be so selfish?

'OK.'

Stroking Joshua's hair, she watched his eyelids droop before gently manoeuvring him back onto his pillow. She kissed him on the forehead again and retreated back into the hall.

* * *

Hugging her cup, she let the warmth from her hot chocolate radiate into her hands and stared blindly at the TV, the vivid colours on the screen dancing in front of her.

Maybe he had changed. Maybe Mike had meant what he had said and that he really did want to make it up to Joshua, to her.

She tapped her index finger against her mug. Who was she kidding? Why should she believe him, even for a moment? Mike was selfish and incapable of thinking about anyone besides himself. He had proven that time and time again, and this time would be no different.

16

'Here you go, sir, a pancake tower as ordered. May I interest you in strawberries with cream to drizzle or some, sticky but tasty, golden syrup?' Placing the tray on the table in front of Joshua, Pippa gave him his plate of pancakes and spooned on strawberries as indicated. 'More cream?'

'No, that's enough thanks, Mum.' Joshua pierced a large piece of pancake with his fork and lifted it to his mouth. 'Why are we having pancakes today? You normally say no on a school day.'

'If you're complaining, I'm happy to eat yours when I've finished these.' Pippa waved her fork over her plate.

'No, no, it's OK.' Grinning, he looked down at his plate and then scrunched up his eyes. 'It's to take my mind off Daddy coming yesterday, isn't it?'

'What? No.' Lying her knife and fork on her plate, she looked at Joshua. 'When did you get so clever? I just want you to know that I'll always be here for you. I'm not going anywhere and I never will.'

'He's not coming back, is he? He was lying to me.' Joshua

used the back of his hand to wipe the tears that were dribbling down his cheeks.

'Come here, poppet.' Patting her knee, Pippa held out her arms, enveloping them around Joshua's small body. 'I don't know if he's coming back or not, but we were doing just fine by ourselves anyway, weren't we? So, you know that even if he can't come back to visit, we'll be OK, don't you?'

'I know we will, but I still want my Daddy.'

'I know. I know.' Pippa gently rocked him back and forth and bit her bottom lip, why would a father do this to his own child? Why would anyone leave and then come back only to promise the earth knowing full well that they wouldn't be able to give it?

A quiet tapping noise came from the front door.

'Who's that? It might be Daddy!' Peeling himself out of Pippa's arms, Joshua slid off her lap and ran to the door.

'I think it's probably Carol.' She was early though, but then again, maybe she needed a break from her sister.

'It's Daddy! It's Daddy, Mummy! It's him.' Joshua let the red blind slap back on the glass of the door and ran towards Pippa, pulling her by the hand towards the door. 'Quick, quick, open the door before he thinks we're out and goes again.'

'OK.'

'Morning. How're the two most gorgeous people in the world?' As soon as the door was open, Mike slid through and picked Joshua up into a hug. 'Why the long face, Joshie boy?'

'Mummy said you wouldn't come back.' Joshua buried his head into Mike's shoulder.

'Did she now?' Mike looked from Pippa to Joshua and back. 'Well, Daddy hurt Mummy's feelings when I had to go away last time, so Mummy thinks I'll let you both down again.'

'Do you, Mummy?' Joshua looked towards Pippa.

'Well, I...' When did Mike learn the art of understanding?

'It's OK, Joshie. It's Daddy's fault. I just need to let Mummy know that I'm not going to have to go away again.'

'You mean you're staying? You're really actually going to stay here?'

'You bet, buddy.'

Rolling her eyes, Pippa grabbed Joshua's book bag from the table and held out her hand. 'Come on, time for school, kid.'

'But I want to stay with Daddy. I don't want to go to school.' Joshua clung on to Mike's neck.

'I don't think Miss Camberly will accept that as a reason for not going to school. Besides, Daddy will be able to come round to see you after school, won't you, Mike?'

'Of course, I will. Your mum's right, you need to go to school. I'll see you later.' Mike lowered Joshua to the floor.

'Can you come to drop me off, Daddy? Please?'

'Not today, poppet. Daddy needs to pop to the shops now, don't you, Mike?'

'The shops? Yes, of course. I'll see you later, Joshie.'

Pippa held the door open and Mike went through first, giving Joshua a high five on the way.

* * *

'Hey, you, wait up.'

Pippa slowed down and paused, waiting for Joe to catch up. 'You were late. I've already dropped Joshua off and spent five minutes telling his teacher about Mike.'

'We were. All my fault, of course. Or at least, according to Harley it was. I overheard him telling some of the other kids that I hadn't got out of bed on time, he omitted telling them that he'd thrown the mother of all tantrums because we'd ran out of his favourite cereal.' Joe shook his head and laughed. 'Are you worried about Mike's reappearance having an effect on Joshua?'

Nodding, Pippa held the school gate open for Joe. 'We've already had tears at breakfast because he asked if he was going to see his dad again and I told him what I thought was the truth and that Mike might not come back. Anyway, just to prove me wrong, he turned up at the café before we left.'

'You think he'll stick around then?' Joe let the gate gently swing shut behind them.

'I didn't. Hand on heart, I didn't think he'd turn up again this morning, but he did.'

'That'll be good for Joshua, then? Having his dad around.'

'Maybe.'

'What's worrying you?'

'He's not got a great track record. He left us for another woman after running up stupid amounts of debt and almost making us homeless. I just don't trust him.'

'He might have changed?'

'That's what he says.'

'You don't sound so sure?'

'No. I don't know, maybe I'm just being harsh. Anyway, how are things going with Harley's mum?'

'We've made up an access schedule.'

'Carol said you were trying to sort one out. How's it going?'

'Surprisingly well. She's kept to it so far. No more turning up on the doorstep all the time at least.'

'That's good then. Right, I'd better hurry or your mum will be left to serve breakfast on her own.'

'OK. Pippa?'

'Yes.'

'I'm here if you need to offload, OK?'

'Thank you.' Pippa tried to crush that familiar warmth rising from her belly, she knew Joe just wanted to be friends and it was sweet of him to listen to her moan, but that was all he could ever be, friends, and she had to remember that.

* * *

'Pippa?' Mike sprang up from the patio table he had been sitting on outside the café and ran down to her on the beach. 'Was Joshie OK?'

'Yes, fine.'

'Can I just have a quick word?'

'I need to open up the café and cook the breakfasts.' Swerving around him, she continued walking towards the café.

'Please? Just give me a minute. There's an older woman in there. Is she one of your employees? I'm sure she'll cope for a few minutes.' Mike grabbed her wrist.

Looking from Mike to the café, Pippa shrugged her shoulders. 'Five minutes.'

'OK. Five minutes. Let's sit down for a bit.' Mike dropped her wrist and found a dry patch of sand a little way up the beach.

Settling beside him, Pippa watched as he trailed his finger in the sand drawing a house, sun and trees. 'What?'

'I want to apologise properly for how I treated you and Joshua when I left.'

'What about how you treated us before you left? Or don't you remember gambling all our money? Oh, I'm sorry, my money, the money I went out and worked my arse off to pay for the flat and food and everything. Don't you remember the way you used to do sod all around the house, even though you had all day doing absolutely nothing, so that I had to come home exhausted after a twelve-hour shift and cook, clean and take care of Joshua?

And don't you remember the way you used to speak to me? Like I was a piece of rubbish?'

'I'm sorry.' Mike held his hands up as if in defence. 'I know I treated you badly, really badly and I'm not proud of that but I can't change the past. If you let me though, I'd like to change the future. I'd like to make it up to you.'

'How? How the hell do you propose you can make it up to me? How are you going to make up for eleven years of sponging off me, shouting at me and treating me like a second-class citizen? Not to mention running off with your mistress?'

'Nothing will be an easy fix, I know that, but I'd like you to let me stick around so I can prove to you and Joshua that I'm getting my life in order and you both are my priority.'

'Mike, I'd like you to be part of Joshua's life. I'd like you to stick around for him, to have regular contact, but I can't trust you.' Looking across to the ocean, Pippa dug her hands into the sand. There, she'd told him what she was thinking. It wasn't nice, but she had good reason.

'I'm not expecting you to trust me straight away. But one day, I'd like to earn your trust again. And then, maybe, you never know, you may find it in your heart to give me another chance.' Mike leaned forward, his lips colliding with Pippa's.

'What the hell are you doing?' Jumping up, Pippa backed away.

'Pippa, don't go.' Mike caught up with her and took her hand. 'Sorry, it was too soon, but I've been wanting to do that since I clapped eyes on you again. You've got to admit, you have too.'

'What? No, no I haven't.'

'You have. I felt it when I kissed you just now. You didn't pull away straight away.'

'You caught me by surprise, that's all.' She paused and looked Mike in the eye. 'I don't think you know how seriously you hurt me when you left. You can't just waltz back into our lives and pick up from where you left off. Now, I really do need to get back to the café.'

'Can I still come by and see Joshie later?'

'You're his dad.' Turning on her heels, Pippa jogged the short distance back to the café. She needed to see Carol.

17

'Is it time to go now?' Joshua hurtled down the stairs from the flat.

'It certainly is. As soon as Daddy comes we'll get a wriggle on.' Pippa took one of Joshua's hoodies from the coat hook. Although it was summer, come the evening there was still a chill in the air. 'Here pop this on.'

'Is he here yet?' Joshua shrugged into his superhero hoodie and shot to the front door. 'Look, is that him coming up the path? Harley's going to the fair tonight too. Do you think we'll see him? Can we go now and meet Daddy on the path?'

'One second, let me make sure my purse is in here or you won't be going on any rides.' Pippa rummaged in her bag, yep, there it was, hidden at the bottom as usual. 'OK, let's go.'

'Daddy!'

By the time Pippa had locked the door and joined them, Joshua was high up on Mike's shoulders.

'Evening, Pippa.' Mike pecked her on the cheek. 'Right, which way? Where's this fair then?'

'It's in the nearest town, Claychester.' She patted the pocket of her jeans, double-checking she had her mobile before subconsciously wiping her cheek. 'So, if we follow the beach to the left we should get there in about twenty minutes.' That's what Carol had told her earlier anyway. She hadn't been able to afford to take Joshua to the local fair in London last year so they had both been looking forward to this for weeks now.

'Off we go then! Joshua, you keep an eye out for the bright lights of the fair and let us know when you can see them, deal?'

'Deal.'

* * *

'I see it! I see it!' Joshua's screech pierced the rhythmic sloshing of the waves.

'Yay! Fair, here we come!'

As they approached, Pippa smiled, the fragrance of warm doughnuts and burgers seeped through the warm muggy summer's air and the bright flashing lights of the rides accompanied the signature loud music and the hubbub of excited chatter and laughter. Stallholders' shouts enticing people to 'Throw the hoop to win a giant teddy!' and 'Only two pounds a go, prize every time!' were intermittently drowned out by ride operators telling everyone to 'Hold on tight' and 'We're going faster!' over their sound systems.

'Can I get down now? I want to get down.' Joshua's legs twitched with excitement against Mike's shoulders.

'OK, but hold on to my hand. It's really busy and we don't want you getting lost.' Pippa held out her hand.

'Can I hold Daddy's hand instead?'

'Of course, you can, buddy.'

She watched as Joshua slipped his small hand into Mike's. Ever since Mike had turned up, Joshua had become a real little daddy's boy, always wanting Mike's attention and to be close to him. It still hurt, even though Carol had assured her it was because Pippa was the constant and Joshua knew she would always be there with him, whereas Mike had left once before. Carol had told her that subconsciously, Joshua was trying to lap up all of the attention Mike could give him each day he stuck around whilst also trying to show Mike that he was needed so he would stay.

'Sorry.' Pippa stood aside to let a mum run after her toddler and watched as she scooped him into the air and ran back to her husband who greeted his son with a bag of candyfloss. Looking ahead, she followed Mike and Joshua at a slight distance as they weaved in and out of people and fairground rides and stalls. Every time they passed a stall, Mike bent to speak to Joshua who kept shaking his head and pointing ahead. He obviously had his heart set on a particular stall or a particular prize.

She hugged her arms around her, they looked so solid, so together, just like a little family in their own right. Shaking her head, she told herself she was being daft, she knew she was, but for such a long time now it had been her and Joshua against the world. They had been their own little team and now, to see Mike with Joshua, it made Pippa feel almost surplus to requirements, as if Joshua didn't actually need her any more.

'Mum? Mum?'

'I'm right here, Joshie.' Maybe she wasn't an extra part, after all, maybe Joshua needed them both. She gripped Joshua's hand just as a group of teenagers hurried past, giggling and calling to each other.

'This is it! Jonathan at school said you could win superhero masks on one of the stalls and it's this one! Look!' He grinned and pointed.

'So it is!' Delving into her purse she gave him a two-pound coin. 'Here you go. Ask the lady for a hoop.'

'It was a good idea of yours to come here, Pippa.'

Smiling, she watched as Joshua threw one of three blue plastic hoops towards their target, narrowly missing once, twice.

'Here, let me have a go for you, buddy.' Mike took the remaining hoop from Joshua's hand, threw it and cheered. 'There you go, lad, which one do you want?'

'The Batman mask! The Batman mask!' Joshua jumped from one foot to the other, pointing at the masks hanging down from the roof of the stall.

Maybe it had been for the best that Mike had come back. Pippa watched him give Joshua a high five before helping him take the mask from the packaging and gently sliding it down over his face. He had changed, in that moment she was sure of it. She couldn't remember him ever participating in Joshua's life like this before, not for a very long time at least.

'Mummy!' Joshua jumped up in front of her, his mask pulled down over his face.

'Joshua! You scared me there!' Laughing, Pippa reached down and swung him onto her hip.

'That's what Daddy told me to do. To scare you! He said you were a million miles away. But you're right here, silly Daddy.'

'Sorry.'

'What were you thinking?' Mike leaned in so Pippa could hear him as they passed the Twisters.

'That I think I might be beginning to believe that you have changed.' Yes, it was good for Joshua to have his father back in his life.

'Harley!' Sliding down from her arms, Joshua ran towards Harley, Joe and Mia, who she recognised from the playground, who were stood in line for the Dodgems.

'Hold on.' Too late, by the time she caught up with him, he was already jumping up and down in front of Harley showing off his Batman mask, leaving Pippa face to face with Joe and Mia.

'Pippa, Mike, hi. Harley was hoping to see you here. This is Harley's mum, Mia'

'Nice to meet you.' Pippa smiled, her cheeks hurting with the strain.

'And you. Joe speaks very highly of you.'

Pippa accepted the manicured hand proffered to her, glad that it was too dark for her own bitten and ragged nails to be seen. Why would Joe have spoken about her? Was she being sarcastic? Maybe Mia had noticed the blush flushing her cheeks which, unfortunately, seemed to happen every time Joe was in close proximity.

'And you must be Mike? Pippa's partner?'

'Don't say that to her, I used to be. I'm working on it though.' Winking at Mia, Mike nudged Pippa's shoulder.

'Mum, it's our turn!' Harley pulled his mum towards a red car.

'Dad, can you come on with me?' Looking up at Mike, Joshua took his hand before looking over his shoulder at Pippa. 'Do you mind, Mum? You can come on the next ride with me.'

'Of course not, poppet. You go and have fun.' She watched as Joshua led his dad around the ride, finally settling on a bright blue car. Moving across, she leaned her elbows on the metal railings and watched them.

'Looks like we get two minutes break.' Joe joined her, his elbow touching hers.

'Yep.' She looked at him, his silhouette illuminated by the bright lights. 'So how are you finding it with Mia back in your lives?'

'It's OK. It's good, good for Harley. How about you with Mike?'

He'd said it was 'good' does that mean they were back together then? She wouldn't blame him, she was gorgeous, tall, with glossy hair, a professional aura, everything Pippa wasn't. She shrugged. 'He seems to have changed. He's not drinking, or else I haven't smelt it on him anyway. And he's here. He's not upped and left again.'

'So, you're giving it another go with him then?'

Pippa could see the lights reflecting in his eyes as he looked sideways at her. 'No. Why did you ask that?' Was he jealous?

'Just the way he answered Mia, I assumed you were giving it another go. He said he "was working on it" or something.'

'Yes, well he can work on me all he wants. I'm glad he's come back into Joshua's life, as long as he doesn't mess up again, but as for me and him? I could never trust him again after how he hurt me.'

'Right. Trust needs to be earnt. It's important to do what's right for the kids though.'

'Obviously.' The muscle in his cheek twitched, why was he clenching his teeth? He thought she was pathetic, didn't he? Was he thinking she should give it another go with Mike? Why, because she wouldn't ever be able to get anyone else or because it would be better for Joshua? She pulled her T-shirt down over her stomach and shook her head, she was imagining things. 'It's not best for Joshua that I get back with him. When he ran off with his slapper leaving us in a ton of debt and almost homeless, he didn't think of Joshua. I shan't put him in a situation where Mike can have that much impact on his life again. Plus, I don't love him.'

'I didn't mean for you to get back with him.' Joe touched Pippa's arm, his hand warm against her cooling skin.

'I need to pop back to that stall. Can you tell Mike to ring me when they get off please?' Biting down on her bottom lip, she pushed herself away from the bar, letting her hair flow down in front of her face.

'Pippa, I didn't mean anything.'

Pushing her way through the crowds, she weaved past teenagers on the fast rides, laughing as they gripped onto each other as they were tossed this way and that through the air. Past a mum giving her husband a thumbs up as he squashed himself into a miniature fire engine on a merry-go-round, their daughter clinging on to him for dear life. Past families huddled together eating candyfloss and toffee apples by the stalls.

Soon, she was back out on the beach, the cool air slapping her in the face, her trainers sinking into the sand. She made her way down to the ocean, the music and chatter growing fainter and fainter until it was merely a whisper in the distance.

The moonlight reflected on the water, dancing on the surface every time a wave bobbed up and down. Pippa watched as a dredger puffed along slowly in the far distance. That was it. Joe had made it definite. Of course, she had known it was anyway, but saying what he had made it crystal clear. There was no her and him. And there never will be. Stiffening her jaw, she closed her eyes against the salty wind.

But if there was one thing she was even more certain about, it was the fact that she wouldn't let Mike wheedle himself into her life, not romantically. Asides from the fact that the love she had once felt for him had been shredded and, she was certain, would never return, she wouldn't put Joshua through that again. Even though Mike had changed, it didn't mean he wouldn't change back, that he wouldn't be tempted by the bright lights of the arcade on the pier or the soothing tones of the presenter on late night casino TV. It didn't mean that he would never turn to drink again to dull the money worries, that he would never start an argument for argument's sake or slip back into his old habits of letting her do everything from being the breadwinner to the bread maker.

No, she knew what was right for Joshua and that was for her and Mike to continue to be civil to each other, friends one day maybe, but nothing more. It was up to Joe if he thought it was best for Harley to have both parents living together. That was his decision to make. It didn't mean she also didn't have her son's needs at heart.

The cheerful 'Beside the Seaside' ringtone of her mobile trilled through the rhythmic lapping of the ocean. Tugging it from her jeans, she plastered a smile on her face, hoping it would reflect in her voice.

'Mike. Hi. Whereabouts are you? By the Twisters? OK, I'll be there in a minute.' Replacing her phone, she trudged back towards the bright lights and loud music.

* * *

'Are you being serious?' Pippa looked down at Joshua standing next to her, his hand gripping the rail by his side. 'You want me to go on the Twisters? You let Daddy go on the relatively tame Dodgems and I get the Twisters?'

'You're funny, Mummy. It's not that fast. Look. They're not even the big adult Twisters. They're the little ones for children.'

'Still, they look fast to me.' She was sure they were bigger than the children's rides back at their old local mop fair. 'Right, come on then, let's be brave!'

'I'll look after you, Mummy.' Joshua held out his small hand, waiting for Pippa to join him on the stairs up to the ride.

Smiling, she followed him to a red cart.

'Look, there's Harley again. His daddy's just won a big teddy.'

Squinting through the bright lights, Pippa could make out the silhouette of Joe, Mia and Harley at the Hook-a-Duck stall.

'Joe's giving it to Harley's mum. Do you think Daddy will win you a teddy Mummy?'

'So he is. No, I don't think so. Besides, where would we put a big teddy like that in our flat anyway?' Pippa shifted in her chair and looked at Joshua. 'Are you enjoying yourself tonight?'

'Yes, it's great! I love coming to the fair!'

* * *

'These are good chips, aren't they, buddy?'

'Yes, they are, Daddy.' Joshua gripped his polystyrene cone of chips in one hand, piercing each one with his tiny wooden fork with the other.

As they walked further along the beach, the moonlight and the gentle lapping of the waves replaced the bright lights and music of the fair. It had been a good night, a successful family outing. They could do this, be a family unit although not together. Her and Mike could work together for Joshua's sake.

'I don't want any more.'

'Are you full, Joshie? Why don't you see if Daddy wants them?' Putting her arm around him, Pippa squeezed his shoulders.

'Daddy, do you want the rest?' Joshua leaned into Pippa's side.

'Are you tired, poppet?'

Nodding, Joshua dragged his feet across the sand.

'Here, pop the rest of your chips with mine and you can have a piggyback ride, if you like?' Mike bent down, his knee in the sand, and waited for Joshua to clamber up to his shoulders. 'I really enjoyed tonight. Thank you for letting me come along.'

'Thanks for coming.' She popped her last chip in her mouth and scrunched up her cone.

'You enjoy having me around, don't you, buddy?' Mike patted Joshua's foot and glanced up.

'Umm.' Joshua closed his eyes, his head nodding slowly and slumped forward.

'I think he's fallen asleep,' Pippa whispered to Mike and pointed above him to Joshua.

'Pippa, wait a moment.'

She paused, letting Mike catch her up before walking again at a slower pace.

'No, stop a moment.' Mike grabbed her hand and gently pulled her back. He leaned into her until their lips touched.

'What the hell do you think you're doing?' Pulling away Pippa stepped backwards.

'You've just told me you liked me coming tonight, I thought...'

'Yes, it was nice that you came for Joshua. Not me. We've been here before. Nothing's changed.' Tucking a piece of stray hair behind her ear, she shook her head.

'I've told you, I've changed. Plus, with all the mixed signals you've been giving me, it's no wonder I got the wrong end of the stick.'

'What mixed signals?' What had she said or done which had even made him think he had a chance to get back with her? 'Anyway, how am I supposed to know if you've changed or not? I've only got your word that you have and you've always been a good liar.'

'That's low, even for you.'

'Even for me? Low? What's that supposed to mean? It's you

who was having an affair behind my back, it's you who kept spending all of the rent money, the money that I'd earnt while you'd been busy sleeping with your mistress.'

'Pippa, we've spoken about this, you know how emasculated I felt, you having the job and being the breadwinner when I couldn't even get past the application process, let alone an interview. You know how much it hurt me to watch you work your arse off.'

'Application process? I only remember you applying for any jobs in the first week after you were laid off. After that, you used to tell me it was good for a woman to be working.' Batting away a tear, Pippa stared into the ocean. She should have seen this coming. Especially after the comment he'd made to Mia. How stupid could she have been? She'd just thought he was joking. She thought he knew where things stood.

'Look, I'm sorry. I shouldn't have tried to kiss you. I shouldn't have expected anything other than what you've already given me. Maybe, given time, you'll come to realise I really have changed.'

'Please, don't.' Pippa shook her head.

'Can we just forget it?'

She nodded. All she wanted to do was run towards the café and shut the door behind her, but with Joshua asleep on Mike's shoulders, she knew she had to walk with him.

'Did you want me to take Joshua so you can get back?' She indicated towards the steps that led from the beach up to the centre of the village.

'It's OK. I'm not that way anyway. I'll walk with you back to the café.'

'OK.' She knew there were two B&B's near the village green. Unless he wasn't staying in the village, she'd just assumed he was because he never seemed to drive anywhere. 'Whereabouts are you staying?'

'Staying? Oh, this place along the main road, somewhere that way.' Mike waved his hand ahead.

'Right.'

* * *

'Here we are. I'll come and lay him down then.'

Pippa unlocked the café door and held it open as Mike ducked through the doorway, Joshua still slumped on his shoulders. 'Thank you.'

'He's down. Still in his clothes, but he's asleep.' Mike closed the door to the flat and joined Pippa at the counter. 'Aren't you going to ask me to stay for a drink?'

'I'm really tired. I just want to go to bed, if that's OK?' She pushed herself off of the stool to standing.

'OK, I get the message. You've had enough of me for one day.'

'Mike, don't be like that. I'm just tired.'

'If this is about that friend of yours, Joe...'

'What about him?'

'You batting me away when I tried to kiss you, even though we both know there's still chemistry between us.'

'You ran off with the tart downstairs leaving me and your son all but homeless and up to our eyes in debt. There's nothing between us.' Why wouldn't he just get the message? Even if she did feel something for him, which she didn't, there would be no way on earth that she'd get back with him. It would be an open invitation for him to hurt her again. No way.

'Don't call her that. She has, had, a name. And I've seen the way you look at him, you can't deny that.' Mike thumped his fist on the counter, the dull thud resonating in the quiet of the café.

'OK, whatever, she'll always be a tart in my head. What kind of a woman goes after another woman's man? But, you're wrong, there isn't anything going on between me and Joe.' Not any more, anyhow. Did she really look at him in that way?

'There are reasons for everything, Pippa. Just because you see everything as clear cut, it doesn't mean it is. I was lonely, remember? You worked all the bloody hours that boss of yours gave you and I was left at home, forgotten about. You can't blame me for looking elsewhere for a bit of company.'

Coughing, it took her a minute to catch her breath. 'You were lonely? I drove you to have an affair because of all the hours I worked? Are you being serious? Do you actually remember what it was like? Do you remember the bills, the final warnings? I worked to pay for us to live. I worked to put food on the table and a roof over our heads. And to keep up with your gambling addiction. Or don't you remember that? Don't you remember why it was me working and not you? Don't you bloody remember being fired from your old job for stealing?'

'That's it, you play the martyr. That's what your good at, isn't it? There are always two sides to each story, but not once have you asked what my side was.'

'Please, just go.'

'I'm going already!' Mike pushed his stool aside, bouncing it against the counter and stalked to the door, turning around as he yanked it open, the blinds flying into the air before crashing back down on the glass. 'If I were you, I wouldn't waste your time pining for that Joe bloke, I saw him snogging Harley's mum when you'd gone off for your little hissy fit.'

Turning the lock in the door, Pippa twisted around, her back against the cold glass, She had forgotten what he could be like. How he could blow up when he didn't get his own way. How had she forgotten that? Looking down, she held out her hands, they were shaking. She wasn't used to it any more, the arguing and accusations. Before, when they were together, she'd just let his words roll off her back, but there was no shouting in her and Joshua's world any more. And she was determined to keep it that way

18

'Are you OK, love? You look a bit peaky.' Carol placed a latte in front of Pippa as she sat slumped on a stool, her arms crossed on the counter.

'I'm OK, just a bit tired. I couldn't sleep last night. Thanks for this.' Pippa held up the latte. 'Sorry, I'll just have a sip then I'll come and help.'

'Don't be silly, it's almost done. There you go, the last plate cleared from the breakfasts.' Carol wiped her hands on a tea towel and got herself a coffee. 'We should have a break before the toddlers and their parents descend.'

Pippa smiled, Rachel and her friends from Toddler Group were regulars twice a week now. Since the school's Spring Fayre, their customer base was continuing to grow. 'I've been thinking, what do you think of the idea of us starting to offer birthday party packages for kids?'

'I'd think that it sounds intriguing, tell me more.' Carol pulled herself up onto the stool next to Pippa's and took a sip of coffee.

'I thought we could help the children make little pizzas and cupcakes and things and then they could eat what they've made for their party lunch and maybe play some party games with them while things are cooking. What do you think? Do you think anyone would actually like that sort of thing?'

'I think that's a great idea. Get planning and we can get that little printing shop on the corner of the High Street to design some leaflets for us.'

'OK, cool. I'll look into the costings and that. We'd have to provide decorations and maybe a little present for the birthday boy or girl.'

'That would be a nice touch. Are you sure you're feeling up to working today? I can hold the fort if you want to go and lie down for a bit?' Carol touched Pippa's arm.

'I might go and take some tablets, if that's OK? My head's splitting.' Pippa laid the palm of her hand across her forehead and let the heat from her hand offer some relief.

'Have a little lie down too, if you like. Things will be quiet here until the toddlers arrive. Maybe you're coming down with something.'

'Maybe.' Sliding off her stool, she made her way up the stairs. A couple of tablets and a half hour lie down should do the trick.

* * *

'Pippa, love? Sorry, I didn't want to wake you but Mike is downstairs, he says he needs to speak to you.'

Opening her eyes, she shielded them from the sunlight piercing the room and cleared her throat. 'OK, I'll be down in a moment.'

'I'll get you a latte ready.' Carol bustled out of the room, a tea towel thrown over her shoulder as always.

Pushing the pink throw off her legs, Pippa sat up and

checked the time. She could only have been asleep for twenty minutes or so but already her throat felt furry. She blinked against the sunlight, at least the tablets had dulled the headache slightly.

* * *

'Mike?' Walking behind the counter, she made her way over to Mike.

'Pippa, I'm so so sorry about our disagreement yesterday.' He pulled a large bouquet of garishly coloured flowers from his lap.

'Disagreement? The argument, you mean?'

'Well, I'd call it a disagreement but, if you like, yes, our argument. These are for you.'

'Thank you. You shouldn't have.' Taking the flowers, she put them at the end of the counter.

'I'm sorry I let my temper get the better of me last night. It's because I feel so strongly about you that I got so passionate.'

'Right.' How did he do that? How did he manage to turn something that was clearly his fault into being hers? He'd always had the knack of making her feel like everything was her problem, her fault, when they had been together. Him losing his job, yep, her fault. Him having an affair, of course, she could be the only one at fault.

'Can we forget about yesterday? Not the fair, that was lovely. But can we forget about the disagreement?'

'You really upset me.'

'I know but that's only because you still care, isn't it? So, me making you upset, that's a good thing, right? If you didn't still have feelings for me then you wouldn't have felt anything.' Smiling, he took her hand in his.

'No, I was upset because of the way you spoke to me.' Pulling her hand away, she crossed her arms.

'Fair enough. I am sorry though, and it won't happen again. I won't try to kiss you again. I'll respect the way you feel about me, but I will show you I have changed.'

'OK.' Pippa pinched the bridge of her nose.

'I need to go now, but I'll be back after you've picked Joshua up from school, if that's OK?'

'Yes, fine.'

'What was all that about?' Joe called from the other end of the counter where he stood near Carol.

'Joe? I didn't see you there. You OK?'

'Better than you by what I see. Is he giving you grief?' Sliding onto the stool Mike had occupied moments ago, he indicated the flowers. 'Or is he trying to make up for giving you grief?'

'Yes, I think so. We had an argument, or as he puts it, a disagreement, last night after the fair.'

'Oh right. Is everything OK now?'

'I guess so. I need to grab a glass of water. Here, you can give these to Mia.' She dropped the flowers into Joe's arms.

'Why would I do that?'

'Don't play games with me, Joe, not today, I'm really not in the mood.'

'Hey, I wouldn't play games with you. You know me better than that.'

'You're back with her. It's fine. You told me in your encrypted way when you basically told me to get back with Mike for Joshua's sake.' Taking a gulp of water she could feel the pain move behind her right eye, sharper than ever. She needed to lie down before it turned into a fully-fledged migraine.

'I didn't say anything of the sort.'

'You did, you said to think of the kids. You didn't think I was thinking of Joshua by not getting back with Mike, but I can't do it, it wouldn't be the best thing for him, for any of us. I know you see things differently with Mia, and I'm happy for you. I really am, so please, take the flowers.' Placing her glass carefully back onto the counter, Pippa turned away.

'Hey, I didn't mean it like that.'

She felt Joe's hand on her forearm, the warmth comforting. If she had the energy she'd tell him that Mike had seen them kissing. But she didn't. What was it to do with her anyway? He probably didn't want it to be common knowledge. She didn't blame him, not really, he was just trying to protect his relationship while it was still early days. Yes, she'd thought he'd be able to confide in her, obviously not.

'OK, whatever. Excuse me.' Her throat stung as stomach acid rose up, cupping her hand to her mouth she ran upstairs, making it into the bathroom just in time.

Sinking to the floor, Pippa hugged the toilet bowl, she'd not had one this bad in ages. Since they'd moved down here, in fact.

'It's OK.'

She felt one of his hands on the small of her back, while he held her hair back with the other. Finishing, she pulled a tissue from the roll and wiped her mouth. Twisting around on the tiled floor, she leant against the cool plastic of the bath.

'Come on, let's get you to bed. You should have told me you felt ill.' Joe curled his arms under her armpits and walked her to her bedroom.

'I can't. We've got the Toddler Group gang coming in soon.'

'I'll stay and help my mum. You need to rest. I'm guessing by the way you're clutching your head it's a headache or a migraine or something?' Joe lowered her to the edge of her bed and pulled her trainers off her feet.

She nodded. 'You can't do that. You've got your own work.'

She let herself sink into the crisp cotton pillowcase and closed her eyes.

'It's fine. I'll ring and postpone. Mrs Wedley's outdoor tap can be fitted tomorrow instead. Now, you sleep and you'll feel better.'

'Thank you.' Closing her eyes she let sleep pounce on her.

* * *

Stirring from sleep, she heard voices outside, excited voices. Joshua and Harley. How long had she slept for? Lifting her eyelids, she was met by the dim light of the sun seeping in through the purple curtains. She twisted her head this way and that experimenting, seeing if the migraine had gone. It had, a muzziness being left behind.

She pushed herself to sitting and looked over at her alarm clock, squinting to make out the red neon numbers. It was 6:15. Joe must have picked Joshua up.

* * *

'Hey, you. Are you feeling better?' Twisting to face the door as Pippa walked through, Joe paused, a jug of squash in one hand and a tower of glasses in the other.

'Yes, yes I am. Thank you, Joe, and thank you, Carol.' She walked into the café and slumped onto a stool. 'Thank you for collecting Joshua. Where is he?'

'Him and Harley are playing footie with Mike outside. I've just come in to get refreshments.' Joe grinned and held up the jug. 'Glad you're feeling better.'

'How did the Toddler Group lot go?'

'Great, there's certainly some little characters in the group, isn't there?'

Pippa nodded and smiled. 'Thank you for stepping in.'

'No need to thank me. I'm afraid I had to help myself to a couple of your fudge cupcakes though.' Joe looked down at his stomach and pulled a worried face.

'You had to, did you?' Pippa laughed.

'Well, I was wasting away, all that running back and forth to the tables. I don't know how you and my mum do it all day.'

'Pippa, love, you don't half look better.' Carol looked up from the open till, money bags surrounding it on the counter as she counted their takings. 'Look, I don't want to worry you, but have you taken any money out of the till today? Did you maybe mean to go to the wholesalers before you got ill or something?'

'What? No. I was going to go tomorrow. Why?'

'I think we have a problem then, love. Of course, it might just be my rubbish counting skills. Here, can you double-check it for me, please? I'm coming up a hundred quid short and I've already counted it twice now.'

'Oh, right.' Sliding off the stool, Pippa joined Carol in front of the till and began counting the notes and coins.

'Hopefully, it's just me. Joe knows how bad I am at accounts and that sort of thing, don't you, Joe?'

'No, you're right. We're one hundred pounds down. How did that happen?' Pippa creased the top of her nose.

'I don't know. We've been busy, but there's always been someone behind the counter. Even when the parents and tots came and we were rushed off our feet, there was always me or Joe behind here. Always. Apart from...' Carol looked down at the floor.

'Go on.'

'When you went and had that lie down this morning, I went and got you, do you remember?'

'Yes, Mike had wanted to speak to me.'

'That's right, he'd said it couldn't wait and he'd asked me to go and get you.'

'You can't think it's him. You do, don't you?' Pippa looked from Carol to Joe and back again. 'He wouldn't do that. He wouldn't rob from his own son's home.'

'You've got to admit, it does look a bit dodgy, doesn't it?' Joe placed the glasses and jug on the counter. 'And from what you've told me, it wouldn't be out of character.'

'That was then. He's changed now.'

'Have you got any proof that he's changed, love?'

'Well, he's told me. He's promised me he's changed. Plus, before it was our money that he took, this is completely different, this is mine. We're not together or anything. No, he wouldn't. I'm sure of it.'

'If you're sure.' Pippa saw Carol look over at Joe. 'Shall I call the police then?'

'No, no. It might just be a mistake. I have been feeling really rough all day, maybe I did take some out or something.' Pippa shook her head, he wouldn't do this to them. There must be a logical explanation. 'Let's just see if it turns up.'

'If you're sure.'

'I'm sure. Just drop it, please? My head's been all over the place today, it would just be like me to have picked it up and put it down somewhere or something. Joshua's just got his dad back, I don't want a silly mistake of mine to jeopardise that.'

'OK, I won't say anything. But, be careful, won't you?' Joe held his hands up, surrendering to Pippa's wishes.

'Everything OK?' Mike entered the café, football under his arm, Joshua and Harley just behind him.

'Just getting the drinks, mate.' Joe looked at Pippa and rolled his eyes before following them back outside, jug and glasses in hand.

* * *

'Mum?'

'Yes, sweetie, I'm still here.' Pippa put her hand on Joshua's car splattered duvet and found his foot, cupping it as she used to do when he was a baby.

'I'm glad you're feeling better.' Pushing his hand from underneath his duvet, Joshua reached for Pippa's hand.

'So am I. It was just a little headache though. Nothing to worry about.'

'I know, but I was thinking...'

'Go on...'

Joshua shifted his pillow and sat up. 'It was lucky that Daddy was here.'

'How do you mean?'

'To look after me while you were poorly and asleep.'

'Yes, I guess it was.'

'I think it's safer to have two adults about, isn't it? So that there is always someone about if the other one gets sick.'

'Hey, you don't need to worry about things like that, Joshie. It was Joe that picked you up from school and Carol who cooked you dinner anyway, so even if your dad hadn't been here, you would have been fine and looked after.' Pippa bit her tongue, Mike had only played football with him.

'Yes, but, it would be easier with two adults, wouldn't it?' Joshua tugged on Pippa's hand.

'Maybe, but we do OK, don't we? We've got friends around, like Carol and Joe and Harley. It's good to have your dad here too though. Why have you thought about this now?'

'When you were sick and me and dad were talking about it being lucky he was here and that he can look after me when you get poorly.' Joshua lay back down and turned to face the wall, pulling his duvet to his chin. 'And he said, when you let him move in he'll be able to help you look after me all the time.'

Move in? What was he playing at saying something like that to a five-year-old? She'd made it perfectly clear on the way home from the fair that she didn't want to get back with him, that there was no chance of a romantic reunion between them. She had, hadn't she? She had made it perfectly clear. She was sure of it. So why would he build Joshua's hopes up like that? Unless it was some sick way of making her feel guilty and change her mind. No, he wouldn't stoop so low.

'Mummy?' Joshua sat back up in bed, crawled towards her and sat next to her, his legs dangling over the side. 'Did I say something wrong? You look sad.'

'No, I'm not sad, but I do need to talk to you, OK? Now that you are a big boy I need you to understand something, OK?' Pippa put her arm around Joshua's shoulders, pulling him close to her.

Nodding, Joshua looked up at Pippa.

'It's lovely that Daddy is back in our lives and can visit us, but me and Daddy aren't going to get back together, you know that, don't you?' Why did she feel like the cruel one when it had been Mike who had left them in the first place and Mike who had, by the sounds of it, told Joshua that he would be moving in with them? Joshua deserved to, no needed to, know the truth before he got his hopes up even further.

'But... why?'

The tears filling Joshua's eyes broke her heart. She took a deep breath, she was doing the right thing by setting him straight. It just didn't feel like it. 'Do you remember when we used to all live together in the flat back in London?'

'Yes.'

'Well, do you remember that me and Daddy used to argue a lot?'

'Yes, when Daddy used to come home walking funny and banging into things you used to tell me to go to my bedroom, but I could hear you and Daddy arguing and Daddy shouting still. I used to hide under my duvet.'

'I'm so sorry you heard all of that. That's why me and Daddy won't be getting back together.'

'Because of me?' Joshua's voice quivered as he buried his head into Pippa's dressing gown.

'No, no, not because of you. Look at me, Joshie.' Holding Joshua by the shoulders she gently pulled him away from her and looked him in the eye. 'Me and Daddy didn't split up because of you, you need to know that, sweetheart. We broke up because we're better as friends because when we live together we don't get on and we argue. And that's why we're not going to live together again, because we're happier being friends and not living together. Do you understand?'

'Yes. I don't want you and Daddy to argue again. You smile more with me and you living here.'

'Exactly. We have the best of both worlds. We have our home here where we are happy and Daddy can visit and we can be happy seeing him.'

'Yes, let's stay like this.' Kneeling up, Joshua hugged her. 'I love you, Mummy.'

'I love you too, Joshie, more than you will ever realise.'

'But Daddy won't be sad that he can't live with us, will he? I don't want Daddy to be sad,' Joshua whispered in Pippa's ear, his voice muffled by the towelling dressing gown.

'No, Daddy won't be sad. Daddy will be happy that we're happy and happy that he can get free ice cream when he visits us. Now, why don't you lay back down and try to get some sleep?

You've got PE at school tomorrow, so you need all the energy you can get.'

'OK, night.' Crawling back into bed, Joshua smiled as Pippa kissed his forehead.

* * *

Pippa pressed the volume button on the TV, turning it up as loud as she dared without it waking Joshua. She needed to drown out the thoughts in her head, needed to stop the questions from going around and around.

She just didn't understand what Mike was playing at. She'd made it clear to him how she felt, completely clear. And, he'd understood. Yes, they'd ended up having a massive argument, but he had understood there was no future for the two of them, so why would he plant the idea in Joshua's head?

Her phone pinged, vibrating across the coffee table, telling her she had a text. It was from Joe.

Hey, you OK?

I'm OK ta. Thanks again for helping with Joshua and the café earlier. You?

Anytime. No bother. Thought any more about the police?

Pippa breathed heavily through her nose.

No. It will probably turn up. No evidence otherwise.

Just trying to look out for you.

I'm fine. I can cope by myself.

She threw her phone back onto the coffee table and then picked it up again.

Sorry. I appreciate it. Thanks. Just tired.

OK no worries. I just care that's all.

Right, you care so much about me that you broke up with me for no apparent reason other than your ex-wife left her boyfriend. Staring at his last message, Pippa took a deep breath. What was it with men and her? She was obviously destined to be single forever. And that was fine. Her and Joshua worked well with just the two of them. They didn't need anyone else.

Shaking her head, she switched her phone off. She didn't need anything else to think about. She'd speak to Mike, again, when he came in tomorrow. Actually, maybe she'd ring him up, it might be easier to spell it out to him over the phone. Plus, if he started shouting she was in control and could just end the call. Yes, that's what she'd do.

19

'Carol, do you mind if I just pop upstairs, please? I need to make a call.'

'Of course not, we're quiet here. You go.' Joining her behind the counter, Carol put the last of the dirty breakfast dishes in the dishwasher and patted Pippa on the shoulder.

'Thanks.'

Sitting on the edge of her bed, Pippa listened as Mike's phone rang and tapped a pen against her bedside table.

'Hello?'

'Mike? Hi, it's Pippa.'

'Pippa? Right. Sorry, I didn't recognise your number.'

'That's OK.' She shifted the phone to her other ear, she could hear the dull bass of music through the line. 'Are you OK to talk?'

'Sorry, what was that?'

'I said, are you OK to talk?' Pippa raised her voice and rolled her eyes. Why didn't he just turn the music down?

'Yes, of course. One moment.'

Straining, Pippa could hear muffled voices before a gentle

thud and relative silence, the rhythmic thumping of bass dulled now. He must have gone outside, maybe. And he wasn't alone. Where was he?

'If it's inconvenient I can ring back later?'

'It's never inconvenient when it comes to you.'

'Right. Are you at your place?' How could she ask where he was? Why did she even care?

'Just at the shops, babe.'

'OK.' Yes, of course he was, shops always burst out loud music, of course, they did. Maybe he was at a pub and didn't want Pippa to know. And how had he made friends already? It had taken Pippa ages, and yet here he was, having to talk to someone, maybe to say where he was going, when he'd only been here a couple of weeks. She shook her head. It was none of her business.

'What did you want to talk about?'

'I... Joshua spoke to me last night. He seemed very confused.'

'What about? Is he OK?'

'Yes, he's fine, but he seems to think we're going to get back together. Did you say something he may have taken the wrong way?'

'No, of course not. It's only natural for a kid to want their parents to be together. Why do you think I said anything?'

'Joshua mentioned that you'd told him you were moving in here, to the café.'

'Are you accusing me of trying to twist his little mind or something?'

'No, I just wondered if you'd said something and he'd taken it the wrong way, that's all. I just want us to both be on the same page when it comes to him, I don't want him being stuck in the middle getting different messages from each of us.'

'Whoa there. Careful what you're saying. I don't want little

Joshua to be confused either. I may have mentioned that things would be easier if you let me move in, that's all.'

Pippa cleared her throat, she could hear his voice getting louder which only meant one thing and that wasn't her intention. She didn't want to annoy him, she just wanted to make things clear.

'OK, look, I'm not having a go, I just don't want Joshua to think we're getting together again when we're not. You do remember what I said on the way back from the fair, don't you?'

'Yes, of course I do, I'm not thick.'

Biting down on her bottom lip, Pippa didn't want to ask the next question because she could already hear Mike getting wound up, but she needed to know the answer. She breathed deeply through her nose and out through her mouth. 'Why did you tell him you were moving in then?'

'He was clearly worried what would happen to him if you got ill again so I wanted to reassure him, OK? Is that so bad of me to want to reassure our little boy that he will always have someone to look after him? If it is, well, I'm sorry.'

'Mike, we coped pretty darn well when you ran off with your tart and I was coping yesterday, Joe picked him up from school and Carol fed him, so he was absolutely fine.' How dare he imply that she can't cope? He hadn't given them a second thought when he'd upped and left, and they'd actually needed him back then. Now, she had learned how to cope on her own. She could do this now. She didn't need, or want, his help any more.

'I've told you before, don't call her a tart. Besides, it says quite a lot about the state of our relationship if I had to run off with someone else, doesn't it?'

Standing up, Pippa paced to the window and looked out. This was supposed to be her and Joshua's safe place, their retreat. Why had he had to ruin that? 'Don't you dare blame me for what you did. What you did was unforgivable and I think you know that really. If you don't, then there's clearly something wrong with you.'

'I'm just saying there's always a reason for things.'

'A reason? Yes, the reason was that you were drinking and gambling all our money away.'

'You were never there though. I was lonely. What did you expect me to do all day cooped up in that tiny flat by myself?'

'Oh, I don't know. The cooking, the cleaning maybe? The things that I had to do after my twelve-hour shift at that pretentious restaurant. I only worked because you couldn't be bothered to try to get another job, or had you forgotten that? Had that been erased from your memory somehow?' And they were back here, again arguing about the past.

'For Pete's sake, Pippa!'

Even holding her phone at arm's length away from her ear, Pippa could still hear him yelling. He had proven one thing at least with this phone call. His temper was still alive and kicking.

Suddenly the phone went quiet. Pippa raised it to her ear and listened. She could hear voices, muffled though as if he had his hand over the mouthpiece.

'Pippa? Are you still there?'

'I'm still here.'

'I'm sorry I lost my rag, I just really care about you and Joshua. I want the best for him and I don't want to let him down again. I want to be the best dad I can be.'

'OK. I didn't say you didn't want to be a good dad.' His tone was soft now, a little clipped but nothing Pippa would have noticed if she hadn't been attuned to him.

'No, no you didn't.'

There was a slight pause in conversation again.

'Truth be told, I'd like to move into the café with you and

Joshua. Just for a while. I think it will build some bridges between us.'

'I don't think that's a good idea. It would just confuse him even more.' Did he really think she would say yes?

'I understand why you're thinking that, but look at it from my perspective. I haven't been in Joshie's life for so long and now I've found him again, I want to be able to get to know him again.'

'That's what you're doing when you come round though, isn't it? You don't need to move in for that. You've been seeing him every day anyhow.'

'It's not the same though. I don't know what his favourite bedtime story is any more, I don't even know what he likes to eat for breakfast. If I could just stay for a bit, a week or two at the most, then I could really bond with him again.'

'Have you not got anywhere to stay? Is that it? Or is your money running out or something?' She ran her fingers through her hair. As far as she knew, he hadn't even read to Joshua when he'd lived with them and he used to put him to bed when she'd been working. She'd often got home to find Joshua awake still, Mike in the living room asleep on the sofa, a can in hand.

'I have somewhere to stay. Somewhere pretty nice, thank you. I'm just trying to be nice and trying to be a good dad, if you'd just let me.'

'OK, I'm glad you've got somewhere nice to stay. I can't let you stay with me and Joshua though, I'm sorry, but it would just be too confusing.'

'Right, OK.' The line went quiet.

Putting her phone down on the windowsill, Pippa looked out. There was a group of surfers she hadn't seen before, probably down for their holidays. Hopefully, they'd call in for their lunch later.

Dropping to her bed, she sat still and listened to the noises from outside, the excited chatter mixed with the sloshing of the waves. She was doing the right thing not letting Mike into their home, wasn't she? She smoothed the edge of the duvet cover. She knew she was. This was *their* home. Not Mike's. They'd come here to get away from all of his drama. There was no way she'd let him ruin that for them. Plus, it *would* confuse Joshua, really confuse him.

No, she needed to be strong on this one.

* * *

'Daddy's coming! Daddy's coming!' Joshua jumped up from the table by the window, his Watch Table as he called it because if sat at it the whole of the bay in front was visible from the pier at one end to the jagged rocks at the other.

'OK, that's nice. Why don't you go upstairs and play for a bit? I need to have a quick talk with Daddy.'

'Do I have to? I want to tell him about the class assembly next week and see if he can come. You think he will be able to, don't you?'

'I can't see why not.' Pippa shrugged, as far she was aware he was still living off savings from his previous job. It was anyone's guess when he'd get a job down here. 'Now up you go, just for a couple of minutes, please?'

'Too late!' Joshua grinned at her and ran to the door, jumping up into Mike's arms as soon as the door opened.

'Do you want to come to my class assembly next week, Daddy? Do you?'

'Why not? Even more exciting than that though, is what I've got here.' Mike patted the pocket of his jeans.

'What's that? What have you got?'

'Let's go up to Mummy and I can tell you both together.' Mike lowered him to the floor.

'Pippa, hi.'

'Hi.' Pippa wrung the dishcloth out under the tap and turned to face him. Would he have another go at her? If he did, then he could go.

'Daddy's got a surprise for us!' Climbing up onto one of the stools at the counter, Joshua swung his legs shifting the stool back and forth.

'Careful on there! Has he indeed?'

'Yes, I have. Joshua, let's have a drumroll please?'

Laughing, Joshua did as he was asked and thundered out a drumroll, his small hands slapping against the counter.

'Here.' Pulling an envelope from his pocket he passed it to Pippa.

'What is it?' Taking the envelope from him, she turned it over in her hands.

'Open it and see. It's my way of apologising.' Resting his elbows on the counter, he leaned his chin on his hands.

'OK.' Slowly she opened the envelope and pulled out two tickets. 'Circus tickets?'

'Not just any circus, they're for The Grande Olde Circus. I had to pull a few strings to get them, but it's supposed to be the best circus there is around.'

'Oh, wow. Thank you. Look, Joshua, circus tickets.'

'There's something else in the envelope too. Have a look.'

Pippa passed the tickets to Joshua who looked at them intently and pulled out a sheet of paper. 'You've booked a hotel?'

'That's right. The circus is about an hour away on the train, so I thought I'd treat you both and you could stay over, a mini holiday if you like.' Mike grinned.

'Mike, you've booked a double room. I thought you understood.' Pippa looked at him and then back at the booking confirmation. Had he not listened to a word that she'd said earlier?

'I understand exactly what you said earlier. The room is for you and Joshua. I'm not going to the circus. This is my treat to you both.'

Taking the tickets from Joshua, Pippa slid them back into the envelope along with the hotel booking confirmation. 'Thank you. It's a really lovely thought but I can't accept them.'

'Why not?' Mike straightened up, placing his palms on the counter.

'They must have cost an awful lot. Plus, I've got the café to think about. If I don't open up, I lose money. I can't afford to do that. I really do appreciate the thought though.' Putting the envelope on the counter, she pushed it towards Mike.

'Carol?'

'Yes, can I get you anything, Mike?' Carol made her way behind the counter, a stack of plates and cups balancing precariously on the tray in her hand.

'Are you busy on Saturday? Would you be able to look after this place so Pippa can take Joshua to a circus a couple of towns away?'

'Mike, no, I couldn't ask Carol...'

'Of course, I can. Those two deserve a break.'

'That's settled then. You can spend Friday night at the hotel and then go to the circus on Saturday.'

'But they must have cost you a ton. I can't accept that.'

'As I said, it's my way of apologising and showing you that I'm serious about building a proper relationship with Joshie here.' Joshua grinned as he ruffled his hair. 'And the money, well, I had it left over from a job I did before I came down here. Just view it as one of the child maintenance payments I owe you.'

'OK. Thank you.'

Mike slapped his hands on the counter. 'Right, who's for a game of footie? Joshua?'

'What was that in aid of?' Carol nudged Pippa as they watched Mike walk out of the café, Joshua running at his heels like an excited puppy.

'Honestly? Yesterday he basically told Joshua he was moving in so I rang him today to tell him, again, that there was nothing between us and he had a real go at me. This, apparently, is his way of apologising.'

'An expensive way to apologise. If you ask me, he's up to something. He's more than likely trying to woo you back.'

'Woo me?' Pippa laughed. 'I don't even think Mike knows what the word means. Maybe he's just being straight with me now.' Pippa shrugged and put the envelope behind the till.

'Just be careful. From what you've said, he's bad news, you don't want to let him back in. Once a cheater, always a cheater.' Carol turned to Charlotte, who had just come in. 'Hello, Charlotte, dear. Is it your usual you're after? Go and take a seat and I'll bring it over.'

With Charlotte's back turned, Carol whispered in Pippa's ear. 'You don't want to end up like that one. Again.'

* * *

'Right, I'm off. I'll catch you later, buddy. Thanks for dinner.' Mike stood up from the table, scraping his chair back and gave Joshua a high five.

'You're welcome. It's the least I can do. Thank you again for the circus tickets.'

Mike waved his hand dismissively before leaving.

'Right, let's get this cleared up, shall we?' Pippa stood up and piled their plates on to the tray. 'Why don't you go on upstairs and get changed for bed while me and Carol lock up? That way we can watch something together before story time.'

'OK.' Standing up, Joshua leaned in for a cuddle. 'I like it when you and Daddy get on.'

'All right. Off you go then, Joshie. And remember to clean your teeth for the whole three minutes.'

Placing the tray of dirty plates on the counter, Pippa began loading the dishwasher. 'How's your sister doing?'

'She's fine. Still complaining she's in pain but she got the all clear from the doctors yesterday, so I think it's probably just the fact that she likes to have something to complain about more than anything.'

'That's good she's recovered from her fall. Is she heading home soon then?'

'No, she's staying put.' Carol opened the drawer underneath the till and pulled out the small plastic money bags. 'She's selling her place and moving down here full time. Do you want to tally up the takings or clean the floor?'

'I'll clean. That's good then. That's what you wanted, wasn't it? Your sister to move in, I mean, not for me to clean the floor.'

'Yes, it is.' Carol laughed and pinged open the drawer of the till. 'It's been nice to have some company of an evening.'

'That's what I miss most, having someone to talk to in the evenings. Someone to share how my days been and to find out about theirs.' Pippa knocked the mop to the floor as she pulled out the broom. After propping the mop back in the cupboard, she began sweeping the floor. The parents and children after Toddler Group had been in again today so, as usual, there was an array of crayons, paper and crisps that had got kicked to somewhere obscure. It wasn't as though they didn't sweep straight after they'd gone, but there was usually something that had got missed somehow.

'Yes, that was the hardest thing to get used to after Joe's dad passed away. The house was just so quiet. Don't you go thinking about letting Mike move back in for the company. You know that's not what he's after.'

'I know. I wouldn't. We didn't really have that kind of relationship anyway. By the time I'd gotten home from work, he was usually too drunk to string a sentence together, let alone hold a conversation.'

'There you go then.'

'He doesn't seem to be drinking now, though. Although, when I spoke to him on the phone earlier I thought he was at the pub, there was a lot of noise in the background, but he didn't act like he'd been drinking when he came round, did he?'

'No, I guess he didn't.'

'I'm glad for Joshie that he's grown up and seems to be taking his responsibilities seriously for once, but I would never get back with him. Joshie and I are happy here, I wouldn't do anything to jeopardise that. Besides, I really don't see him in that way any more.' Kneeling down Pippa swept the pile of floor dirt into the dustpan, and as predicted she counted three crayons and a couple of small pieces of paper. 'I don't know where those kids hide the crayons and paper. I swept straight after they'd gone.'

'I think they must hide them in the corners of the room or something. Kids are clever like that.' Carol chuckled.

'They certainly are.'

Holding on to the edge of a table, Pippa pulled herself to standing and took it to the bin.

'You're pleased you took the chance and came down here then?'

'Yes, really pleased. Even thinking about what our life would be like in London makes me feel all shaky. We'd be homeless by now, I'm sure of it. There would be no way I'd have been able to pay all of the arrears off. When we left, the estate agents were that close to kicking us out, I've no doubt they would have done so by now.'

'I'm glad you came too. It's good to see this place getting back to its glory days. I'm enjoying working again too. It makes me feel younger again.'

Pippa smiled, thinking back to the situation her and Joshua had been in and how she had felt as though she had absolutely no control over her life, to now. She shook her head, it actually gave her goosebumps just thinking about it. Shaking the dustpan into the bin, she hooked out the crayons, she'd anti bac them and they'd be fine.

'It's funny how life turns out. If you hadn't reopened this place and if Joe hadn't roped me into helping you, I think I'd have been stuck indoors at home for the rest of my life.'

As the floor dirt tumbled into the bin, a piece of paper stuck out. 'What's this? A betting slip? I didn't even think there was a betting shop in the village.'

'There isn't. There's one in the next town though. Someone must have dropped it. It's not a winner, is it? We could claim it and be rich!'

'I doubt it, it's all crumpled up.' Pippa pulled the paper apart. 'Oh, it's not a slip, it's a receipt or something I think. I don't know, I've never even been in a betting shop and I never will because of the way gambling changed Mike. But by the looks of things, someone betted on the horses yesterday.'

'Ooh, did they win?'

'Hang on. Yes, they did.'

'Lucky them.'

'Yes. They put £100 down.' Pippa pinched the bridge of her nose, for once not caring that her hands were covered in dust. 'And there's the name and phone number of a hotel scribbled on the back. I recognise the writing.' Pippa reached behind the till.

'Everything OK?'

'No, sorry, can I just get that envelope Mike gave me? Yes, that's the one. Thanks.' Pulling out the hotel confirmation Pippa leaned against the counter. 'I thought so. It's the hotel Mike booked for me and Joshua.'

'What is, love?'

'The name of the hotel scribbled on the back of this betting slip. It's the same one. It must have been Mike.'

'What must have been him?' Carol joined Pippa, looking over her shoulder at the betting receipt. 'Oh. The one hundred pounds?'

'Yes. He must have taken it and put it on the horses. He bought me and Joshua those tickets and hotel room out of guilt.'

'Oh, love, are you sure?'

'I can't think of another explanation, can you?'

'No, no I can't. What are you going to do?'

'I don't know.' Pippa reached her hand to her forehead. There it was again, that niggly headache starting. She jerked her head up, looking at the till. 'Is it down again today?'

'No, not today.'

'That's something then, I guess.'

* * *

Pippa waved Carol off, watching until she'd turned the corner up towards the road before locking the door and pulling down the blinds.

How could she have been so stupid? Why had she trusted him again? She'd known what he was like and how he had treated her and Joshua before, why had she let him back in?

Joshua would be devastated if he knew his dad had stolen from them. And he'd find out if Pippa confronted him. Maybe she shouldn't confront him. Maybe it as just a one-off, he'd wanted to surprise her and Joshua with the circus tickets and he'd taken the hundred pounds for that. Maybe. But even if he had, it didn't make it right.

After making herself a tea, she slumped into a chair. If she didn't call him out on this, it would only happen again. He would only steal again and again.

Plus, he had lied. He had promised he wasn't gambling any more, and he clearly was. What else was he lying about? She *had* to confront him, she didn't want his and Joshua's relationship to be based on lies. Should she even let Mike see Joshua any more? Or was this something completely separate? Joshua enjoyed having Mike back in his life. It would be completely unfair of her to stop him seeing his dad, but then again if his dad was a liar and a thief, what kind of role model was he to him?

20

Sitting up, she tucked her hair behind her ears, she must have fallen asleep here at the table. There it was again, the tap, tap, tap on the door. Was it Mike? Had he realised she'd found him out? What did he want?

Maybe if she stayed really still he'd think she was upstairs asleep and would go.

'It's Joe.' His deep voice, though muffled, was unmistakable.

'Joe, what are you doing here?' She pulled open the door.

'Can I come in?' He walked past her, turning back to lock the door again before looking at her. 'Sorry, did I wake you?'

'No, well yes, but I'd fallen asleep at a table.' Pippa indicated the table with the half-drunk cup of tea on and the chair pulled out and patted down her hair. 'So it's probably a good thing you woke me.'

'My mum told me what happened.'

'OK.' Pippa could see Joe's jaw clenching as he stood there, she pulled out a chair and picked up her cup. 'Here, sit down I'll grab you a coffee.'

Waiting for the coffee machine to warm up, she watched Joe

as he paced towards the window and back again, finally sitting down in the chair, his knees bouncing against the underside of the table.

'Here you are.' Placing his coffee mug on the table in front of him, Pippa put her hand on Joe's shoulder. 'Joe, are you OK?'

'Yes, no. No, I'm not OK. I'm worried about you and Joshua.'

'Oh.' Sliding into her seat, she took a sip of her coffee. 'You don't have to worry about us. We're fine.'

'No, you're not. My mum said that it had been Mike who had stolen from you. How can you be OK with that?'

'Well, obviously I'm not.' She placed her mug carefully down in the centre of a coaster. 'I'm not OK with it, but what am I supposed to do? If I confront him, Joshua loses out on having his dad around. If I don't, I can never trust him that he has Joshua's best interests at heart. I'll always be checking he's not stealing from us again.'

'Then what are you going to do?'

'I'm not sure yet. But what I'm not going to do is let him walk all over me again. I just need to figure out how I can word it so he knows I know and he won't try anything again but also so that he doesn't just walk out of Joshua's life again.'

'You can't want him to be a part of Joshua's life now, surely? Not after he's stolen money from you? Money that, ultimately, is to keep a roof over his son's head.'

Pippa looked down at her coffee, swilling the deep brown liquid around the white of the ceramic. 'Yes, I think I do. Joshua has been so happy to have him back in his life and I can't be the reason that bond breaks.'

'It wouldn't be you. It's him. He broke that bond as soon as he put his dirty hands in your till. You must be able to see that?' Joe gripped his mug so tightly that the tips of his fingers turned white.

'No, he broke my trust, not Joshua's. You must see that. Say, Mia breaks your heart again, you wouldn't stop her seeing Harley, would you?'

'I wouldn't give her a chance to break my heart again, believe me.'

'OK, maybe you trust her this time around and, you're right, she probably has learnt her lesson and will stay faithful this time but...'

'Hold on, what do you mean "this time"?'

'Now that you're back with her.'

'I'm not back with her. Why would you think that?' Joe looked Pippa in the eye. 'Is this about what you were talking about when you were ill? When you gave me those flowers for her?'

'Yes, no. Kind of.'

'I told you then that I hadn't meant it like that. I'm not back with her.'

'It was something Mike said as well. I just assumed...'

'What did Mike say?'

'That he saw you two kissing at the fair.'

Joe spat the coffee he'd just sipped back into the mug. 'What? I can assure you there certainly wasn't any kissing at the fair. We were there together because Harley insisted we both went.'

'Oh, OK. But you gave her a teddy you'd won? Sorry, it's none of my business at all. You don't need to answer that.'

'I gave her the teddy because Harley wanted it to go in the room she's making up for him at hers. She wants to have him overnight, starting with Friday night. Tomorrow.'

'I'm sorry. I didn't mean to pry. I just assumed... well, I believed Mike when he told me I guess.'

'See, there you go. More evidence that he's still lying to you. He had no reason to make something up like that.'

'No, yes. But that was different. He wanted me to get back with him and I said no. I think he'd seen that we were mates and put two and two together so told me you were back with your ex.'

'You can't trust him, Pippa. Look, I know it's not any of my business, but Harley told me that Joshua had said he was moving in here? If you're telling me the truth, that you don't want to get back with him, then I think it's a rubbish idea. It'll give him the wrong signal. Plus, you can't let him now that he's done this. No way.'

'Excuse me. First off, Joe, yes, he said that to Joshua but I've told Mike there's no chance of that. Second, it was not as a couple, he just wanted to move in for a bit to get to know Joshua.' Pippa counted the reasons off on her fingers, her face reddening with each one. 'And thirdly, the biggest one, why the hell do I have to justify myself to you? This has absolutely nothing to do with you, Joe.'

'Well, I'm very sorry, but I don't agree. It does have something to do with me.'

'How? Whatever I do with my life is my business. Not yours. Mine! Mine! Mine! Plus, how thick do you actually think I am? I'm not going to trust Mike again. Ever. After what he put me and Joshua through, even if I had complete proof that he had changed I wouldn't trust him again.'

'I'm just trying to look out for you. I'm not saying you're thick. Just that love can screw with your emotions sometimes.'

'Love? I don't love him. Even when we were together I hadn't loved him, not for years. Give me some credit, I know what he's like. I know he's not changed.'

'So, what are you going to do about it?'

'I'm going to talk to him.'

'When? I'll make sure I'm around.'

'What? No! I don't need your protection. I think you should

go now.' Scraping back her chair, Pippa made her way to the door, holding it open for him. How dare he? How dare he try to control her life and tell her what she should do about Mike?

'Pippa, please?'

'Just go. You've made it perfectly clear what you think of me.'

He looked at his feet and stepped outside. Turning around, he looked at Pippa as she closed the door behind him.

Flinging the mugs into the sink, Pippa rubbed her eyes. How could he make her feel like this? Not that she should care what he thought of her.

'Mum? Who's here?' Joshua's head peered around the door to the flat.

'No one, Joshie. It was Joe. He'd just popped round. He's gone now.' And he probably won't be back for a while, not after the way she'd spoken to him. But he had deserved it, hadn't he? Pippa swiped the tears away from her cheeks before turning her head and led him back upstairs.

21

'Hi, I got your message.'

Pippa rested the wooden spoon against the side of the blue ceramic bowl, cake mixture dripping from the edges, and turned around. 'Hi, Mike, thanks for coming.'

'What did you need to talk to me about?' Jumping onto a stool, he rested his arms on the counter.

'Um, do you mind if we talk outside?' She looked around the room at the customers eating scones and cake. 'Carol, are you OK if I take a quick break?'

'That's fine.' Carol looked over and nodded.

'Thanks. You go and wait outside, I'll grab us both a coffee.' Pippa watched Mike leave to find a table on the patio outside and swallowed. This was going to be so awkward.

'Pippa, stay at the tables where I can keep an eye, please?' Carol tugged Pippa's T-shirt as she walked past.

'It'll be fine. Honestly.' Picking up the coffees, she made her way outside. The tide was out and the beach seemed to go on for miles until it eventually reached the water.

'This one OK?' Mike called her over to the metal bistro set furthest away from the café door.

'Perfect.' Placing the coffees down, she slipped onto the chair opposite.

'I think I know what this is about?'

'You do?' Why had she assumed that he didn't think he'd be found out? He must have realised.

'Yes. You've changed your mind. You think it will be a good idea if I move in for a bit after all.' Mike grinned and leaned across the table, his hand on hers.

'No.' She slid her hand from his grasp and put her hands in her lap. 'I know what you did.'

'Hang on, you sound like one of those bimbos from the horror movies.' Mike laughed and shifted in his seat.

'Our till was down by a hundred pounds the day before yesterday.'

'Right, well you do have all sorts of people passing through, it must happen a lot.'

'No, no it doesn't happen a lot. In fact, it has never happened before.' Pippa tapped her foot against the concrete slabs. 'I also found a betting receipt.'

'OK, I'm not sure what this has got to do with me. Loads of people bet a hundred quid. It's a nice round number.'

'I didn't say the bet was for a hundred pounds, Mike. I know it was you. I just don't understand why you would steal from us? And then to use that money to place a bet, which you had told me you weren't addicted to any more.' She shook her head.

'Pippa, you can't go around accusing people of something like this. That is what you're doing, isn't it? You're accusing me of stealing and using your money to gamble.'

Pippa looked him in the eye, his voice was very low and controlled. She knew she had to tread carefully. She didn't want him shouting and turning the customers away. 'Mike, I just want you to tell me the truth, that's all. A hundred pounds went missing. The only time the till was left unattended was when you popped in and insisted on seeing me when I was sleeping off that headache. You asked Carol to come upstairs to get me. That was the only opportunity someone would have had to take it.'

'So, you are accusing me then? I knew it!' Mike slammed his mug down on the metal tabletop, coffee spilling over the top, the brown liquid forming a pool at the base of the mug. 'There must be other times someone could have taken it. You can't just blame me because I'm easy prey.'

'I'm not. On the back of the betting receipt was the name and number for the hotel that you're treating me and Joshua to.'

'Circumstantial, that's all it is. You can't prove the betting receipt was mine. Besides, I don't gamble any more.'

'Is this not your writing?' Pippa pulled the slip of paper from the pocket in her apron, smoothed it out and pushed it across the table.

'No, yes, but who's to say I used the money from your till?'

'Well, you said a moment ago that you hadn't gambled and now you're saying you did?'

'Yes, OK I hold my hands up, I placed a bet. I wanted to treat you and Joshie. I had a moment of weakness and placed a bet. OK?' Mike held his hands up.

'So you're admitting to stealing the money?'

'No, I didn't steal the hundred quid.'

'It's a bit of a coincidence that a hundred went missing and you gambled with a hundred pounds too, isn't it?'

'For goodness' sake, Pippa! If you'd let me move in half of it would be mine anyway. Half of all the damn café would be mine.'

'You what? *You* left *me*. You left me. Remember? Not the other way around. You ran off with the tart downstairs.'

'Don't call her that.' Mike thumped his fist on the table, the cutlery clattering in the pot in the centre of the table.

'Whoa.' Pippa reeled back. 'You're still with her, aren't you? That's why you don't like me calling her a tart?' Why hadn't she seen it before? It was so obvious now. She took a shallow breath, the air hardly touching the sides of her lungs. How could he still be with her? Was it her who he'd been talking to when she'd rang him? Why?

'No. It's not really any of your business, is it? You don't want me back anyway, remember.'

'What? I don't understand. Why would you have asked to move in with us if you were still with her? You asked me to take you back.' She gripped the side of the table, standing up and backing away. It all made sense now. He'd been trying to wheedle his way back in, and his tart was in on it too. Pippa swallowed the bile rising to her mouth.

'Do you know what, Pippa? It's all a bit confusing, isn't it? You wait until I left you because you were never around, may I remind you? You waited until I had gone and then this money maker mysteriously lands at your feet.'

'What are you saying?'

'I'm saying, I'm entitled to half of this. Half of all the profits you make, half of the whole damn place.' Mike waved his arm, indicating the café.

'You have got to be kidding me? I inherited this. *Me*. Not you, not us. There wasn't even an "us" when I inherited it.'

'That's what you claim. I'd like to know what a solicitor would say.' Mike scraped his chair back, knocking it to the floor, the dull sound of metal on concrete filling their ears.

'Are you being serious?' Pippa held on to the back of her

chair.

'You know what? Yes, I am. I'm being deadly serious. You always land on your feet, you do. Ever since I've known you, it's been me having no money and having to ask you for money. And I'm bloody sick of it.'

'Hold on. Me with money? Yes, because I worked for it. I worked twelve-hour shifts six, sometimes seven, days a week and you know it. I hadn't hidden this place away whilst I was missing my son's first assembly or his first day of school. I found out about the café after you left, months, no over a year, after you left in fact. This has nothing to do with you. Nothing.'

'I spent the best years of my life with you, Pippa. I deserve something from it.'

'No, you don't.' A hollow laugh escaped her throat, had he really just said that? 'You made mine and Joshua's lives a misery for so long and like I said before you decided to leave.'

'You're pathetic. Do you know that? Absolutely pathetic.'

'Oi. Don't you speak to her like that.'

Looking across towards the bottom of the slope leading to the café, Pippa saw it was Joe, he was running towards them. Biting the bottom of her lip, she blinked her eyes, she would not show Mike what he was doing to her.

'You, mate, don't need to get involved.' Mike yelled, his eyes wide and fixated on Joe.

'I think you should leave.'

'You do, do you? Is that what you think too, Pippa? Or are you going to get your grease monkey to speak for you too?'

'Mike, please go. I'll text when you can visit Joshua.'

'You what? You think I want to spend any more time with that snivelling complainer? Get lost, Pippa, you'll hear from our solicitor.'

'Don't you dare talk about your son like that. You know what?

He's better off without you. Go back to your tart. I don't want you anywhere near us again.' Pippa could feel her heart banging through her chest, she gripped tighter on to the back of the chair, her wrists hurting with the strength of her grip.

'You heard her. Go!' Joe was next to her now. Pippa could feel the warmth from his body against her side.

Pippa ducked as Mike's coffee mug flew through the air, landing on the floor inches away from her feet.

'Get away before I make you!' Joe yelled and punched his fist into the palm of his other hand.

Standing side by side, they watched Mike slope away, no doubt going back to his mistress to tell her they'd get no more money from Pippa.

'Pippa! Are you OK? I saw what happened and rushed out as fast as I could.' Breathless, Carol joined them.

How could he have said that about Joshua? His own son? Had he really been playing the daddy role to get money?

'Pippa, love?'

Pippa could feel Carol's touch on her arm but couldn't seem to pull herself away from watching Mike's figure getting smaller and smaller in the distance.

'I'll take her for a walk, if you're OK for a bit, Mum?'

'Of course, take as long as you need.'

'Pippa, come with me.'

Joe's arms enveloped her shoulders, strong and safe, and she let herself be led away from the café. They walked down the slope away from the patio and onto the sand. She let herself be guided in the opposite direction to where Mike had stormed off until they reached a small outcrop of rocks.

She watched as Joe wiped a piece of stray seaweed from one of the rocks and lowered Pippa to sitting. Sensing him sitting down next to her, she let the warmth from his body penetrate her skin. In a rock pool at her feet, a small crab walked around the perimeter, waiting eagerly for the tide to return to collect it. They listened to the waves splash mesmerisingly against the sand of the shore.

* * *

Pippa didn't know how long they'd been sitting before the tears came. She felt them against her cheeks and then on her hands in her lap. She let herself be gently pulled into Joe's arms, laying her head against his broad shoulder.

'He had only come back for the money, hadn't he? He didn't really want to get to know Joshua again.'

'I don't know what to say.' Joe's breath tickled the hairs on her head.

'You don't need to say anything. You tried to warn me when that money went missing. I should have seen him for who he was. He's not changed one bit, and yet I let him twist me around his little finger. Again.'

'Here.' Joe passed her a tissue. 'You're not at fault. I didn't like the fellow but, even I couldn't have predicted that he would use his own son to try to get money off you.'

Wiping her eyes with his tissue, she shook her head. 'What am I going to tell Joshua?'

'Why don't you say that he's had to go away with work or something?'

'Good idea. I don't want him finding out about this.' Twisting on the rock, she faced Joe. 'Thank you for stepping in. I know I said I didn't need your help with him yesterday, but, thank you.'

'You're very welcome.' Taking her hand, he looked her in the eye. 'If I'm honest, my mum rang me and told me you were speaking to him.'

'Oh, right.'

'Don't be cross with her, she was just worried about you. It was my fault, I had asked her to let me know when he turned up.'

'Well, thank you.' Even if all Joe wanted was to be friends, he was a good friend to have around. She squeezed his hand. 'I guess we should get back.'

'Yes, I guess so. Are you going to go to the hotel and circus tomorrow?'

'No, I don't think so. It wouldn't feel right. I don't want anything to do with Mike again, let alone his gambling habit.'

22

'Mummy! The doorbell! Is it our takeaway? Is it?' Joshua knocked incessantly on the bathroom door.

'It might be. One moment.' Looking at herself in the mirror, Pippa padded her index fingers across the black bags under her eyes before pinching the bridge of her nose. She hadn't slept a wink last night and even Joshua had asked if she was ill.

'It was. It was our pizza! Joe's got it. Quick, Mum, before we eat it all.'

'OK, sweetie. You go and make a start. I won't be long.'

'I'll save you a pot of dipping sauce.'

'Thank you.' She listened to him padding down the hallway and sat on the toilet lid, her eyes fixated on the back of the door, a small smudge of make-up was on the door handle. She should clean it off.

Taking a sheet of tissue paper, she patted her eyes, she would not cry again, she'd only just reapplied her make-up. She wanted to go and join in the film night and pizza. Joshua never ceased to surprise her. When she'd told him they couldn't go to the circus or hotel any more, he hadn't even asked why, instead he'd immediately started asking if they could get a takeaway instead.

She shook her head, they'd get through this. They'd got through worse when he'd left before. At least, this time, they had their home.

'Pippa.'

She gently slapped her cheeks, trying to bring a little colour out. 'Yes?'

'Are you OK? Open up, I have a slice of pizza with your name on it.'

Standing up, she opened the door and stood back as Joe stepped in, a plate of pizza in his hand.

'Now, we could eat pizza in the bathroom, or you could come and join us. Joshua is desperate to start playing the film and he's insisting on waiting for you because, apparently, it's not a real film night if one of us is locked in the bathroom.'

Smiling, Pippa held her hand out to Joe's outstretched arm, allowing him to lead the way. 'Come on then. That pizza smells good.'

'It certainly does, but I don't think we can order you pizza every time you lock yourself in the bathroom!'

'Very funny.'

* * *

Thanks for coming tonight.

You're welcome. Was fun and took my mind off Harley being at his mum's.

We should make it a regular thing when Harley can come too.

Boys would like that. So would I.

Leaning forward to put her mug on the coffee table, she then snuggled back into the cushions of the sofa, tucking the blanket in around her. She should probably go to bed, but she was too exhausted to even think about cleaning her teeth and getting ready.

Glad you enjoyed it. You've been great recently. Thank you.

Stop saying thank you. I've not done anything.

You have.

Laying her head back on the cushion, she let her eyes close.

* * *

Forcing her eyes open against the heaviness of sleep, she listened again. Something had woken her. She was sure of that. Was there a noise?

She lifted her head and leant her body on her elbow.

Yes, there it was. There was definitely something. Tapping. Maybe Joshua had woken up.

Making her way across the landing, she paused at Joshua's bedroom door and watched as his duvet rose and fell with his breathing. Maybe she had imagined it. She had been having a really weird dream after all, about opening a bird sanctuary of all things. She smiled, she always had the most vivid dreams when she was exhausted.

Sitting back on the edge of the sofa, she picked up her mobile. Joe had left a couple of messages, she must have dropped off halfway through a conversation. The last one was only ten minutes ago, she couldn't have been asleep long then. She stretched her arms up, it felt like a long time.

No I haven't.
Have you fallen asleep on me?!

Typical Joe.

Sorry. Yes, I had fallen asleep. You still awake?

She jerked her head up, there it was again. Noises. This time a rhythmic dull banging. It was definitely coming from downstairs, she could hear that now.

Yep. Did you have a good sleep?

Woken up by noises from downstairs. Did we leave the dishwasher running? Think may have a plumbing problem!

Shaking her head, she tried to clear the fuzz from sleep. She must have put it on when she'd let Joe out. Something must have worked loose. That'd happened before, she'd dropped a teaspoon which had worked its way towards the bottom of the dishwasher, clattering its way against the metal.

You think you have a leak? Want me to come over?

Last time it was just a teaspoon that had escaped the cutlery tray! Should be fine. Will go and sort it before noise wakes Joshie.

You sure?

Picking up the jumper she'd worn earlier, she pulled it over her head and stood up before making her way towards the stairs.

An almighty clatter stopped her on the top step. What the hell had that been? If it was a spoon loose, the dishwasher would defiantly be broken now. It sounded like metal being flung. There it was again and again.

She tiptoed down the steps until she was halfway down. It must be the dishwasher. There was no other explanation. Another crash, ceramic this time. As though something had fallen and smashed.

Hammering in her ears, her pulse quickened and she tried to slow her breathing. There was someone in the café. It must be someone, a person. The noises were too loud for it to be the dishwasher. Holding her breath, she listened. She could even hear the thud of boots or shoes across the lino now.

Her phone pinged in her hand. Bringing it up to her eyes, the writing flickered in the dim light.

Is it leaking?

Her hands shaking she typed back.

Someone in café.

Sinking to the carpet, she gripped her phone in the palm of her hand and switched it to 'silent'.

Don't go down. Ring police and stay where you are. I'm coming over.

Her hands were clammy. She tapped 999 into her phone.

Another huge clatter resonated up the stairs as something fell against the floor startling her. She watched as in slow motion her phone slipped from her hand, bouncing down the steps until it landed with a thud against the tiled hallway floor.

Gripping the handrail, she held her breath and listened. Nothing. Pulling herself to standing, she tiptoed down the remaining steps, kneeling on the hard floor to reach her phone. Looking up at the door only inches away from her, she prayed she had remembered to lock it. She normally did.

She could hear another noise through the door now. It began softly at first, a sound similar to the soft crushing of newspaper. Growing louder and louder.

'Pippa?' A sharp yell came from the café.

Looking up at the door handle, she let out a deep breath. Mike. It was *Mike*. She stood up. What the hell was he doing here?

How had he got in? She was sure she'd locked the front door. Had he broken in? Was he after money from the till? Seriously? He had stooped low before, but this was a completely different level. No, there must be a logical explanation. Maybe he'd left his mobile in the café or something. That'd be a logical explanation. There must be. But he should have checked with her first. What gave him the right to force his way in?

Her hands began to shake and not from fear this time. Standing up, she unlocked the door to the café and swung it open.

'Mike! How the hell did you get in?' It was the stench that made her stagger back, bashing her shoulder on the door. She heard the dull thud as it slammed shut behind her.

She coughed as the smell seared up her nose. She knew that smell. Petrol. Why would there be petrol in the café? And then she saw the fire, flames springing up in the few seconds she stood there, jumping from table, to chair to floor. Spinning across the café tiles.

Turning the torch on her phone on, she swung the light around the room, chairs had been overturned, the coffee machine pulled off the counter and, yes, the till drawer left open. They hadn't had much in there, just a float for the next day. Mike was standing the other side of the flames, his silhouette dancing in the smoke.

'Mike. What have you done?' Her voice sounded frantic, high and loud above the rustling sound of the fire.

'You're supposed to be at the hotel. Why the hell are you not at the hotel?' The urgency leached through his voice making it crack, sounding unfamiliar.

Joshua! Her mind was whirring, she had to get Joshua out. He was still asleep. He was in bed. She was here. Mike had started the fire. Why had he started the fire? Why was there petrol? She had to get to Joshua.

Twisting on her heels, she grappled at the door handle, the metal of the knob warming already. Why wouldn't it open?

Calm down, a voice shouted in her head, reminding her that the door stuck sometimes, locking itself when it closed heavily.

'Mike! Mike, help us!' Holding her hand to her mouth she began to gag, all she tasted was the dusty smoke filling her mouth along with the acidity of the petrol. Where was he? Why couldn't she hear him any more? Had he left her? Left them? Left, knowing that Joshua, his son, was upstairs asleep? Would he do that? Even Mike?

Thoughts swam around her mind so quickly she struggled to grasp onto any, to make any coherent sense of anything she was thinking. The deafening shrill of the fire alarm kicked in.

Tugging again at the door, she leaned backwards, her full weight on the handle. Nothing, it wouldn't even budge a millimetre. Twisting around, she swung her torch from one side of the room to the other. The brilliant orange of the flames twirled around her, now filling the café from wall to wall.

Holding on to the door handle, she pushed her feet against the wall and hung, pulling down on the handle, still nothing. The latch must have slipped into place. It was locked. She covered her mouth with the top of her jumper and screamed.

She needed to get to Joshua. She needed to get to Joshua.

Blinking, she tried to clear the white spots dancing in her sight. It was a fire door, wasn't it? It must be. It would definitely be a fire door between here and the flat. There was some regulation or something that would have made it be a fire door, there was. It was. Joshua should be OK. Joshua would be fine for a while. He must be.

Unless it wasn't or unless the fire went through the ceiling. Could it do that? Sinking to the floor, Pippa squeezed her eyes tight shut, trying to rid them of the incessant stinging. Digging her nails into the palms of her hands, she coughed, a hacking cough that she couldn't satisfy, she couldn't get enough air into her lungs to cough properly.

Think! Think!

The key! They kept a spare key in the till. The flames were beginning to leap against the side of the counter now. She didn't have long. Trying to keep her breathing slow and shallow, she pulled her jumper up over her mouth again. Keeping as low as she could, she crawled across the floor, the tiles cooler than the air against her skin. She was almost there. Her knees stung from the shards of ceramic tearing at her pyjama bottoms.

She must be there now. Peering upwards she made out the dark shadow of the till against the fierce light of the flames.

She was there! Kneeling up, she reached her hand up to the

till drawer, pulling it away sharply as the poker hot metal touched her skin.

Whimpering into the material of her jumper, she leaned against the hot counter. It was now or never, if she left it any longer the till would be engulfed by the fire. She could already see it dancing on the lip of the counter.

Biting down hard on her jumper, she reached out her hand again, reaching into the till drawer. An intense pain travelled up her arm, her fingers turning numb. Knocking the tray out of the drawer, Pippa scrambled about in the coins that collided across the floor. The key, she needed to find the key.

As she rummaged through the small mounds of coins, her fingers closed around the square head of the key. She had it!

Another sound added to the mix of the roar of the fire, a smash, glass falling. Curling into a ball, she shielded her head with her hands.

The windows. The fire must have blown the windows out. Joshua's room was above the door. What if his window smashed too? His bed was next to the window. He would get covered in glass. Had he even heard the fire alarm? It would have surely woken him by now. He'd be terrified. Her little Joshie would likely be huddled under his duvet, not knowing what to do. She had to get to him. She had to.

'Joshie, Mummy's coming.' The fierce rasp scratched her throat as she spoke the words, inaudible above the crackling of the fire.

Staggering to her feet, she half ran, half tumbled to the door just as the fire leapt above and across the counter, swallowing where she had been.

Gripping the key, she tried to jam it into the lock. She could hardly feel the key in her fingers. It slid out of her grasp, falling to the floor.

'No, no.' Her voice cracked, lost in the thunder of the fire. Feeling across the floor with her good hand, she found it.

Trying again, the key slotted in, she twisted it. The door fell open in front of her. Sobbing, she crawled through, reaching up and pulling the door shut behind her.

Taking breath after breath, she coughed, again and again. Her breathing shallow, her lungs tight, her chest heaving. The air was still smoky but the hall was not full of the grey fog as it had been the other side of the door.

She needed to get Joshua into the living room at the back of the flat and out of the window.

'Joshua!' She couldn't raise her voice higher than a hoarse whisper, her throat tightening around every syllable. The stairs loomed above her, swaying in her vision. She needed to get to Joshua. They should have made a fire escape plan when they'd moved in. They had made a plan in London. The firefighters had gone into Joshua's school and that had been their homework, to make a fire plan. Why hadn't they made one here?

Reaching out her fingers to grapple with step after step, she pulled herself up. Every movement was a struggle, every single muscle in her body seemed to be working against her, flinching in pain, in protest to the lack of oxygen.

She couldn't do it. She couldn't get to the top. Speckles of light shifted in and out of her vision. Every breath was a war that she had to fight for. She couldn't fight any longer. Her eyelids closed. The darkness comforting.

* * *

'Mummy!'

Joshua! With the last ounce of strength in her body, she forced her eyes open. Her head swaying, she tried to focus on the small fuzzy being in front of her. Joshua was there. Joshua was OK. He was standing on the landing just above her, clinging onto to Teddy.

'Go!' She flung her arm out in the direction of the living room. 'Window.'

'No, Mummy! You need to come! Please, Mummy! Come with me!'

'Go!' She could hear her voice cracking. He had to go. He had to.

'I'm not leaving you.' Sitting down next to her, Joshua put his arms around her shoulders, his small body shaking against her.

'Leave! Go!'

'Pippa!'

'Mummy, I can hear someone.' Joshua looked towards the living room door.

'Go. See.'

'OK.' Joshua coughed. The smoke was beginning to get thicker here now. The air around them foggier. 'Look after Teddy. I'm coming back for you.'

Pippa watched as Joshua went into the living room. She could hear the slight whisper of him shouting but couldn't work out what was being said. Unclenching her fingers, she wrapped them around Teddy. The soft fur a welcome relief to the searing pain in her skin.

'It's Joe! He's coming to get us! He's getting his ladder from the top of his van.' Joshua knelt down next to her, stroking her hair. 'It's OK, Mummy. Joe will save us.'

Straining her neck, she looked up at Joshua. The lights were out but she could still make out his features, the curve of his chubby cheeks, his button nose, his heart-shaped lips.

'I love you, Joshie.' Joe would save him. Joe was always there for them. If things were different maybe they could have made it work. They would have made a lovely little family.

'Mummy! Wake up, Mummy! You can't go to sleep now, you always say I can't sleep when we're having visitors and Joe's coming.'

23

'Hey, you. We've been waiting for you to wake up.'

Joe's voice pierced through the fuzziness in Pippa's head, faint at first and then getting louder. Was she still on the stairs to the flat? She took a deep breath. No, the air wasn't thick with smoke here. There was something hooked onto the bottom of her nose, though. What was that? It was tickling her skin every time she breathed. Reaching her hand towards her face, she tried to swipe it away. She couldn't feel her face, her fingers felt puffy and huge. There was no sensation. What was going on?

'Leave that. It's just a tube giving you a little oxygen, that's all.'

Oxygen? The fire! She remembered now. Lifting her eyelids she blinked against the brilliant white of the lights above her. Hospital. She was in the hospital.

'Joshua! Where's Joshua? Is he OK?' Pushing herself to sitting she groaned, pain pulsing through her body.

'I'm here, Mummy!'

It took a while for her eyes to focus, to focus on him, but she could see him now, he was sat next to Joe by her side. She brought her hands into view, the hand that she'd touched the till with was all bandaged up. That's why she couldn't feel things properly.

'You're OK? I love you, Joshie.' He was fine. He was alive and fine. Tears slid down her face, her lips trembled. She shouldn't think about the 'what ifs'. He was safe.

'Joe carried me down over his shoulder. Just like a fireman! I'm going to tell all my friends at school! They won't believe me!' Joshua sat up a little taller, puffing his chest out.

'Joe, how can I ever thank you?' Pippa lifted her hand and patted Joshua's cheek before reaching across to Joe's hand.

'He got you out too. He went back up and got you out before the fire engine came!' Joshua jiggled on his chair.

'Joe, I...' Pippa bit down on her bottom lip. She could feel the sting as her eyes filled with fresh tears. Things could have turned out so differently.

'Come on, Joshua, let's go and get one of those chocolate milkshakes from the cafeteria that I promised you.' Twisting her head around, Pippa saw that Carol was there too. She now stood at the bottom of the bed holding her hand out to Joshua.

'Yay! See you in a bit, Mummy.' He flung himself at Pippa, his small arms circling her neck and landed a sloppy kiss on her cheek before running to Carol.

'Let's wipe those tears away.' Joe gently patted Pippa's cheeks with a tissue.

'Thank you. Really, thank you.'

'Shhh.' Standing up, Joe leaned into her, his lips soft against hers. 'I'm sorry it's taken me nearly losing you to realise how much you mean to me.'

Lifting the index finger of her good hand to her lips, she circled them. He had kissed her.

'Sorry. Sorry, I shouldn't have done that, not with you in here.

Sorry.' Joe slumped back into his chair and rubbed his hand across his face.

Pippa stared at him. His chin was more stubbly than usual, his frown lines deeper and his eyes were bloodshot as if he'd been crying.

'Are you OK?'

'Me? Yes, of course! It should be me asking you. You're the one that was trapped in that fire, for goodness' sake.' Joe smiled a smile that didn't reach his eyes.

'I think I love you, Joe.'

'I know I love you, Pippa Jenkins.' This time his eyes sparkled as his face cracked into a grin. He reached for her hand, his fingers interlocking with hers.

'The café?'

'Yep, it's all but ruined. Still standing, but ruined.'

'Ah.' Taking a shuddering breath, she realised that it didn't matter, not really. She could have lost so much more.

'The insurance will cover the repairs though, and I've called in a few favours so we can get it back up and running as soon as possible. My mum's cleared the spare room at hers for you and Joshua to stay and she's already talking about setting up a temporary stall. She describes it as an open-air pop-up café, whatever that's supposed to mean.' Joe shrugged his shoulders. 'She says that way you won't lose your regulars while it's being rebuilt.'

'Your mum's thought of everything.'

'She certainly has.'

'What about Mike? Did he get out?' She sat up on her elbows.

'Mike's fine. The CCTV at the café caught everything that happened. He was arrested this morning.'

'Right.'

'He reckons he thought you and Joshua were at the hotel. It sounds like he had it all planned, the hotel and circus treat was just to get you out of town so he could burn the place down.'

'Why? I don't understand.' Even if he hadn't meant to hurt her or Joshua, he'd still meant to burn the café down.

'Apparently he was planning on getting his grubby hands on some of the insurance money. Don't worry about him. Now close your eyes and get some sleep.' Joe held her hand as she let the fog of sleep envelop her.

EPILOGUE

Peeking through the blinds, shivers ran up her spine.

'I can't go out there. Have you seen how many people there are?' Pippa stepped back and shook her arms out, hoping the nerves would flow out of her body.

'Yes, you can.' Joe turned away from the window and grinned. 'Harley! Joshua! Are you both ready?'

'We are!' They called back in unison, standing behind the counter. Harley lifted up a plate full of cupcakes while Joshua stood beside him, a plate of iced biscuits in his hands, both boys grinning from ear to ear.

'Go on, Pippa. Let your customers in.'

Pippa smiled at her mum who stood with Carol behind the counter. She'd come down after the fire to visit and hadn't gone back. When the flat had been made safe Joe and Harley had moved back in with them and her mum had taken over Joe's tenancy at his house. It was early days in their relationship, but both Pippa and Joe had struggled to think of reasons why they shouldn't and millions of reasons why they should.

'OK. Wish me luck.' Taking a deep breath, she looked around the newly decorated café, they had kept the décor very similar to how it had been before, and opened the door.

ACKNOWLEDGMENTS

Thank you, readers, for taking the time to read The Little Beach Café. I hope you've enjoyed reading about Pippa's journey to her new life by the sea and her romance with Joe as much as I enjoyed writing her story.

A huge thank you to my wonderful children, Ciara and Leon, who motivate me to keep writing and working towards 'changing our stars' each and every day. Also to my lovely family for always being there, through the good times and the trickier ones.

And a massive thank you to my amazing editor, Emily Yau, who reached out and believed in me – thank you.

Thank you also to Shirley for copyediting and proofreading The Little Beach Café. And, of course, Clare Stacey for creating the beautiful cover. Thank you to all at Team Boldwood!

MORE FROM SARAH HOPE

We hope you enjoyed reading *The Little Beach Café*. If you did, please leave a review.

If you'd like to gift a copy, this book is also available as an ebook, paperback, hardback, digital audio download and audiobook CD.

Sign up to Sarah Hope's mailing list for news, competitions and updates on future books.

https://bit.ly/SarahHopeNews

Why not try *The Seaside Ice Cream Parlour,* another heartwarming novel from Sarah Hope…

The Seaside Ice-Cream Parlour

SARAH HOPE

ABOUT THE AUTHOR

Sarah Hope is the author of many successful romance novels, including the bestselling Cornish Bakery series. She lives in Central England with her two children and an array of pets, and enjoys escaping to the seaside at any opportunity.

Follow Sarah Hope on social media:

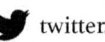

twitter.com/sarahhope35
facebook.com/HappinessHopeDreams
instagram.com/sarah_hope_writes

Boldwood

Boldwood Books is an award-winning fiction publishing company seeking out the best stories from around the world.

Find out more at www.boldwoodbooks.com

Join our reader community for brilliant books, competitions and offers!

Follow us
@BoldwoodBooks
@BookandTonic

Sign up to our weekly deals newsletter

https://bit.ly/BoldwoodBNewsletter